T0130076

"I'm not laughing at you, Lissa."

Matthew's voice was tender.

"Apologies accepted," Lissa replied. Her spirits bobbed up like a ball that has been held under water.

Having seen the complexity that lay beneath such a beautiful surface, Matthew found Lissa all the more attractive. As she tilted her wineglass to her lips, the candlelight played along the ivory column of her neck, the underside of her chin, and down her throat. Matthew couldn't remember ever having seen anything lovelier.

With Lissa still beaming at his apology, he growled out, "Exactly how old are you, anyway?"

"Exactly?"

"You are out of your teens?"

"Of course I am," she snapped. "Why?"

"Before you ask me questions like that, I'd better warn you about myself. I have a very bad, very unbreakable habit of always telling the truth."

"Good, because that's what I want to hear," Lissa said. What she was feeling was the tiniest bit frightened. An invisible cord of menace seemed to stretch between her and Matthew. It bound her to him and was drawing her closer to him and to the danger she sensed. She repeated her question. "Why?"

"Because I want to make love to you."

ALSO BY TORY CATES

Different Dreams
Cloud Waltzer
Where Aspens Quake
Handful of Sky

A HIGH, HARD LAND

Previously published as *A Passionate Illusion*

TORY CATES

POCKET BOOKS

New York   London   Toronto   Sydney   New Delhi

Pocket Books
A Division of Simon & Schuster, Inc.
1230 Avenue of the Americas
New York, NY 10020

This book is a work of fiction. Any references to historical events, real people, or real places are used fictitiously. Other names, characters, places, and events are products of the author's imagination, and any resemblance to actual events or places or persons, living or dead, is entirely coincidental.

Copyright © 1986 by Tory Cates
Previously published as *A Passionate Illusion* in 1986
by Silhouette Books.

First Pocket Books paperback edition June 2014

POCKET and colophon are registered trademarks
of Simon & Schuster, Inc.

For information about special discounts for bulk purchases, please contact Simon & Schuster Special Sales at 1-866-506-1949 or business@simonandschuster.com.

The Simon & Schuster Speakers Bureau can bring authors to your live event. For more information or to book an event, contact the Simon & Schuster Speakers Bureau at 1-866-248-3049 or visit our website at www.simonspeakers.com.

Designed by Lewelin Polanco
Cover illustration by Craig White

Manufactured in the United States of America

10   9   8   7   6   5   4   3   2   1

ISBN 978-1-5011-3762-4
ISBN 978-1-4767-3263-3 (ebook)

A HIGH,
HARD LAND

Chapter 1

Jeannie tried to keep her gaze trained on Quaid's face. It was the only way to combat her nervousness. Each time her eyes slid a degree or two to the left or the right of those rugged planes she knew so well, her concentration was destroyed. She had to erase everything from her mind except the face she'd loved since girlhood and get on with what had to be done, and done as well as she possibly could do it.

She stared down at the worn roughed-out suede boots on her feet planted directly in front of Quaid's spit-shined Tony Lamas and drew in several deep, calming breaths to compose herself. Quaid's strong, sure hands went to her shoulders to help her steady herself. It was just the touch she needed. All her doubts and apprehensions fell away. She knew once more exactly who she was and what the situation was.

She was Jeannie Duncan, born September 5, 1930, on

the small, remote New Mexico ranch she'd inherited when her father had died the previous year. And she loved Quaid Dawson. Had loved him ever since she'd first seen him ten years ago dancing his horse through a brilliant rodeo spotlight, doing fancy roping tricks. Since then he'd ridden in and out of her life more times than she could count. And each time he seemed to tear away a larger chunk of her heart to take with him as he followed his wanderlust to the next county, the next state, the next country—to the next rodeo always farther and farther away.

Well, she thought, she had the power now to keep him anchored to her. He himself had given her that power in a magic night of lovemaking. Even as they stood there, his strong hands on her trembling shoulders, a child grew within her. Quaid's child. A child that would be born in 1950. Jeannie liked that. Liked the fact that the world would be half done with the century when her baby came. It was a good sign. All that remained was for her to tell Quaid that in less than seven months' time he would be a father, and he would not leave her. Or so she hoped. What was making her nervous was thinking of all the times she'd heard Quaid scorn the ordinary life she cherished. How he pitied all the poor fools who spent their lives stuck on one dreary plot of land while he, he was free to roam the earth.

But surely, Jeannie reassured herself, surely that would change with a baby. The sun was just beginning to set. This would not be the night of farewell and parting that was the start of another long, lonely rodeo season that would take Quaid from her. It would be the beginning of their life together.

His hands moved up from Jeannie's shoulders, cradling her jaw and forcing her to look up into his face. Behind him was the immense, rapidly darkening New Mexico sky, which opened up so magnificently above the high mesa they stood on. It was their special spot. They had ridden up to it tonight, Quaid thinking they would be parting, Jeannie adrift with plans for the future they would share. She stared deep into his eyes as if they were pools she wanted to drown in. He felt her distress.

"Darlin'," he drawled, in the rumbly baritone that could still send shudders of excitement skittering up her spine, "I've got to be moving on. I hope the season'll be short and I can get back to help you with roundup in the fall."

"You say that every year," Jeannie said softly. "And every year the season keeps getting longer. You know I never see you before the snow starts to blowing."

A flicker of guilt shot through Quaid's eyes at the accusation. He was the one who decided how long the season was, and he could never make himself quit until the spotlight had dimmed at every rodeo on the circuit. Still, even with the stinging words of reproach fresh upon them, Quaid could not resist the plump temptation of Jeannie's lips. She tried to pull away from him, but he held her firm in his grip until his mouth found hers and overcame her with the sweetness of his kiss.

This was the moment. Jeannie knew it would never come again. With their mouths fused in a recollection of the passion that had sired the child she carried within her, Jeannie took Quaid's hand in hers. She placed his warm palm against her belly, against the spot where their child slept. Quaid pulled his mouth from hers, his hand still spanning her womb.

Jeannie's heart stopped as she slowly raised her eyes to meet his. It almost didn't start again when she saw the expression on Quaid's face. In her fondest fantasies, she had imagined him melting with solicitous tenderness at this moment. Insisting that she lie down. Asking what he could bring her, the mother of his child, and demanding to know what the earliest date was that he could marry her. In her more realistic imaginings, she had figured that Quaid would take the news with bittersweet resignation. More sweet than bitter, though. She had never foreseen the reaction that actually greeted her: stunned disbelief.

Even as the evidence of Quaid's reaction spread across his handsome features, he began to pull physically away from Jeannie, denying the message she had given him.

Jeannie Duncan had spent a lifetime eking out a spare living on a harsh land. She'd survived a lot: the deaths of her mother and father; years when disease almost wiped out the herd; drought, snow, hail. She had brought calves into the world and seen them off to slaughter. Only nineteen years of such a life could have prepared her to face

Quaid's rejection and to keep on living. As she looked into his eyes, searching in vain for the love and commitment she'd hoped to find there, her heart broke and re-fused into a hurt and twisted lump that could only barely keep life pumping through her. All within the space of two blinks of an eyelash.

"Jeannie, if you've got something to tell me," Quaid warned, "you'd better come right out with it because I've got to be getting on down the road."

Getting on down the road. The words rang brutally in Jeannie's mind. To Quaid they stood for the freedom of a never-ending trail of possibilities. To her they represented a prison of loneliness in which she would have to bear and raise her child all alone. She knew that Quaid was giving her the chance to say straight out what he already knew. But Jeannie would never do that. If he was going to force her to say the words "I am carrying your child," like a judge pronouncing sentence, then she did not want him with her. Her silence was the reprieve Quaid had been waiting for. He backed away from her.

It was April, but in the high desert of northeastern New Mexico that meant very little. As the sun continued to lower, a bitter wind blew through Jeannie's jacket. She did not feel its chill, however, for she was locked in a place where even cold could no longer reach.

Quaid pulled his horse in close and swung up into the saddle. "Come on, ride back down with me." He offered her his hand so that she could swing up into the saddle ahead of him. "We can lead your horse back down." There was a soft, caring tone in his voice, which was Quaid's signal that he wanted to talk more. But it was too late, far too late, for Jeannie.

She could not force any words past her choked throat. If she had been able to, she would have told Quaid Dawson to get on down whatever road he felt compelled to follow. To chase his foolish dreams of freedom and never to come back. She didn't ever want to see him again. Didn't ever again want to feel the pain that was suffocating her.

"Go" was all she could force out. Just one cold syllable of irrevocable finality. She turned away from Quaid and stared out to the distant spot where the last sliver of sun made a golden pink hump above the horizon.

Quaid looked at her uncertainly, his horse circling in its eagerness to head back down to the bin of hay and grain waiting at the stable.

"Go!" This time Jeannie commanded his departure. All she had left was her dignity, and she vowed to guard that as ferociously as she would guard the child within her. When Quaid didn't move, she ripped a branch from a stubby juniper tree and switched the horse's rump, sending it skittering off down the trail. Of course a master horseman like Quaid could have stopped the animal's flight with ease. But he didn't. He chose not to, Jeannie reminded herself bitterly. How could she have loved such a man? she wondered as his broad back shrank in the distance. But the question: how could I love him still? was the one that finally devastated her. That finally unblocked the rage and grief welling within her.

Jeannie sank to her knees, dissolved by the tears she could hold in no longer. Waves of pain washed through her. She grabbed for the one thing that had been constant throughout her life. The one thing that had always been there to comfort her through hardship and death. She grabbed a handful of the earth that had been her father's and was now hers. It was all she had now in the world. That and her child. A surge of strength shot through her as she promised her unborn child that she would survive. She raised that fistful of dirt up to the sky as if flinging a challenge to the cruel fates that they could cast her down, but they would never break her spirit. A smile of triumph broke across Jeannie's face.

"Cut! Cut! Cut!" The disgust-laden voice rang out clearly through the mountain air.

Lissa Bauer felt herself brutally ripped from the character of Jeannie Duncan and flung back into the harsh artificiality of moviemaking. The transition was far too abrupt. All those cameramen and lighting people. Jack, the director. Stan, his assistant. Elsie, the script assistant. Jerome, the makeup man. They suddenly seemed like the kind of gore-seeking vultures who stop to gawk at the injured when there's a car crash. But the worst of all of them was the man who had destroyed the scene, Matthew Briggs, the novelist who had adapted his bestseller,

A High, Hard Land—a novel that had become an international phenomenon—for the screen.

"My God, woman," Briggs was saying to her, "if you're going to do Scarlett O'Hara, why don't you just go all out? 'There will always be a Tara.'" He did a swooning imitation of the heroine of *Gone With the Wind*, complete with southern accent.

Behind him the director, Jack Myers, was covering his head with both hands and all the technical people were rolling their eyes in pained disbelief. Lissa herself was still too stunned to react. It was only the second day of shooting. She'd been nervous enough about working with Shaun Douglas, the actor playing her lover, Quaid. Shaun Douglas had been her first screen crush and the magic had never dimmed. It might have flickered a little, though, when she'd first met him the day before and discovered that, upon close inspection, the fabled golden locks of Shaun Douglas had distinctly graying brown roots and the secret of the actor's much-vaunted youthfulness might be told by the fine line of face-lift scars hidden at his hairline.

Just as Lissa was collecting herself to respond, Shaun galloped back up. "Great take, huh?" he asked the director.

"We might be able to salvage parts of it," Jack answered with an icy glare to Matthew Briggs, who had gone back to his seat and was thumbing through the script, oblivious to the hostility being directed his way by disgruntled crew members who were already starting to set up again to reshoot the scene.

"Parts of the scene?" Shaun echoed, dismounting stiffly and wincing as he landed a bit too hard on the foot he'd had a bunion removed from.

"Parts," Jack reaffirmed. "Seems Mr. Briggs here"—he swept his hand out in a gesture of mock courtliness to indicate the novelist—"was not happy with the interpretation Lissa was bringing to the role and yelled for a cut."

"You what?" Shaun asked angrily, turning to Matthew Briggs. Briggs looked up.

"*You* called for a cut?" the irate actor repeated.

Briggs eyed him calmly for a moment before standing up.

Lissa watched him rise. His movements were deliberate and unhurried. He was not in the least intimidated by the irritation of either an international star or an entire movie crew. His imperviousness to those things fascinated Lissa. She was aware of a tendency, which she fought in herself, to be too eager to please. The annoyed crew on the set stopped chattering as everyone felt the charge of anger leaping between the two men. They were both tall, each a couple of inches over six feet. But even though Shaun Douglas probably outweighed Briggs by a good thirty pounds, Briggs still seemed far more threatening as they squared off. He had a tightly wound energy that made Shaun Douglas seem slack and unfocused. Everything about the man seemed to bristle, Lissa thought, her own irritation vanishing as she watched Briggs spring to the defense of his work. There was a ferocious intensity about him that Lissa couldn't help but admire.

"That was a perfect take you mucked up, fellow," Shaun bellowed with the belligerence of a wounded water buffalo.

Briggs tensed, ready and waiting for Douglas to make his move. The writer's large features, now animated by a smoldering rage, seemed sharp and aggressive. He had dark, almost black hair that refused to lie flat against his head. He had too little meat on an expansive frame. Bones and hard knots of taut muscle protruded from his jeans and denim jacket.

"It might have been perfect for your chew-up-the-scenery style of acting, Douglas," the writer answered. "But to anyone who cares about the story behind that scene, the acting stank out loud. Yours as bad as hers."

Lissa was so absorbed by the force of Matthew Briggs's intensity that she had forgotten she was at the very center of the drama unfolding in front of her. It was her acting he was cutting to ribbons. All she could think about was how incredible it was that the writer wasn't cowed by Douglas's celebrity. Or by much else, it appeared.

"Buddy, you've just stepped a little too far over the line here," Douglas said, letting the Western accent he'd used as Quaid slip back in to drawl out his words. "Now either you apologize or . . ." The actor balled up both his hands into huge fists and leaned back to pull one behind him.

"Or what?" Matthew Briggs sneered. "You'll hit me? Forget it, Douglas, I'm here to see to it that no pat

A High, Hard Land

Hollywood solutions are inflicted upon my novel. Save the duke-outs for the paying fans. I'm not interested."

As Briggs turned to leave, however, Douglas unleashed his cocked fist, bringing it around in a wide arc. Briggs caught the motion out of the corner of his eye and ducked away, leaving Douglas to land his haymaker on empty air. Tossing the targetless punch threw the beefy actor off balance. Trying to save himself, he landed hard on his bunionectomy and howled out in sudden pain.

"You see, Douglas," Matthew Briggs admonished the actor coolly, "Hollywood solutions just don't work in reality, and if there's one thing we have to have in this film, it's reality. Without it we'll just end up with a sappy, overwrought Western."

Briggs turned to the crew watching the performance in goggle-eyed amazement. "Now," he asked them, "none of you wants that, do you?" Heads jerked automatically to answer in the negative.

"What about you?" He turned for the first time to Lissa, who had gone to help Shaun Douglas, letting the actor, wincing in pain, lean on her shoulder.

She glared at the man who had humiliated both her and her costar as his gaze came to rest upon her.

"Is that what you want?" he badgered her.

"Is what what I want?" she demanded tightly. As far as she was concerned, Briggs was rapidly approaching the line that separates an artist defending the integrity of his work from a prima donna having a tantrum.

"Do you want to end up with a typical piece of Hollywood tripe?"

"Of course not," she sniffed.

"Well then, can I expect you to stop acting like the damned Spritzi Soda Girl?"

In the sudden silence that fell, a muffled giggle was clearly heard. Lissa felt herself go cold with rage. Briggs had indeed crossed the line. Whatever admiration she'd felt for Matthew Briggs for defending his work vanished. His reference to a past she was trying hard to put behind her was both unkind and uncalled for. With all the control she could muster, she turned to Jack and asked, "Will you and Mr. Briggs please come with me to Sidney's trailer?"

The two men silently followed Lissa to a waiting Jeep and drove to the trailer where the producer of *A High, Hard Land* was embroiled in a dispute with the local teamsters union. The three entered the trailer as Sidney Feldman screamed, "You thugs are a curse on the film industry!" He then slammed the phone down and reached into his top desk drawer for an antacid tablet. At the sight of his female lead, director and screenwriter, all looking as if their best friend had either just died or would shortly, he grabbed a second tablet and popped them into his mouth.

"Yes, my children," he said, greeting them with a chalky smile. "What can I do you for?"

Lissa brought herself up to her full five foot four inches and announced calmly, "Either Mr. Briggs is banned from the set or I will be unable to work." Lissa hadn't known until she spoke just what she would say. Once the threat was out, though, she realized it was true. She couldn't go on being Jeannie in front of a man who jeered her.

"Banned from the set?" Sidney asked, standing up to his full five foot four and leaning across the mammoth desk that took up nearly all the floor space in the trailer. "It's only the second day of principal photography and you're talking 'banned from the set'? You should be talking 'what a wonderful picture we're all going to make together.' You should be talking 'be my child's godparent.' You should not be talking 'banned from the set.'" Throughout his monologue, Sidney, who was as fine an actor as any he'd ever employed, let his voice rise dramatically until it reached a crescendo on his last four words.

When he had captured the attention of all the injured parties, Sidney slumped theatrically back into his chair, playing the put-upon producer to a tee. "Tell me now," he asked with weary patience, "what is the problem?"

Feeling like three naughty schoolchildren in front of the principal, no one spoke. Lissa finally broke the silence. "Mr. Briggs ruined a perfectly good take because he was unhappy with my performance."

"Is that true, Matthew?" Sidney asked.

"Partially. If I'd felt the take was 'perfectly good,' I wouldn't have ruined it. It wasn't. So I did."

Lissa turned to Matthew Briggs. All the anger was gone from him. He had stated his opinion with such conviction that he'd made it sound as if he were explaining something terribly obvious and fundamentally irrefutable. His steadfastness unsettled Lissa. In her mind, the memory of her performance began to echo with a hollow, tinny ring. It had none of Matthew Briggs's resounding conviction.

"So, it's just that simple, eh?" Sidney interjected with a sigh. Turning to his director, he asked, "Was the take any good, Jack?"

"I don't think that's the question," Lissa interrupted, shaking off the doubts Matthew Briggs had planted. "The question is, why should this, this"—she waved her finger in his direction—"this man be allowed to make that decision?"

"And a very good question it is," Sidney agreed, shaking his head. "The answer is not so good. The answer has to do with lawyers and deals and other not-so-good things. What it comes down to, Lissa, my love, is that Matthew had one nonnegotiable demand in his contract. Didn't you, Matt? Would you please tell Lissa what that one demand was and why my hands are now tied?"

Matthew Briggs turned and looked at Lissa Bauer, really looked at her for the first time. Close-up she looked much younger, smaller, more vulnerable than she had under the harsh glare of the artificial lights. She also looked nothing like the annoying Spritzi Soda Girl, her most popular commercial incarnation, in which she'd embodied that product's effervescent sweetness with a cloying sugariness of her own. Oh, she still looked like what she was: a movie starlet whose star was rising. She had the requisite mane of tawny curls, the whiter-than-white teeth, the perfectly adorable chip of a nose, the cornflower blue eyes, the figure designed to stir the fantasies of every man who saw her. But, at the moment, all that physical glory was shadowed by something that Matthew Briggs was distinctly surprised to see: hurt. For a moment, his outrage cooled; he had hurt the small woman beside him.

He wobbled for a moment on the verge of apologizing, of retracting everything he had said. Then he remembered the other Jeannie, the real one, the one he had written his novel about, and he knew that he couldn't take back even one of the hurtful words he had said. To do so would be to betray the real Jeannie, her life and her bravery. If he caved in now, Matthew told himself, he might as well chuck it in and start writing sitcoms for television.

"I am legally entitled to remain on the set," he finally answered. "It's in my contract. If I'm banned, the script and my novel go with me."

"Look, Mr. Briggs," Lissa said, struggling to keep her voice even. "You may be legally entitled to be on the set, but you have no right to fire off whatever critique happens to spring into your mind."

For a few brief seconds a battle raged within Matthew Briggs. He honestly did not want to hurt the woman beside him. She had surprised him. It was clear that she was something far different from the vapid screen personality he had expected. There was a strength in her that drew him. She was most definitely not the Spritzi Soda Girl. He'd miscalculated that much about her and miscalculated it badly.

That was unlike him. He had spent most of his life analyzing people, figuring out what drove them and why. He'd done it even as a boy, long before he'd started writing novels. When he was younger, he'd met each person as an individual, free from any occupational stereotypes. As he'd gotten older and his inventory of acquaintances had grown, he'd come to see the wisdom in stereotypes. He'd found lawyers to be, by and large, careful, meticulous people. Professors were more likely than usual to be absentminded. And actors. Actors had to be the type of people who enjoyed displaying themselves. Of the actors Matthew had known, this turn of the temperament was almost invariably associated with a certain shallowness. That was what he had expected from Lissa. That was not what he was getting.

Like any man, he was not immune to a lovely face or a graceful figure, but he always demanded more. With each word that this confounding starlet spoke, Matthew knew that there was indeed a great deal more to Lissa Bauer. She had a depth that aroused his interest, that intrigued him powerfully, that he wished he were in the position to explore. But he wasn't. His first obligation had always been, must always be, to his work. That was what, finally, impelled him to speak.

A High, Hard Land

"The critique I fired off did not just 'happen to spring into my mind,'" he answered her levelly, with an earnest voice. He had something important for her, and her alone, to hear.

"My book," he continued, "is about courage. The courage of one woman to live a hard life in an unforgiving land exactly the way she wants to live it. But it's a quiet kind of courage. It doesn't force itself on anyone."

Lissa felt him struggle to communicate the essence of his work to her. His intensity compelled her to extend herself to him, to reach out for the message he was sending. She nodded and he continued.

"The people of the high plains have to scrape to survive. They can't allow themselves the luxury of big, showy emotions. Their emotional lives are played out on a subdued, internal stage. Do you understand what I'm saying?"

Lissa nodded. She wished she'd flown out earlier to Alta Mesa, New Mexico, where they were filming, so that she could have gotten more of a feel for the land and people. But she had been cast at the last moment and had barely had time to pack and find someone to come in and feed her cat.

"So," Jack Myers, the director, spoke for the first time. "Everything's settled. Lissa plays it a little smaller and everyone's happy, right?"

Matthew turned to Jack with something approaching pain searing his eyes. "That's exactly the kind of simplistic Hollywood thinking that I'm here to guard against.

Just 'play it smaller' and that solves everything? Well, it doesn't, Mr. Myers. What we should be after here is truth. Isn't that what art is all about?"

"Gentlemen, gentlemen," Sidney interrupted before the director could deliver a snide put-down. "Come on, we've got a lot more to agree about than disagree about. You, Jack, I know you loved Matt's book and his script. It was just what you were looking for. You wanted a change of pace from your usual. Something with a little less emphasis on action and a bit more on character. That was your major incentive for signing on. And you, Matt." He faced the writer. "You've told me you've admired Jack's work in the past. *Gain the Earth. A Fine Compulsion. Back for Seconds.*" Sidney reeled off a list of some of the director's better movies, carefully skipping over the car-crash epics that were all Jack had been directing for too long.

"And you, Lissa." The producer turned to his female lead.

Lissa's stomach lurched. She knew her reasons for being on the set of *A High, Hard Land* and didn't particularly care to have them described in detail. Not in front of Matthew Briggs. Since the days of the Spritzi Soda ads, she had painfully inched her way up the acting ladder, scrambling for the only parts offered to her—ingenues in bawdy teen sex comedies. To date, her entire cinematic career had depended on how she filled out a bathing suit. She knew she hadn't been anyone's first choice to play

Jeannie Duncan, the beloved heroine of Briggs's best-seller. She had groveled for a chance at it; studied with a coach to get the high plains accent down cold. Four times she had tested for the role before it had finally gone to another, slightly better known actress, trying like Lissa to pull herself into the front ranks. Only at the last moment, when the other actress had developed a serious case of mononucleosis, had Lissa been cast as Jeannie Duncan.

Even now, Lissa felt that she was barely hanging on to the role of her life by her fingertips and that Matthew Briggs was threatening even that precarious hold. She certainly did not want her acting career recapitulated in front of him. Sidney, master of diplomacy that he was, realized that and said only, "And you, Lissa, you're involved in this picture because you want a chance to grow. To stretch a little."

"Matt." He turned to the novelist. "With all modesty, you confided to me that I was the reason you signed on."

"That's true, Sidney," Matthew Briggs agreed, his demeanor warming. "*The Forgetting Pond* was one of the few movies I've ever seen in my life that truly had an impact on me," he said, naming a film that Sidney Feldman had written, produced and directed. "It's still my all-time favorite."

"Mine, too," Lissa added, surprise and the memory of the film overcoming her hostility. "I saw it when I was eleven years old and have never been the same since." She looked over in amazement at Matthew Briggs. It was difficult for her to believe that Sidney's tender story about a lonely black girl growing up during the Depression could have affected him as powerfully as it had her.

"There, you see," Sidney said, beaming at them, "you two have something in common. You both love me. So go on, get out of here. Go start a Sidney Feldman Fan Club and I'll send you eight-by-ten glossies. Autographed, no less."

Reluctantly, Lissa stood. She still had not forgiven Matthew Briggs for his outbursts. Or for his arrogance. Or, and most painfully, for his low opinion of her talent. But she found it hard to completely dislike anyone whose favorite film was *The Forgetting Pond*. Besides, nothing in her life had ever come easily. She had fought for everything she'd gotten. If she now had to fight to win approval from the man who had created the character she was playing, so be it. Before this movie was in the can, she thought with determination, she'd force Matthew Briggs to admit that she *was* Jeannie Duncan.

*C*hapter 2

Did Sidney ream that jerk's butt?" Shaun Douglas pounced upon Lissa the moment she walked out of the producer's trailer.

"It's in his contract that he can stay on the set," Lissa answered, giving the pertinent fact about Matthew Briggs and his presence.

"You mean we can't get the guy booted out?" Shaun moaned.

Lissa shook her head. "No," she said, adding optimistically, "but he could be good for us." Shaun eyed her dubiously. "Who knows?" she asked. "He might come up with some insights into our characters and all. I mean, who knows them better than the man who created them?" But Lissa's thoughts were not on character insights; they were on Matthew Briggs. Was there really something quite remarkable about him or had she just been around film people for too long? Film people seemed to live in a world of infinitely elastic standards and principles. By comparison, Matthew Briggs, with his firm notions of what was and was not good, seemed solid and real and unbudgeable in a way that Lissa hadn't experienced for a very long time.

"Frankly," Shaun replied sourly, "for all I care, Briggs can save his insights for the Literary Guild."

Lissa heard the trailer door creak shut behind her and turned to see Matthew Briggs emerging. He had to bend a little to keep his head from banging on the low trailer door. In that position, his head crooked a bit to the side, he paused to look at her. His stare made Lissa uncomfortable. There was too much knowledge in his dark eyes. In one glance, he seemed able to take in more about her than she cared to expose. And then he was moving again, coming toward her.

"Look, my outburst today was tactless and I'd like to make it up to you. Can I buy you dinner?"

Lissa was surprised by the apology and disarmed by his forthrightness. He certainly didn't have the glibness of the people she usually associated with. Film people had a way of twisting everything into a joke, taking the importance out of everything with a knowing laugh or an ironic comment. Matthew Briggs did not have that talent, or failing. Lissa hesitated for a moment, not sure if she wanted to spend an entire evening with such a difficult man. Shaun noticed her hesitation and seized upon it.

"Sorry, friend," he interrupted belligerently, "but Miss

Bauer and I already have plans for this evening. Right, Lissa?"

Lissa stumbled for a response. "Uh, right," she stammered.

"Another time then," Matthew said. And then he did something even more remarkable. He smiled. He was clearly not a man who smiled easily. He was like the people of the high plains that he wrote about, with his emotions closely guarded, dispensed rarely and with extreme discrimination. She felt honored to have had one of his smiles bestowed upon her. The expression offered a brief glimpse into another side of the savagely intense man. For the few seconds that it played upon his face, Lissa saw that he was capable of experiencing feelings from the lighter side of the spectrum just as deeply as those from the darker. She had been wondering since she'd first seen him whether he was a good-looking man. That smile erased the question from her mind. It was irrelevant. Matthew Briggs looked the way he was meant to look. Too thin, too intense, but it all came to life when he smiled. As his smile faded and Matthew turned and left, regret nipped at Lissa. For a moment, she was sorry that Shaun Douglas had come to her rescue.

But then, she reminded herself, it was Shaun Douglas she would be having dinner with. That would be something she could tell her grandchildren about. Or at least her mother. Amanda Bauer was the movie star's biggest fan.

"What a perfect opportunity for me to get to know my little costar," Shaun Douglas burst out, wrapping a burly arm around her shoulders. Lissa felt odd having him touch her so familiarly. For her, what they had done that day as Jeannie and Quaid had happened to two other people. Obviously, Shaun hadn't been quite as professionally detached. She slipped out from under his arm and they walked side by side back to the hotel.

The entire crew of the movie was staying at El Portal since it was Alta Mesa's only hotel. The rambling structure had once been an elegant Victorian mansion financed by the vein of silver that flashed through one of the mountains ringing Alta Mesa. The vein had been played out nearly a century ago, and the old house abandoned when the townspeople recovered from their brief bout of silver fever. They returned to the subsistence ranching and farming that had kept them alive since the area was settled in the sixteenth century by the conquering Spaniards, who had made the town the last stop on their push to the north.

Only in the last decade had the people of Alta Mesa discovered an alternate source of revenue: tourists. By beautifully renovating the town's one mansion and dividing it into rooms furnished with authentic period pieces, they had a tourist draw lovely enough to compete with the primitive beauty of the high plains.

Lissa and Shaun paused inside the lobby. It was a lushly appointed space with tall, white columns rising up to the ceiling three stories overhead. Banquettes covered in brocade curved around the base of each column. Crew members sat around waiting for dinner dates and reading *Variety* or talking loudly about other shoots they'd been on and the abominable behavior of this or that major star. A wide marble staircase rose up at one end of the lobby. At the other end was the hotel dining room.

"Shall we try the dining room?" Shaun asked.

"It's either that or drive a hundred miles to the next town," Lissa reminded him.

"So, you want to meet in the bar in, say, an hour or so?"

"Suits me," she agreed, turning toward the staircase.

Upstairs in her room, Lissa flopped down on the canopy bed. She was exhausted. The emotionally wrenching scene with Shaun, followed by the confrontation with Matthew Briggs, had drained her. She lay motionless for several minutes while unbidden thoughts of the novelist whirled through her mind. How did he think she should play Jeannie? she wondered, beginning to wish that she had accepted his dinner invitation. A moment later, she sprang back up, then sat down on the floor with her legs spread out in front of her. Every muscle in her body felt tightly wound with tension and her head was beginning to throb. She leaned her slender torso forward, reaching out to grab the foot extended in front of her. She hoped a few minutes of stretching would relax a few of the kinks and empty her mind of the disturbing doubts that were cropping up. She didn't like the way that Matthew Briggs was undermining her confidence.

Lying down on her outstretched leg she turned her head up. Automatically, her body executed the series of stretches it had perfected long ago in the endless rounds of dance classes that she had taken as a child. Her mind, though, was still occupied with thoughts of Jeannie Duncan and the man who had created her. Strength. That quality ran through both of them in abundant measure. Gradually, the tightness left her body. Still pondering all that Matthew Briggs had said, she showered and put on makeup. Her thoughts returned to reality only when she confronted her open closet.

She had built her career on being something of a lovable kook with a smart, sassy appeal. That appeal had grown naturally out of her own style, which she had emphasized by dressing in stylishly bohemian clothes. That image had served her well. It was a major reason why the Spritzi Soda people had chosen her to represent their product.

But even before she had gotten the part of Jeannie, Lissa had been itching beneath the pert and perky confines of that image. Now, to change out of the jeans and boots she would be wearing every day on the set and into one of the trendsetting outfits in her closet seemed too jarring. She wished she'd brought clothes that fit more with the lost elegance of this hotel or the rugged simplicity of the land. She wished she even owned clothes like that.

A High, Hard Land

With a sigh, she slipped into a pair of striped jeans that had more zippers and pockets on them than a test pilot's flight suit. Over that went a baby tee and an undersized jacket in a glaring citron. She belted it with something that would have looked at home on a Mexican bandit, plopped a beret on her head, and set off.

Downstairs in the bar, Shaun Douglas was holding court. A mob of technicians, all female, surrounded him, encircling the table he sat at with a ring three deep. Lissa stood at its periphery and tried to catch Shaun's eye. The sandy-haired actor's voice carried easily throughout the lounge.

"Oh, God, yes, working with Dina was a dream. A very bad dream."

The crowd of adoring women tittered appreciatively as he dropped the movie queen's name, encouraging the famous voice to rumble on.

"Fortunately, she was with Archer at the time, so at least I didn't have to go through the obligatory charade of an infatuation. Stud service used to be required of all Miss Dina's leading men, doncha know."

As she heard his voice slur, Lissa counted the empty glasses in front of Shaun. She figured at least half a dozen of them were his. As Shaun looked up to signal the waitress for a refill, Lissa caught his eye. He flashed one of his patented heartbreaker grins at her and tapped his glass to signal, "Just one more." Then he went on regaling his audience.

"God, though, shooting in Puerto Vallarta in those days was marvelous. Just marvelous! Charlie, Charles Norton, the director, had a villa there and we lived like kings. Of course, Anthony, my costar, was just in heaven with a parade of local beauties marching through his bedroom. And I don't mean the senoritas, if you catch my meaning." The group around him laughed in lascivious delight at the naughty tales.

Douglas tossed back the drink the waitress slid in front of him while the women coaxed him to go on with his mildly scandalous banter. As the waitress cleared away a trayful of empty glasses from the table, Douglas gripped her by the elbow and ordered another.

"Make it a double!" he called after her. The actor then glanced up to where Lissa stood waiting and held up his hands, gesturing to the raucous crowd around him, indicating that he was helpless, he couldn't possibly leave and disappoint all his fans. Looking back to his admirers, he threw an arm around Elsie, the script assistant, sitting next to him. The pretty, curly-haired brunette beamed up into Douglas's face.

Lissa slumped into a chair at the periphery of the group, debating whether to go back upstairs and have room service send something up or just to skip dinner completely. She was too tired to face the hotel dining room alone tonight. She had already observed the way that a crew filming on location turned into a pack of high schoolers. Cliques rapidly formed with whoever was the most celebrated star or director elevated to the position of head cheerleader or captain of the football team. There were even class clowns, rebels and nerds. It wasn't a scene that appealed to Lissa even when she was in high school, and she was even less eager to participate in it now. With Shaun Douglas by her side, she could have disappeared into the woodwork and happily let him deflect all the attention. But Shaun was occupied. She was halfway out of her chair, ready to head back upstairs, when she heard the voice.

It was a deep male voice and it called her name in a low undertone that still managed to cut cleanly through the brittle chatter. She turned around, surprised that there was anyone behind her in the dim area to the rear of the bar. She knew immediately, of course, who the voice belonged to: Matthew Briggs.

"What are you doing hiding off here in a darkened corner?" she asked, joining him in the shadows.

"Just watching," Matthew answered. "Please. Have a seat." He rose and pulled out the chair next to him.

There was another one on the opposite side of the table. For a moment Lissa debated taking it. How silly, she reprimanded herself. She took the chair he held out. The table was small and pressed Lissa close to the writer. The sense of intimacy was heightened by the darkness that cloaked them. She felt as if she and Matthew Briggs were an audience of two, sitting in a very tiny theater watching the performance on a very large, very busy stage.

"He's quite the raconteur, isn't he?" Matthew asked, jerking his chin in Shaun's direction. The actor was keeping the group spellbound, his hands moving through the air to emphasize points in a story that Lissa could no longer hear. From where she sat, next to the writer in his quiet corner, Shaun and his fans seemed suddenly remote, their antics a bit silly.

"Notice the way he pauses, but keeps his hand held aloft in the air." In the shadows next to her, Matthew imitated Shaun's gesture, holding his own hand out in front of them. It wasn't the hand of a writer. The fingers were strong and capable, the skin weathered and calloused across the palm. The white curve of a scar flashed silver across the fleshy base of his thumb. Lissa was wondering how a writer would have gotten a wound deep enough to have left such a scar, when Matthew went on. "You see, he's symbolically holding his audience's attention. The pause is for dramatic effect and the gesture signals exactly that."

"Do you always dissect people?" Lissa asked, prickling anew at the memory of Matthew's public dissection of her earlier that day.

"Always," he confirmed. "Who knows? I may need a character like Shaun someday. A man who has no sense of himself without an audience."

"You certainly do condemn people awfully quickly," Lissa said.

Briggs whirled around in his seat to face her. "That

was not a condemnation, Lissa." Again there was that quality he had of stating his opinions with such assurance that they seemed irrefutable. "People are miraculously complex beings," he went on, his eyes darkening as they filled with intensity. "Take me. There are reasons, many and deep, why I'm the way I am. Why you're the way you are. Why Douglas is the way he is. Who knows what those reasons might be? Maybe his parents had no love to give him. Maybe they ignored him. Try as hard as he could, maybe young Shaun Douglas, or Delbert Castleberry, as his name was back then, maybe young Delbert could never win his parents' love, approval, even their attention. What must that be like for a child?" Briggs asked, his voice filled with a deep compassion that encompassed all children who suffer so.

"Like they didn't exist," Lissa answered, fascinated by his conjecturing.

"Right," he affirmed, pleased with her power of empathy. "Like they didn't exist. Then, let's say, young Delbert is chosen to be Joseph in the school Christmas play. There he is, sick with nervousness, but determined not to shame himself. He goes out onstage wrapped in his mother's bedsheets and delivers his lines. And, surprise of surprises, an entire auditorium of people listens to him, to what little Delbert Castleberry has to say. And maybe he picks his parents out there beyond the glare of the footlights. And, lo and behold, they're listening, too. And when he's through, they clap! For the first time in his life he feels as if he really exists for them. Then, in that one instant, and for all the years and reasons that preceded it, an actor and a dominant personality trait are both born."

"Did Shaun tell you that story?" Lissa asked, spellbound by the ring of truth that chimed out from the tale.

"No," Matthew shrugged. "It's my story. I made it up. It only represents whatever the truth of Shaun Douglas's life is. The truth of a lot of people's lives who have to have an audience to make their lives seem real to themselves."

"What's the truth of your life?" Lissa asked, unable to resist the question.

When Matthew laughed, there was a warmth in it that Lissa liked. It told her that he was not so serious about himself and his work that he couldn't laugh at both. "With any luck," he answered, "I'll know the answer to that question just a little before they lower me into the ground. And just so that somber event doesn't happen prematurely, how about coming with me for some dinner before I starve. It doesn't appear that your dinner date is going to break away anytime soon."

Lissa glanced over. Douglas now had his arms around the script assistant and the costume supervisor and was beginning to sag noticeably between the two. "I'd have to agree. But I don't know if I'm up to the scene in the hotel dining room."

"Glad to hear it. Listen, if you promise not to tell, I'll take you to the best restaurant in the area."

"I didn't know there was another restaurant."

A High, Hard Land

"Then you're in for a pleasant surprise."

La Fonda was exactly that. It was a country inn a few miles outside of town run by a local Chinese family. Their ancestors had made the long journey from California to work in the silver mine, then stayed on when it played out.

"I cannot believe," Lissa said, putting her fork down after the first few eager bites, "that I am eating the best kung pao chicken I've ever tasted in my life here in the middle of the high desert."

"Their Mexican food is just as good. They had to learn enchiladas and flautas in self-defense."

Lissa smiled, astonished to find herself feeling comfortable and relaxed. She glanced around at the cozy, nearly empty, dining area. The walls and ceilings flowed softly into one another with the curving grace of all adobe architecture. A few classically elegant Navajo rugs and pottery pieces enhanced the clean, simple lines. A fire crackled in the corner. The spicy scent of piñon wafted through the room on the waves of warmth pulsing from the burning wood. In the next room, a flamenco guitarist played the fiery songs of love and loss brought to the New World by the conquistadores. The tunes, gentled by distance, reached Lissa as the plaintive distillations of desire.

"That one's from Andalucia," Matthew said, listening to the muffled lyrics. His eyes roamed the corners of the room as he strained to make out the words. "It's about a man who loses his heart to a gypsy. Her dancing inflames him; it is like the pelting of rain on trees . . ." Matthew paused and listened some more. "The flash of sunlight on water. He desires her as a man desires the beauty of the rainbow . . ."

Lissa, caught up in the story, waited for Matthew to go on. But the pause lengthened until something changed in his expression and she saw that he wasn't going to continue. "What happened?" she asked, laughing lightly, joking in the way she'd learned from the film people. "Do the gypsy and the singer live happily ever after?"

Matthew smiled back, trying, as she had, to make light of the song, but his eyes remained dark. "No, once she has his heart, she leaves with her band, vanishing like dew in the sunlight and leaving him to sing his song of sadness, to sing that the man who dreams of holding love dreams of holding the rainbow," he said, finishing the translation. "Do you believe that?"

"That love is a rainbow?" Lissa asked, wishing she could ward off the question.

"That love is an illusion." His eyes held hers.

"It probably is as often as it isn't," she answered, hoping that her answer sounded wiser than it really was.

"But I imagine that love with a gypsy is always an illusion," Matthew probed.

A strange heat rose through Lissa as he stared at her, waiting for an answer. She didn't require a translation to divine the meaning of his question, to figure out who the gypsy might be, arriving with her traveling band to dance for coins and display herself. She suddenly felt that whatever she said would be important, too important. She didn't want that. Not yet. She deflected the dangerous undercurrents of the conversation with just the sort of ironic comment that would have made her a great success at a Hollywood dinner party. "Yes, it's all done with mirrors."

But it didn't seem to win any points with Matthew Briggs. She sensed a gulf opening up between them and knew that Matthew Briggs had probably dismissed her as a shallow creature of the film world, unable to comprehend the majestic depths of his soul.

They ate in silence for several minutes as Lissa fumed. Finally, she glanced up, ready to tell him just how wrong he was and how infuriating his condescension was. But the sight of him stopped her. The angles of his face were etched in gold by the light from the candles flickering on their table. He had a high forehead that ended in dark brows sweeping off above his eyes. Only the tips of his dark lashes caught the candlelight. His eyes were lost in shadow as he tilted his head down. His cheekbones jutted forward to pick up the light, as did the strong ridge of his nose and hard planes of his jaw.

As if her gaze were a palpable touch, Matthew glanced up from his plate and caught her staring at him. Lissa was shaken by the fire that leaped within the ebony depths of the eyes suddenly trained upon her. Matthew Briggs seemed to see and to feel so much more than most people. She felt exposed in front of him and wondered what he would guess to be the truths of her life. The certainty that he would be wrong amused her.

"You're smiling like a woman with a secret," Matthew observed.

"Am I? I guess I was wondering about your impressions of me and how accurately they would match up to the reality of my life."

"Is that a challenge?" Matthew asked, putting his fork down.

"It's whatever you make of it," Lissa answered enigmatically.

"Okay, I'll take a stab at it." He cocked his head and subjected her to a clinically thorough scrutiny. His expression of detachment masked an entirely different internal response. For a moment, all Matthew was aware of was the way the candlelight played across Lissa's lips. They were parted ever so slightly to reveal the bottom edges of white, even teeth. He was sure those lips would feel soft beneath his, and taste sweet.

Mentally chastising himself for being such a pawn to stereotypical symbols of beauty, he turned his mind to the task at hand and gave Lissa the evaluation she had asked for. "Because looks count for so much, too much, in our society, I'd have to guess that yours bought you a fairly easy passage through girlhood. You're bright, but obviously from the way you dress, you're rebellious. So you rejected what your family wanted you to do, which was go to college. Instead you struck out for New York and immediately hit it big with this Spritzi Soda thing. Now you're laughing. Was I that far off?"

"Don't take it too hard," Lissa said teasingly, pleased to have so completely eluded whatever net the novelist used to capture characters. "Everyone figures I was the golden princess drifting through life until Spritzi Soda vaulted me to stardom."

"So what's the real story?" Matthew asked.

As his eyes captured, then held, hers, Lissa's laughter died. The "real story" wasn't one she told many people. Not that she was ashamed of what she had come from; it was more that she was protective of her roots. She didn't want her past becoming fodder for a publicist to patch together into a studio bio. She had never lied about it but had just stuck to the bare facts and let the publicists embroider whatever they wanted to around them. But, for some reason, it was different with Matthew. She wanted to tell him about herself, her family. To prove to him that she wasn't the vacuous creation of commercials and cheapo movies that he assumed her to be.

"You're right," she started off. "Looks do count for too much in our society, but money counts for more." She'd tried to keep her voice light and casual. To glide over the subject of her past. But there were too many sharp edges on too many memories to hook her. "And money was one thing my family was always woefully short of. I was the baby, the last of five children. There were six altogether in my family. Four boys, one girl. One mother." Lissa deliberately skipped over an accounting of her father. Matthew would get the truth, just not the whole truth. Not the parts of it that were still, and always would be, too painfully raw. Which meant anything that had to do with her father.

"The very first thing I can remember was bouncing up and down in my crib trying to sing 'Too Darn Hot' along with my mother, who was rehearsing for a dinner theater production of *Kiss Me Kate*."

Matthew's smile welcomed the memory and eased Lissa into a warmer perspective of her early years.

"My mom, Amanda, and my father met while they were both in the road company of *South Pacific*. The manager of the troupe absconded with company funds and left everyone stranded in Minneapolis. Most of the cast made it back to New York, but my parents stayed, got married and decided to bring culture to the provinces. Culture." Lissa's mouth crinkled into a wistful smile. "We had culture coming out our ears. Every one of the little Bauers could play an instrument or dance or sing or do all three. My oldest brother is with Ballet Repertory in New York now and the youngest just signed a contract with the Santa Fe Opera for the summer season. Another brother paints and the fourth one is a photographer. So there was always culture, just no money."

As Matthew listened, he saw how badly he had misjudged the woman across from him. As her memories swirled about her, her face, the face he had judged to be of a standard Hollywood perfection, took on an entirely different cast. There was a new complexity behind the blue eyes, rosy cheeks and creamy skin. "My family wasn't too well-off, either," he put in, feeling the lameness of his comment, but not knowing what else to say.

"That's how a lot of people translate poor: not being well-off," Lissa answered softly. "But that isn't what it was for us. We were capital P-o-o-r. Tell me, what was your favorite treat as a boy?"

"My mother was pretty good with a German chocolate cake," Matthew answered.

"In my family the big treat was slices of salted raw potato." Lissa saw the look of sympathy flash across Matthew's face and waved it away. "I'm not telling you this for you to feel sorry for me. I wouldn't trade my childhood for anyone's. I just couldn't stand for you to go around with a set of smug assumptions about who I am just because I've done some soda pop commercials. It wasn't sad growing up poor. For example, we couldn't afford a television, so we made up our own programs and acted them out with props and costumes from my parents' trunks.

"I mean, we made do," Lissa continued, basking in the light from Matthew's eyes. It was almost as if he were watching her thoughts. That he could see her and her brothers tossing pretend grenades across the couch-fort at one another in a reenactment of some war drama or staging their own version of whatever musical their mother was appearing in at the moment. "It was that, the making do, not rebelliousness, that determined the kind of clothes I wore back then. The boys all handed down every scrap they ever wore. When it was finally too small for any of them, I would get it. Fortunately, I was a tomboy and quite content to live in old T-shirts and jeans."

"But then came puberty," Matthew guessed.

Lissa nodded. "Right. And the start of the most miserable years of my life. It's astounding how cruel kids can be. Up until then, I'd always been part of this pack of boys that were my brothers' friends. But then in junior high everything changed. Suddenly, the boys didn't want a skinny ragamuffin tomboy hanging around them anymore. So I tried to make friends with some of the girls. It didn't work. Not with my hand-me-down clothes.

"So I started to modify my wardrobe. I turned saggy old T-shirts into minidresses and wrapped every old belt I could find around the waist. I took in the jeans until they fit me like a second skin. I dyed the old shirts with girlish pastel colors. I did everything I could to try and look normal. Stylish. Of course it was a fiasco. I looked odder than ever. After a while, I finally made a few friends, a couple of other kids who were also on the outer fringe. They started dressing like me. We encouraged each other and tried to pretend that it was our choice to be outsiders, that we were proud of being different. It was a lonely time."

Matthew gave a short, sharp burst of ironic laughter. "And then the Spritzi Soda company took you and your madcap image and made it into every pubescent girl's ideal."

"It is kind of funny, isn't it?"

"I'm not laughing at you, Lissa," Matthew said tenderly. "There's no hurt in the world like the kind we go through in adolescence, and yours was worse than most. I retire any and all smug assumptions I may have made about you and offer apologies for the crack I made today."

"Apologies accepted," Lissa said. Her spirits bobbed up like a ball that had been held underwater.

Having seen the complexity that lay beneath such a beautiful surface, Matthew found Lissa all the more attractive. As she tilted her wineglass to her lips, the candlelight played along the ivory column of her neck, the underside of her chin and down her throat. Matthew couldn't remember ever having seen anything lovelier. His groin tightened in response, his body already answering a call that he hadn't consciously responded to. This was not like him. He was not a man to go lusting after starlet ingenues in bandoleros and berets. But that argument exerted no sway over his body. With each gesture she made, each flick of her doelike eyelashes, each beat of the pulse in her neck, he wanted her more. Wanted her until the need became a deep ache within him. That he could not will the ache away infuriated Matthew Briggs.

With Lissa still beaming from his apology, he growled out, "Exactly how old are you, anyway?"

"Exactly?" she asked, startled by his sudden change in tone.

"You are out of your teens?"

"Of course I am," she snapped playfully. "For, let me see." She ticked the months off on her fingers. "For exactly seven years, nine months, three weeks and four days. Is that 'exact' enough for you?"

"You're twenty-seven years old?" Matthew asked, relief flooding through him. It was one thing to want a woman uncontrollably. It was quite another to lech after a poppet. "Why on earth do you go around looking seventeen then?"

"Looking seventeen is my stock-in-trade," Lissa answered icily. "It's what got me into commercials and teen movies, and it's part of what got me into your masterpiece," she sniped.

"Look," Matthew explained, "I'm delighted that you're only six years younger than me."

"Why?"

"Before you ask me questions like that, I'd better warn you about myself. I have a very bad, very unbreakable habit of always telling the truth."

"Good, because that's what I want to hear," Lissa said. Her every sense tingled and she pronounced the words with more courage than she felt. What she was feeling was the tiniest bit frightened. An invisible cord of menace seemed to stretch between her and Matthew Briggs. It bound her to him and was, even now, drawing her closer, closer to him and to the danger she sensed lay in him and in his answer. She repeated her question. "Why?"

Matthew leaned closer to her until she was reeling

from his nearness, her thoughts muffled in the heat and smell of his body. "Because I want to make love to you, Lissa Bauer. To a woman, not a girl. Because your beauty stirs me, but the woman beneath the shell of that beauty touches me in a way that I haven't been touched in a very long time. Perhaps ever."

Lissa had braced herself for Matthew's words, but the potent strength of what he had said overwhelmed and disarmed her. She could not shrink from him and play the coy games he had eschewed. His honesty called forth her own: she wanted him just as badly. She wanted to know the feel of his hard, rangy body on hers, the taste of the mouth that could form such devastating words.

Misinterpreting her silence, he stood, putting his napkin on the table and reaching for her elbow to help her up. "I've shocked you. I'm sorry. It would have been wiser, probably more strategic"—he quirked an ironic eyebrow—"to have pretended indifference." He slapped a stack of bills on the table as Lissa got to her feet.

The drive back to Alta Mesa was an exercise in strained silence. The night was as black as the bottom of a mine shaft except where crystalline pinpoints of starlight pierced the sky. The lights from the pickup truck's dashboard illuminated Matthew's features. In the darkness, Lissa was free to study them. He did scare her with his honesty, his intensity. He was so much his own man and such a real one that he made the men she'd been meeting since she'd started acting seem like pale imitations, copies of the real thing. She had had no trouble keeping those men in a tidy place at the back of her life while her career occupied center stage. But Matthew Briggs was not a man to be tidily arranged. He was a wild, sprawling creature that no man or woman could ever control. And that scared her. Almost as much as it tantalized her. She slid a few fractions of an inch closer to him.

"Why does a novelist drive a pickup truck?" she asked to break the silence that was building a wall between them.

"This novelist drives one to haul horses or grain in and to drive over roads a foot deep in either snow or muck. I own a ranch not too far from here. On the other side of those mountains." He pointed off toward a range lost in the inky black night.

Guided by an instinct that told Lissa there would be just one Matthew Briggs in her life and that he could vanish as suddenly as he'd appeared, she reached out and touched the hand he'd extended. He gave her a hard, piercing look to see if she understood the full import of what she was doing. Lissa understood. Matthew pulled the truck over to the side of the lonely road and stopped.

He took the hand she had offered in his and brought it to his lips. Without ever letting her eyes slip from his, he pressed her palm to his mouth. The touch of his lips against the sensitive flesh of her hand melted Lissa. Electric whorls of sensation spun through Lissa's body as Matthew's tongue laved the tingling skin of her palm.

A High, Hard Land

"Is this what you want, darling?" he asked, pulling her so close to him that his words were a warm caress. He stroked her hair with a gossamer touch she would never have dreamed his large, strong hands capable of. It lulled her into a dreamy haze where thinking became a dreary chore. She wanted only feeling, this feeling of being luxuriously pampered, of being taken care of, to go on forever.

When had she ever felt taken care of? Not when she was a child, playing "little mother" to her unruly tribe of brothers. Not with any of the men she'd ever been involved with. Matthew went on stroking, his hands weaving a magic aura around them. Lissa wanted to be contained in, sheltered by, that wondrously sensual aura.

"I don't know what I want, Matthew," Lissa answered, "I only know what I don't want. I don't want to end tonight with a wall between us."

"So what you're saying is that you'd like a sample before you make your selection."

"Matthew, are you always so hard on people in your life?"

Her question stopped him dead with its unerring accuracy. He was hard. Hard on himself and hard on the women he'd loved. His relationships in the past seemed to have existed in shadows. Lissa was so unlike that. Maybe it was just that, her lightness, her radiance, that drew him. He hungered for that in his life the way a plant hungers for sunlight. Looking at her as she waited for an answer to her question stirred him beyond his ability to analyze and order. Passion flooded through him like a warm, drenching rain that surged to the innermost reaches of his heart. He'd never hungered so intensely for a woman in his life. Not since hot-blooded adolescence had he known this feeling of being absolutely at the mercy of desire. With an effort, he calmed the hunger pounding in his blood. He wanted to capture every second of discovery, wanted their experience whole and undiluted.

Lissa watched, mesmerized by the savage pulsing of the vein at Matthew's neck. And he watched her. She felt as if he were absorbing every particle of her being through his dark eyes. They asked for so much. "Wha . . . what do you want from me?" The question was pulled from her.

"I want to know you," he said softly. His voice trembled with the need he was restraining. "I want to know the look in your eyes the first time we kiss. I want to know the feel of your legs wrapped around me when we make love. I want to know the sounds you make when my love has satisfied you."

Matthew's feverish litany was like a wizard's chant. It brought her further and further under his spell until she too wanted to know all those same things about the man casting such a spell. Her eyes were open as he brought his lips to hers. She saw the stab of almost agonized pleasure that flashed through their fathomless depths as his mouth found hers. She knew that he saw the same surge of emotion register in her eyes, that he saw it turn to a dazed languor as his lips brushed gently across hers, then pulled away.

A High, Hard Land

His lips were parted as he stared at her, his breathing ragged. He savored the expression on her face, just as fully as he had savored that first hint of a kiss. Her lips, just a hairsbreadth from his, throbbed from wanting. Matthew spanned the distance with the probing tip of his tongue. It caressed her lips with an infinitely tender touch, tantalizing her as he ran it over her lips with an intoxicating lightness. She could not resist. His eyes on her became part of the darkness she wanted to surrender to. He was still watching as her eyelids fluttered closed and a soft moan whispered from between her tortured lips.

Then Matthew's lips were fully on hers, taking what they had only teased before. And Lissa gave him her mouth, answering the primitive demands he made. She lured his tongue into her mouth, gliding her own over it in a leisurely exploration that made Matthew's heart lurch violently against her as he pressed her closer. It was a revelation to Lissa that she could wield such power over this headstrong man, that she could cause him to tremble and groan in her arms. She suddenly wanted him to know the effect he had on her, the way she wanted him to know everything else about her.

Lissa parted their mouths with a tinkling peal of delighted laughter. Without thinking, she blurted out the first thing that came into her mind. "I guess you won't be thinking of me anymore as the Spritzi Soda Girl."

"Not if you don't act like her again."

All the careening impulses stampeding through Lissa

braked to a halt. "What do you mean?" she asked, hoping that she didn't already know the answer. "Are you still going to maintain that that is the level I was acting on today?"

Matthew rolled back against the truck seat with a weary sigh and looked up at the truck's ceiling as if he might find the right answer to Lissa's question inscribed there. "Is that what this evening was all about? Convincing me that you're a good actor? Because if it was, Lissa, it didn't work. If I had any sense, I'd know enough to lie to you now. If I did that and somehow managed to keep my mouth shut tomorrow and the day after, and the day after that, I might have a good chance of keeping you with me here tonight and in bed for the rest of the shoot. But I can't do it, Lissa. I can't lie to you. I can't do it tonight and I won't be able to do it tomorrow."

Matthew stopped and looked back down to see Lissa staring up at him. A powerful urge to wrap his arms back around her and to tell her that everything was all right charged through him. He wanted to protect her from hurt. But he couldn't. Too much was at stake. There was genuine sadness in his voice when he finally spoke. "You played Jeannie like the Spritzi Soda Girl today, Lissa. I had to tell you that, and I'll have to tell you tomorrow if you do it again."

Lissa could not believe his words. When she finally realized that they weren't a joke, that Matthew wouldn't be taking them back with a smile and a laugh, they demolished her. They tore through the cozy web of intimacy she had been spinning around them and left her cold and alone. She pulled stiffly away from him.

"Lissa, please," Matthew begged her. "I'm not saying you're a bad or untalented actor. You have something very special to share with an audience. You have the power to be Jeannie. You just need someone to help you bring out that power. Unfortunately, Jack doesn't seem able to."

"Oh, so now you think you should not only be writing this movie, you should be directing it as well." Lissa attempted to hide her pain behind a veil of waspishness.

"No, I don't understand enough about the technical side of filmmaking to direct. All I know about movies is what they have in common with novels. They both create an illusion. If they're any good, it's an illusion with more truth to it than reality. But to get to the truth in the illusion takes passion, the kind of uncompromising passion that first a writer and then an actor must bring to the characters they create and play." Matthew's tone grew heated as he spoke about what lay at the core of his life as a writer.

"What about compassion?" Lissa asked bitterly. "How about bringing a little of that to the people around you?"

"Lissa, I know I seem brutal. Maybe I am. I'm not sure. All I know is that I can't betray either my work or the people who inspired it."

"Apparently, you have no such qualms about betraying what was happening between us tonight. Or was there anything happening, Matthew?" Lissa asked harshly.

"Maybe it was just another one of the 'passionate illusions' you've dedicated yourself to fabricating."

"No, Lissa." The line of Matthew's jaw hardened. "It was real. We both felt its power. I can't deny that and neither can you."

"Can't I?" Lissa asked coolly. Then she laughed, a sharp brittle laugh that sliced through the dark mountain night and shredded away what was left of the gauzy web that had enclosed them such a short time ago. "So, Matthew, you aren't the consummate master of human emotions after all. You've made at least one serious mistake already. You see, I can deny what happened between us because, at least from my perspective, nothing at all happened. It was all acting. What do you think of that, Matthew Briggs? Not bad for the Spritzi Soda Girl, eh?"

Matthew turned grimly away from Lissa and started up the truck. Lissa stared out the window. She had salvaged the tatters of her dignity, but at what cost? she wondered grimly. The stars that had seemed so enchantingly radiant before now looked like distant diamonds sparkling cold and hard in a remote universe. She thrust her chin out in determination. She would not cry in front of Matthew Briggs. She would never again let him see the slightest glimmer of her true emotions.

Then, in the silent finality of unanswerable lies, they drove back to Alta Mesa.

Chapter 3

It was the middle of July for Jeannie Duncan in *A High, Hard Land*, but for Lissa Bauer, filming in Alta Mesa, it was still the raw end of a chilly April in the mountains. She shivered a bit beneath the cotton maternity frock that Jeannie was wearing that day. Even with ample padding—a "prego pillow" to simulate a six-month pregnancy stuffed beneath her dress—Lissa was still cold. A spell of bright, sunny weather had caused Jack to shoot the few summer scenes as quickly as possible. Who knew, the director had explained, when a late spring snowstorm might blow in?

So Jack had assigned a crew of men to hit the street where they would be filming early that morning. Armed with heat lamps, they had managed to melt away most of the snow clumped along the street. Then plastic zinnias were planted in front yards and green leaves meticulously taped to the few bare trees that would be in any of the shots that day. If only, Lissa wished, pulling her jacket more tightly around her, moviemakers could exercise their magic over the temperature.

"Oh, just let me dab on a bit more of that radiance we hear pregnant women have so much of." Jerome, the makeup director, flitted around Lissa, flicking at her with the blusher brush. Lissa smiled away the distraction as he rushed off to check out the other women in the scene. When he had left, Lissa tried to compose herself again. For what was far from the first time, she cursed the source of her discomfiture—Matthew Briggs. She hadn't seen him since that night in his truck a week ago. He had vanished. Probably, she thought, because he had gotten hold of the shooting schedule and knew that she wasn't going to be called upon to do any real acting until today, provided the weather was good. Which it was, if you didn't count the cold that was turning her fingers and lips blue. For the past week, Jack had shot mostly action sequences that had required little of her other than hitting the marks that he laid out.

But today was different. Lissa's stomach flip-flopped as she thought about what lay before her. For the first time since Matthew had interrupted the scene on the top of the mesa, she would have to do some real acting. Though she fought the knowledge, she knew she was nervous about seeing Matthew again after what had happened between them. She might have been able to fool him that night, but she couldn't hide the truth from herself: never before had she been so powerfully moved by any man. He had dominated her thoughts for the past week, during which she had dreaded and longed for the moment they would meet again. Now she simply dreaded it. She was certain that he would reappear today, just when she had one of her toughest scenes to act out.

With a sense of detachment, Lissa watched Jack. Like the rest of the crew, he was almost lost within a billowing down parka, hiking boots and a knitted cap as he ordered about the assistants who were preparing the set. He pointed a commanding finger, and a propman rushed forward to adjust a sign mounted earlier in front of Alta Mesa's one church, Our Lady of Sorrows. The sign he adjusted covered the church's real one and read: First Baptist Church of Plainsville. A fictional church for the fictional town the movie was set in.

Out beside the sidewalk in front of the gracefully spired church, a set of rails had been laid down in the street. A wooden dolly with a camera mounted on it rested on the rails. Behind the dolly on either side of the tracks were two men built like Russian weight lifters, complete with ballooning potbellies. These dolly grips would supply the power to move the dolly carrying the camera, camera operator, camera assistant, director and cinematographer once shooting began.

Jack was on board conferring with the cinematographer, Amado de la Cruz. They each looked through the camera's viewfinder, checking that they had the shot they wanted and that the lighting was right. With his eye pressed to the camera, Amado waved to a grip, and the man brought a tall, shuttered light in closer to the white picket fence that had been built around the church yesterday.

Jack checked the scene one last time, then relinquished the camera to its operator who, because of union rules, would be the only person allowed to actually look through the finder while the camera was running. Then Jack turned to where his leading lady was standing off away from the crowd.

"Lissa," he called. For a second, Lissa didn't respond to the name. She was submerging herself in Jeannie Duncan, becoming the pregnant young woman trying to carry her fatherless child and run a ranch at the same time. Lissa broke free of her reverie and went over to where the director stood on the dolly.

"Have a peek at the setup," he advised her, waving the camera operator away from the finder.

Lissa looked and saw the church and a portion of the sidewalk in front of it neatly framed.

"Okay, we're going to track you up the sidewalk to this point. Got it? You won't get out of frame?"

"Got it," Lissa assured him.

Jack draped his arm around her. "You ready for this, kid?"

"I suppose so," Lissa answered, trying to sound optimistic. "I wish, though, that we could take a minute out to discuss Jeannie's motivation here. I'm probably the only person in America who hasn't read Matthew Briggs's novel. And there hasn't been time for me to do any of the research I usually do to prepare for a role, so I don't feel like I'm on real solid ground with my character."

"You know the scene, don't you?" Jack asked testily. "You've got your lines down, I hope."

"Yes, of course, but . . ."

"Well, no sweat, kid. You'll do great. And what's not great, we'll clean up in editing. Now, let's see if we can't get this in one take. Sidney's chewing my butt about budget and everyone's freezing. So, time is gold and cold, *capiche*?"

"Sure, Jack, but . . ."

The director patted her shoulder and sent her on her way. "Clear the set," he said conversationally to his assistant, Stan Davisbury, an officious young man who had made a profession out of bootlicking and who functioned mostly as an extra set of vocal cords for Jack Myers, yelling all the director's orders.

"Clear the set!" Stan echoed in his best tone of loud authority.

Prop, sound and lighting men scrambled out of the scene that was to be filmed. Lissa went to her first mark on the sidewalk. As she walked, she scanned the faces of the crowd. A surge of relief pumped through her. Matthew was not among them. She breathed in deeply and threw her shoulders back. She'd do this scene beautifully, and she'd do it in the first take.

The wardrobe mistress was waiting for Lissa just out of the frame on the sidewalk. She took the jacket Lissa shrugged off and replaced it with a thin shawl intended more for decoration than warmth. It was Jeannie Duncan's go-to-meeting shawl. Lissa adjusted it around her shoulders and let the ends trail over the padding beneath the thin cotton dress she wore. Lissa cradled what was supposed to be her swollen stomach and tried to reestablish the empathic link she had forged with her character. She reflected that she would have done just what Jeannie was doing: she would carry the child of the man she loved no matter what the cost. Even if that man didn't love her. And she would do it with her head held high.

"All set?" Jack asked her.

She nodded, smoothing the shawl over her stomach and taking several deep breaths so that she wouldn't be shivering with cold and blowing frozen air on camera.

"Camera!" Jack called.

The camera operator started the film rolling. "Camera."

"Sound," he called next.

The sound man, with a set of earphones on his head, waited a beat to sync the recording, then called out a confirming, "Sound!"

"Marker," Jack barked.

A camera assistant held a slate on which a complex set of markings recorded the number of the shot being made, the number of the take of that shot, the number of the roll of film in the camera, the type of film and the names of the cinematographer, director and the title of the movie. "Scene ninety-eight, take one," the assistant said before he struck the clapper against the top of the slate and stepped aside.

Lissa felt like a runner at the starting blocks waiting for the gun to go off. That gun was Jack's voice as he called, "Action!"

Lissa started off, careful to control her walk, to make it into the slight waddle she'd observed pregnant women using. But very slight, she corrected herself, as she felt the mannerism become too pronounced, because Jeannie Duncan's is not an ordinary pregnancy. She is spending every day of it either on the back of a horse or doing the chores essential to keeping her ranch running. With each labored step, Lissa sank further into Jeannie Duncan, into the fears she had about her ability to single-handedly bear a child and keep a ranch running. The church where Jeannie had worshipped with her parents when they were alive was one source of strength she drew upon to combat those fears. She came down from the mountain each week for the comfort she found there. And she had continued to come despite the chilly reception she received, which grew colder as her state of unwed motherhood grew more pronounced.

The two strongmen pushed the dolly along the tracks, keeping exact pace with Jeannie's measured footsteps. The sound man followed, monitoring the levels on his recorder. His assistant walked beside him holding a microphone on a long boom up above Lissa's head, just out of the frame being filmed. The procession came to a halt beside the gate in front of the church.

Half a dozen Plainsville women were gathered out in the churchyard. The gate that always stood open was closed. Jeannie paused. The churchwomen glared at her. She opened the gate and walked in. The women turned to meet her, forming a blockade in front of the church door.

"Morning, Miss Trimble," Jeannie chirped with false brightness. "You mind steppin' aside?"

The churchwomen exchanged uncertain glances that turned hard with group support behind them. The woman directly in Jeannie's path was tall and skinny, with a pinched face that held little understanding and less compassion. "Yes, Jeannie Duncan, we do mind," she said with the conviction of the self-righteous. "All of us mind and we been minding for some time now. We was hoping you'd have the decency to stop coming here once you started showin' so bad. But you didn't do that."

"What would you have me do, Miss Trimble?" Jeannie asked, knotting her trembling hands together beneath the shawl. "Hide under my bed? The Lord's house is for us sinners as well as for saints like you."

"I'll ignore your sass, Jeannie Lee Duncan, because you don't have no parents to tell you any better," Miss Trimble continued sanctimoniously. "We're going to have to do it for them. You can't come here no more. It's setting a bad example for our good Christian young folks."

Jeannie suddenly felt all her strength fail her. She was tired of doing it all alone. Tired of fighting. All she wanted was to be held. To listen to someone tell her he loved her and would take care of her.

"I see," she said, her voice trembling over the words. Unutterably weary, her head drooped as she turned away from the church she'd grown up in. Tears shimmered on her face as she walked back out the gate that had been closed against her and back down the sidewalk.

The entire crew watched Lissa finish her walk down the sidewalk. Jack waited a few seconds after its end, then called out, "Cut! And print! Kill the lights. That's a take, people!"

"Hoorah!" one of the churchwomen called out as she and the others with her rushed off to the warmth of waiting jackets.

"Good going, Lissa," the thin woman who had played Miss Trimble called out to her as she bundled up in her jacket. "I don't think I could have physically survived a second take in this cold. You did good. Real good. I almost teared up there myself for a second."

Lissa smiled in acknowledgement of the praise as others came up to congratulate her for getting a difficult scene in one take. Jack called a break, and most of the crew immediately headed for the catering vans where steaming vats of coffee waited. Which is exactly what

Lissa wanted to do as well, but the costumer who was holding her jacket seemed to have vanished. By the time Lissa had found her and reclaimed her jacket, the set was nearly empty. Only then did Lissa notice that one of the trucks parked outside the church held an occupant. She turned away the instant she recognized the truck, but the door was already opening. She could not escape the voice that called out after her.

"They're wrong, you know. All those people patting you on the back. They're wrong. You're enough of an actor to know that at least."

Lissa stopped dead. Anger boiled through her, and she turned to face Matthew as he strode over, his long legs easily gobbling up the distance between them.

"Why," she asked with as much calm as she could muster, "is everyone else always wrong and you always have the right magic answer? Jack Myers has been making films for thirty years. Half a dozen of them have won Academy Awards. How are you able to see so much more than him?"

"He's an action director," Matthew countered. "He won those awards for sci-fi flicks and shoot-'em-ups. He doesn't know squat about how to get subtle, nuanced performances out of actors."

The nimbus of intensity that seemed to swirl around Matthew Briggs was whirling at full force. It animated him with such a powerful life force that he seemed to vibrate with it, making everyone else around seem like a band of sleepwalking zombies. Lissa felt herself being drawn in again by its mesmerizing force. She turned away from Matthew and the magnetism he exerted over her.

"I have nothing further to say to you," she announced sharply.

A hand calloused from roping and tending a ranch halted her retreat and spun her back around.

"You're not going to flounce off until we talk this through."

"We have nothing to discuss. I've already told you that."

"Personally, that may be true," Matthew allowed. "But, professionally, it's crucial that we sit down right now before you sell this entire film down the river for a few cheap tears."

"What are you talking about?" Lissa demanded.

"Let's go for a ride," Matthew suggested. "It's too cold to talk out here."

"An extremely short ride," Lissa warned. "This break will be over soon."

They drove a few miles in silence, letting the heater warm the interior of the truck.

"Well," Lissa prompted, staring fixedly ahead at the cobalt-blue mountains that ringed Alta Mesa.

"Well, you played the scene all wrong."

"You certainly don't mince words, do you?"

"Not when I care about something, and I care about this film. About Jeannie. And I know she would not have reacted the way you did to those women."

"What was wrong with the way I reacted?" Lissa asked exasperatedly.

"Let me ask you this; how did you react when the girls in junior high wouldn't be friends with you? When they made fun of your hand-me-down clothes?"

"I knew I should never have told you about my life," Lissa said, anger singeing her words. "I think it's despicable of you to use what I told you against me."

"I'm not using it against you, Lissa," Matthew replied, with a pleading note in his voice. "I'm trying to use it for you. To make you see how a real flesh-and-blood person, a proud person like Jeannie is and you are, would have reacted to those women. What did you do in junior high?"

Almost against her will, Lissa found herself drawn back to the unhappy days of her adolescence. She was once again in the main hall of her junior high school, standing in front of her locker. A cluster of girls had gathered around behind her. Lissa knew who they were. They were the popular girls. The ones secure in their family's money and their own insulated clique.

"Ew, someone alert the Fashion Police," she'd heard one of them say. "We've got a major violation here." A burst of taunting giggles had followed the comment.

"Yeah, thrift store drive-by." More cruel laughter and "witty" comments followed.

Lissa had wanted to shrivel up and hide away in the darkest corner of a remote universe. But there was no such mercy available to her. There would be no escape. She'd turned to face her tormentors. As she did, the group's ringleader had "accidentally" sprayed her full in the face with a blast from a bottle of cologne. As the stinging spray had dripped down Lissa's face, the group had waited like hungry vultures for her reaction. Waited for her to provide the punch line to their little joke.

Everything inside of Lissa had wilted at such unprovoked cruelty. What, other than being born into a family with too many members and not enough money, had she ever done to be singled out for their maliciousness? But she'd stanched the tears brimming in her eyes.

Instead, with the theatrical flourish she had picked up from her mother, Lissa had dabbed a finger at the gagging cologne dripping down her cheek and brought it to her nose. "Ah, Kate Spade," she said, patting the finger behind each ear. "Not my favorite, but good enough to kill the stink from you bitches." Then she had strutted off, head held high. It was only when her back was turned that Lissa would allow her tears to fall. Not before. Never before. She'd have been damned before she would have let those assholes see her cry. And so would Jeannie. Matthew was right.

"Take me back," she'd said softly, her voice signaling surrender.

There was no triumph at his victory in Matthew's expression. Without a word, he started up the truck and they drove back into Alta Mesa. As he pulled up alongside the catering vans, Matthew put his hand over Lissa's. "You're cold," he said solicitously.

"It does get a tad bit nippy running around in thin cotton maternity smocks."

He smiled and moved his hand to place it over the padding on her stomach. "You make a beautiful expectant mother." The barbed intensity relaxed as he spoke. To Lissa, it was like seeing a turreted fortress transformed by magic into a warm and welcoming cottage. But she had been lured in by that welcome once before and had found it cruelly deceiving. She would not make the same mistake twice.

Still, the feel of Matthew's hand, the intimacy of his words, sent waves of warm delight radiating through her. The sensations, proof of Matthew's power over her, were a grating irritation to Lissa. She wanted to deny any feeling she might have for a man who had expressed such contempt for her work and, by extension, herself. "Surprise," she sniped. "It is possible for the great man to utter words of praise."

Matthew pulled his hand away as if from a hot stove and reached across her to grip the door handle on her side. He flipped it open and a blast of cold air lashed against her. "Looks like the break is over," he said coldly, staring ahead at the crew members beginning to filter out of the catering vans. "Thanks for discussing the scene with me. I know you'll do the right thing about it, what a real actor would do."

Lissa paused as she moved toward the door. "Why do you always use the word 'actor'? Haven't you noticed my gender?"

"If that's the main quality you're basing a career on, my apologies and 'actress' it shall be henceforth. It just occurs to me that we don't have doctoresses and lawyeresses."

As Lissa slid out of the truck, she was assailed again by a feeling of loss, of opportunity missed. But she shook it off as Matthew drove away. What, she asked herself, was she losing in a man who had nothing but criticism for her and contempt for her professional past?

"Good news," Jack called out to her, pulling on his gloves as he approached her. "The rest of the filming today will be interiors."

"Have you struck the set yet?" she asked tentatively, wondering if they'd taken up the rails and dolly in front of the church and converted it back from Baptist to Catholic.

"They're just starting on it. I let the break run a little over, but so what? You bought us all some time this morning." The director beamed at Lissa as he patted her on the shoulder.

"Could you stop them, Jack?" Lissa asked. "I'd like to do another take."

"You'd what?" The director's manner took a 180-degree change from avuncular approval to peeved outrage.

"I'd like to do another take. The first one was wrong."

"Who says it's wrong?" he demanded.

"I do. Matthew Briggs does," she added reluctantly.

"He does, eh?" Jack looked from Lissa to the set that the grips were just starting to dismantle, then back to Lissa.

"Please," she asked him.

"Are you sure you want to do this?" he asked. "Because if we do, it's going to be on your head." She nodded yes. Sighing heavily, he then yelled out to the crew to stop tearing down the scene. They were going to do one more take.

"Another take?" A collective groan went up from the crew.

"That's right," Jack confirmed. He glanced toward Lissa. "Lissa doesn't like the first one."

Instantly, the crew's hostility was turned toward her. Lissa could feel the wave of animosity generated by the people whom she was forcing back into the cold. "Is that true, Lissa?" the woman who played Miss Trimble asked.

Lissa felt she was at a turning point that Matthew Briggs had forced her to. She could either back down, as Jack and the crew were clearly waiting for her to do. Or she could do what she felt was right for her, for her character. She could do what a true actor would do. What Matthew expected her to do. Lissa chose carefully. "That's true," she answered, regretting that the decision she had to make would mean some discomfort for others.

Jack did not bother to hide his annoyance at her decision. "Okay, you'll get a retake," he said harshly. "But just this time. When this is over, I'm putting an end to these little confabs with Briggs once and for all."

With that threat hanging in the air, Jack restaged the scene. When Lissa played it this time, walking up the the church, the hostility she felt from the women who greeted her was real. Instead of shrinking from it, Lissa let Jeannie use that emotion to free her own. She let it transport her back to that hall in junior high where she'd faced down her tormentors. This time, there were no tears on Jeannie's face until she was well outside the church gate.

At the last minute, though, the take was ruined when the sound man, carrying the microphone on a boom above Lissa's head, let it dip into the frame. Her concentration broken now, Lissa flubbed the next five takes. By that time, she and everyone else in the scene was turning blue from cold, and they all had to retire to a van to warm up. Lissa took the opportunity to psych herself up, and when they went out again, she managed to block everything from her mind except Jeannie and what the scared young woman was feeling.

When she walked back out the church gate and down the sidewalk, Lissa knew that she had nailed the scene perfectly. A kind of elation she had never experienced before charged through her. She'd pushed herself as far as she could to reach for perfection and it had paid off. She hadn't settled for the slightly flawed, but acceptable. The mundane, but workable. Now was when she should get the pats on the back, the applause, she thought.

But there were no congratulations this time after Jack called, "Cut." Instead, the director hurried everyone along. "Hustle, people," he called out. "We're running behind now. We'll lose the light if we don't shake it."

In that instant, with the crew rushing away from her without a word, Lissa saw clearly that integrity could take her down an often lonely road. She shrugged and reminded herself that she wanted to be an actor, the best she could be, not a popularity queen. Clinging to that attitude as best she could, Lissa made it through the rest of the day's shooting.

At the end of the day, she fled to the hotel. Tonight would definitely be a room-service night, she thought wearily. Intellectually she knew she'd done the right thing that day, but, emotionally, she wasn't ready to face a crew that held her responsible for having to freeze outside for a few extra hours. She called her order down to room service—a chef's salad and a large pot of hot tea—and was told that there would be a thirty-minute wait. Room service was being inundated that night by calls from cold, tired crew members.

Time for a bath, Lissa decided, hoping a good hot soak would take the chill from her bones and raise her decidedly drooping spirits. She left her door ajar so that room service wouldn't disturb her.

She had barely begun to relax in the tub when the room phone jangled. An unclothed, sopping wet drip into the next room seemed like too great a health risk to

Lissa. Instead, she submerged her ears underwater until the phone sounded as if it were ringing on another planet. The last ring was just fading into silence when there was a sharp rap at her door. Apparently, room service was dealing with the crush better than they'd predicted. Lissa reached an arm out and opened the bathroom door a crack.

"Come on in," she called out loudly. "Just put it down anywhere. Thank you," she added before shutting the door again. Her chef's salad would keep, and she could always order up another pot of tea and tip the delivery person double then. She heard the outer door open, some shuffling around, a door closing, then silence. She slid back down underwater and let the day's chilled tenseness ebb out of her body.

The water was going cool by the time Lissa finally stepped out of the tub and toweled herself dry. She wrapped a towel around herself and opened the bathroom door, wondering if she should spend the evening studying her lines. The next thought that crossed her mind was "What on earth is Matthew Briggs doing in my room?" The first words out of her mouth were to that effect.

"Is breaking and entering a hobby of yours or do you do this professionally?" Lissa asked, proud of the cool composure she was able to fake. Her chilly reception seemed to have little effect on Matthew, who had installed himself with regal ease upon a high-backed wicker chair.

"You invited me to come in," he pointed out. "Your exact words were 'put it down anywhere.' I chose to 'put it down' here." He gestured toward the chair he sat upon, but his eyes never left Lissa's slender figure.

Lissa felt as if the towel she clutched about herself had shrunk to the size of a washcloth as Matthew's gaze raked over the length of her legs and up to the swell of her breasts where they were threatening to spill out over the terry cloth. Lissa felt as if the scrutiny were some perverse sort of test. To squeal and run from his gaze, to admit that he was a man who deeply unsettled her, would be to fail. With a studied casualness, Lissa looked straight back into Matthew's eyes.

The man's force was centered in his eyes, eyes as dark and potent as the strongest espresso imaginable, Lissa reflected. But what was not there was far more unsettling. There was no hint of lechery, lust or even desire. Instead, a kind of surprised and dazzled wonder washed through them.

"You are even more exquisite than I imagined you would be."

Matthew spoke with an almost childlike innocence that completely sabotaged Lissa's cool, calm, collected pose. It was further subverted when he rose slowly from his chair and went toward her. She was trying to decide whether to scream, fall into his arms or land a strategically placed kick to his groin, when Matthew whisked her robe off the bed.

"You'll catch a cold," he murmured, wrapping it around her shoulders.

Lissa turned away from him and quickly slipped it on, belting it securely. "Just why are you here, Matthew?" she asked in what she hoped was a professional tone.

"Didn't Sidney tell you?" he asked. "He said he was going to call half an hour ago."

Just as Lissa was remembering the call she hadn't answered, the phone rang again.

"Lissa, you're back." It was the producer, Sidney. "I tried to call you earlier, but you were out. I sent Matthew over."

"He's already here," she informed him dryly.

"Good. Okay. Here's the deal. Jack is going to walk if Matthew doesn't stop undermining his direction. The three of us have already talked this through. Jack stormed in here the instant shooting was over today, then I called Matthew in. Legally, our hands are tied. We can't boot him off the set and I can't pay to shoot two versions of this picture: Jack's version and Matthew's version. Do you see what I'm driving at here?"

"Vaguely," Lissa answered. Matthew was roaming around her room, examining the clutter.

"Listen, you two have got to get together. These 'artistic disagreements' are costing me money. So what we all decided was that you and Matthew should take some time off by yourselves and thrash out Jeannie's character together. Do whatever you need to do to come to some kind of understanding on how she should be played. Jack can shoot around you for a day or two. God forbid it should take so long. How's that sound?"

"Lousy," Lissa answered. Matthew, his back to her, was leafing through a photo album filled with pictures of her mother and brothers. He turned and peered over his broad shoulder at her. Already fully aware of what Sidney was proposing, he quirked an eyebrow at her negative response.

"I realize that Matthew is not the world's easiest person to get along with," Sidney continued. "But you're going to have to do this for me, Lissa. It's too early in the game for this picture to get off the tracks. I don't want to make this an order, but, no matter what you decide, I'm ordering Jack not to shoot any scene with you in it for the next day or so."

"So," Lissa burst out, "I can take my pick. Either sit around here and count the roses on my wallpaper or go along with this little plan you've cooked up."

"That's about the size of it. I hope you'll look upon it as an artistic opportunity. Matthew has some great ideas for helping you with the character."

"I'll just bet he does." Lissa stretched the phone cord until she could reach Matthew and plucked her photo album out of his hands.

"See you in a day. Two at the most."

"Two days!" Lissa shouted as the producer hung up. "This won't take two hours." The last words she directed toward Matthew Briggs. "Are you always so good at getting your way?" she asked him as she hung up.

"Just when something is very, very important to me."

Lissa sighed. "Okay, I know when I'm beaten. Looks like I'm your captive. What are these great ideas you have for helping me with my character?"

"A. Come out to my ranch. B. Read *A High, Hard Land.* C. See the country and meet the people that inspired the book." Having outlined his itinerary, Matthew asked, "Is half an hour enough time for you to pack?"

"We're not leaving tonight," Lissa countered.

"Why not? If we leave now, we can be at my place in time to get a good night's rest, then start in fresh tomorrow morning."

"But we can't . . . I don't want to . . ."

"Spend the night with me?" Matthew supplied to end her stammering.

"Exactly."

"I promise you, you will have your own room with a door that will lock securely. I can guarantee that the only way anything the least bit improper will happen is if you simply can't control yourself and come sneaking into my bedroom late at night and ravish me."

"And I can guarantee that that will never happen."

"Never?" Matthew questioned, taunting her with a teasing tone.

"Never," Lissa reaffirmed with a decisive finality.

Chapter 4

They *drove straight into the* towering granite-blue mountains that flanked Alta Mesa. Along the way they left behind the tentative, chilly spring that was trying to thaw out the town and moved back up into the snow-packed winter still ruling the heights.

"What are you raising on this ranch of yours?" Lissa finally had to ask as they continued their ascent into the pine-covered slopes. "Mountain goats?"

Matthew's chuckle was warm. "I run a few head of cattle. Not a major operation by any means. Probably more of an excuse for me to live here than anything else. We'll crest the peak in a bit, then start heading down into some of the finest grazing country around."

"Hmmph," Lissa muttered skeptically. She was still peeved at the power play that had been worked on her, but her irritation was leaking away, absorbed by the magnificence of the country around her. The road zigzagged up the steep incline, until they emerged on a treeless ridge above the timberline that looked down onto a valley. Far off to the west, the sun was setting. Golden rays of fading light lay across the land that spread out below Lissa for what seemed an eternity. Rolling pastures of grass just beginning to turn green were studded with explosions of wildflowers. Long trails of cattle slowly ambled back to a distant pen for the night.

A deep sense of calm stole into Lissa as she looked out over the enchanted vision below. Whatever had brought her to this place, she was now grateful for it. The tension that had been so strong in the truck had gradually lessened as they climbed through the mountains. But as she looked down at the bucolic vista, that tension evaporated entirely. Lissa could actually feel its departure, leaving the atmosphere in the truck immeasurably lightened. When she glanced over at Matthew, she found a very subtly, but very profoundly, changed person. The bristling animation that whirled about him was gone. A look of bone-deep contentment radiated from his features, making them seem less severe, less wary. He was like a warrior who had taken off his armor, laid aside the barbed breastplate and weapons of war and allowed his innate humanity to come forth again. Lissa thought the image was apt. For Matthew, Alta Mesa was a battlefield where he had to fight for the integrity of his work. On this side of the mountain—his side—peace reigned.

A curl of blue smoke rose from a hacienda, tiny in the

distance, which was the one sign of human habitation in this high-altitude Eden.

"Looks like we're in luck. That smoke is coming from Teodora's cookstove."

Even Matthew's voice was different, slower, a bit deeper. It dragged leisurely over the words. Lissa thought that his voice probably would sound the same way after he'd made love. She batted the thought away in the same instant it occurred to her and asked, "Teodora?"

"My housekeeper, the woman who is kind enough to keep me from starving and disappearing beneath an avalanche of books and paper. Well," Matthew continued, as they drove down into the valley, "what do you think of the place?"

There was a boyish eagerness in his question that touched Lissa. Matthew wanted her to like his ranch.

"I can't remember ever being in a more beautiful place," Lissa answered simply.

Matthew didn't bother to hide his pleasure at Lissa's verdict. He looked over, pleased to find her absorbed in the landscape. It gave him a chance to study her. A bolt of yellow sunlight striped her face. It was the perfect illumination for her, Matthew thought, happier at that moment than he'd been in a long time. He suddenly realized just how much he cared about what she thought of his place. How much more he cared than he should. More than was good for him or for the work he was trying to protect.

He forced his attention back to the road that was just

beginning to turn a hazy, violet gray as the shadows of dusk spilled across it. But he couldn't help sneaking one more look at Lissa, one more glance at her face, radiant in the last rays of sunshine. Nor could he prevent the lustily poetic impulse that sprang into his mind at that glance: he would have loved to lick all that buttery sunshine from her cheeks, her neck, her mouth. Abruptly, Matthew caught himself and pressed on the accelerator. The truck lunged forward.

Lissa put a hand out to brace herself against the dash and wondered what the sudden rush was, and why Matthew's features had gone hard again. She warned herself that these were dangerous things to be wondering about since she already knew the tumultuous effect he could have on her. A slash of golden sunlight crossed his lips, reminding Lissa of their feel on hers, their astonishing softness and warmth, their power to disarm her. She would have to be on guard against that power, she determined, and turned away to watch the ranch house they traveled toward.

Once they had arrived, Lissa was surprised by the interior of the ranch house. Matthew's nest, though essentially a very large log cabin, was well-feathered and cozy. The long planks of an old, highly polished oak floor shone up from between earth-colored scatter rugs. Deep bookshelves lined the whitewashed, plastered walls of the living room. Curtains in a warm russet print hung at the windows, scooped up and tied at their waists, while an antique lampshade of ruby glass cast a warm glow in the wonderfully intimate room.

"It's not at all what I expected," Lissa admitted.

"And what were you expecting?" Matthew inquired. "Starkly utilitarian rooms? A couple of straight-backed chairs? A rickety manual typewriter?"

"I don't know exactly. It's just that this is so . . . so cozy."

"A home should be cozy," Matthew averred.

Lissa silently agreed wholeheartedly, still drinking in her surroundings. "It's funny but this is exactly the kind of home I yearned for when I was growing up. My mother didn't ever have the time, the money or, really, even the inclination to do much in the way of decorating. As far as she was concerned, curtains were needless frills and she would rather have spent the money on voice or dance lessons. I'm glad now she made that choice," Lissa maintained staunchly. "But still . . ." Her voice trailed off as she looked around and imagined long, peaceful afternoons curled up reading in a well-cushioned chair.

"Matt-you, you're home!" A Spanish-accented voice called out a greeting, cheerfully mangling Matthew's name.

"Teodora," Matthew said, pulling toward him a round Chicana woman, who was wiping her hands on a towel. "This is Lissa Bauer. She's an actor in the movie they're making in town. Lissa, this is Teodora, without whom I would die of neglect."

Teodora stuck out her hand and shook Lissa's enthusiastically, showing two gold-outlined teeth when she smiled. "He's not joking," Teodora confided to Lissa. "This man, when he sits down at his computer back there, he thinks a person can live on words. He don't need food no more. Well, okay, I gotta go. There's posole on the stove and I made up a batch of tortillas. That ought to hold you for a few days. I'll be back when I can."

"Whenever is convenient for you," Matthew said, helping Teodora pull on a fringed leather jacket and holding the door open for her. She trundled out with a backward wave and got into her own pickup truck. Outside, night had fallen and the nip that was always in the air had chilled down to a seriously cold temperature.

"Let's get a fire going," Matthew said, closing the door. As he laid thick piñon logs in the round adobe fireplace, he explained that Teodora lived nearby and dropped in when she could take time out from caring for her own ranch, husband and family. Lissa liked the way he talked about her and the way the woman had treated him. It was clear that he did not consider theirs an employer-employee relationship. He genuinely appreciated and valued Teodora's help.

"The kitchen should be warm. We can eat out there while the rest of the house warms up," Matthew suggested.

Teodora's stew of beef, hominy and green peppers tasted strange to Lissa at first, but by the second spoonful she could tell that an addiction was developing.

A High, Hard Land

"Hot but habit-forming," she pronounced as she fanned a cooling hand in front of her mouth.

Matthew jumped up to pour her a glass of milk. "Here, drink this," he ordered. "It will put the flames out better than water ever could."

Matthew continued to be warmly solicitous throughout the meal, making Lissa feel like a cherished guest instead of a nuisance actor who couldn't interpret a role correctly.

"Shall we retire to the sitting room?" he asked when Lissa finally put her spoon down.

The room was warm when they reentered it and wonderfully fragrant with the mountain scent of the slow-burning piñon. Matthew offered her a seat on the high-backed leather sofa angled to face the fire. He took the chair next to it, resting his feet on an ottoman. Lissa curled up on the sofa and they both watched the flames in a companionable silence.

As Lissa looked at the fire licking along the stout logs, she realized what was so very peculiar about the evening: she was comfortable, totally and completely at ease. She was relaxed in a way she hadn't been in a very long time, with a man who had succeeded only in putting her on edge before. That was what was so odd. Part of her peace was because Matthew himself was so mellow here in his mountain sanctuary.

But there was another reason as well. Though the air between them was charged with sexual tension,

Lissa knew that Matthew would never make another advance. She was as safe with him now as she would be with her brothers. The realization both calmed and prickled Lissa. She glanced over at Matthew, staring intently into the flames, and was no longer convinced that she wanted quite as much safety as she had demanded. She remembered the night in his truck, his mouth on hers with its boundless promise of need and fulfillment, and the tension that had been dissipated so thoroughly began to mount the tiniest bit within her. Matthew's legs were stretched out before him, his elbows resting on the arms of his chair, hands clasped in front of him. Resting his chin on his hands, he stared ahead into the fire, the flames reflecting in his eyes. His body was so large and powerful, yet she knew how devastatingly tender it could be when caressing, kissing. She could imagine Matthew showing an exquisite control with the right woman. With her? The tension that they were both working so hard to deny mounted a bit higher.

"How long have you lived out here?" she asked. "Alone like this?"

Without taking his eyes from the fire, Matthew answered. "You mean without a woman? I've lived here for six years. Though there have been women under this roof, none with any degree of permanency." He turned to look at her. "If that's what you were asking."

"Not really," Lissa said, though, in fact, it was precisely what she'd been wondering about.

A High, Hard Land

"Well, then, since I've brought the subject up, tell me about your involvements. Anyone waiting for you back in L.A.? Some golden California beach boy?"

"How about one golden California calico? All I have awaiting my return is an overfed cat, Hun. Everyone says what a sweet name for a sweet cat until they see her at feeding time. Then it becomes quite apparent that she was named after the barbarian invaders."

Matthew smiled at Lissa's little domestic tale. "Surely a woman with your looks has more than a cat offering to provide companionship."

"In Los Angeles there's always someone offering something," Lissa replied wearily. "In New York, too, for that matter." To guard her past, Lissa had adopted the habit early in her career of not talking much about her private life. It hadn't been difficult, she'd found, since there were so few people she cared to reveal herself to. Matthew was one of the rare ones. She didn't know why, but she'd already told him more about herself than most people learned in a year or two of knowing her, and she still wanted to tell him more. "I learned pretty quickly that most of the offers came with a lot of hidden strings."

"Hopefully, none that have gotten you too tangled up," Matthew said.

"Not too," Lissa answered, dismissing the handful of affairs that had ultimately occupied so little territory in her mind and heart. "What about your amorous past?"

"I'm not sure I can sum it up as neatly as you've done

yours." He paused and tapped his steepled hands against his chin as he thought. "I'm torn, Lissa," he finally answered. "This horrible habit I have of always telling the truth is inclining me to say one thing. But, on the other hand, some truths are better kept for when two people know each other better."

"I've told you more about myself than I tell most people," Lissa prodded.

"All right," Matthew capitulated. "In my 'amorous past,' as you so delicately put it, I've seemed to favor dark women of dark passions." He thought about Lenore, the poet, with her thick mat of black hair and wild, black eyes. Her need had been inexhaustible, yet he had tried to satisfy it until the night she had begged him to do what he could never do to another human, to hurt her. "I'm captivated by a certain brooding energy in a certain kind of woman, but in the end am left with their discontent, if you understand what I mean."

Lissa wasn't sure that she did. All she was sure of was that Matthew had known secrets she had never been privy to. Secrets that tantalized her.

Matthew watched her face light up like a schoolgirl listening to a more experienced chum tell her salacious tales, and wished he had said nothing. Because, for all the air of weary sophistication that she liked to wear, Lissa was an innocent. She was not someone like himself, who was drawn to the darker, less-traveled paths of human nature, where inexplicable passions lurked. That was not to say that he thought her a virginal prude, but just that her nature, in spite of the hardships she'd endured growing up, had a sunnier turn to it than his did. He found her natural goodness enormously appealing and did not want to do or say anything that would sully it. She raised a protectiveness in him that he hadn't felt in a very long time. The women he had gotten used to were more than capable of taking care of themselves and would certainly not have appreciated any sudden bursts of protectiveness on his part. Not that Lissa would have, either. Matthew honestly couldn't say why he felt this sudden urge to shelter a bright and beautiful creature who had managed to tackle Los Angeles and New York all on her own. Still, there was something touchingly tender about her that roused the damnedest instincts. Even as he was puzzling over the odd urge to protect her, he was aching to part her lips again.

Lissa stretched herself out along the couch, her eyes still holding Matthew's. The ease she felt with him made her bold. She wasn't ready yet to overtly instigate anything, but she definitely wanted to explore the possibility with him a bit further.

As her lovely, long limbs stretched out on the couch and she turned glittering eyes on Matthew, his groin tightened.

"Are you teasing or inviting?" he asked.

"What are you talking about?"

"I'm talking about how you look stretched out like that."

"And just how do I look?" Lissa demanded.

"Like a woman waiting for her lover. Like a woman anticipating the pleasure she will draw from his body and return with her own."

"I didn't think you would descend to this," Lissa retorted.

"Descend? Ascend would be the word I would use. And if I'm too blunt for your tastes, I'm sorry. I already warned you that truth was a bad habit of mine."

"Truth or just a very sophisticated come-on?" she challenged.

"Don't flatter yourself, Lissa. You're right, I know how sweetly seductive your lips are, and I've ached to taste them again. And you would yield them to me, wouldn't you?"

"Don't flatter *yourself*," Lissa snapped.

"I'm not. I don't consider a few kisses to be a trophy worth bragging about."

"And what is the trophy you're after?"

"I'm too old for collecting trophies, Lissa. I'm not interested in symbols of victory, in conquest. I want you. I've said it before and I won't deny it now. But I won't coax and wheedle. I won't be one of the swains that pester you for your favors in the cities you call home."

"So then, what do you have in mind?" Lissa asked, her heart thudding out the answer.

"It's your mind I'm concerned about," Matthew shot back. "There's no doubt in mine that once I taste those lips a second time, no power under heaven will be able to stop me. And so, Lissa, there will be no second time until you ask me for it. And no teasing invitation will do. Do you understand me?"

"Better than you'd care to be understood," Lissa shot back, letting the flash of anger hide the symptoms of arousal that Matthew had stirred in her. She pretended that fury, not passion, was making her breathing ragged and flushing her cheeks.

Without answering, Matthew rose and went to the bookshelf. His shadow, cast by the fire, leaped and danced across the rows of books. His real hand and his dark, shadowed hand converged as he plucked a volume from a high shelf before returning to the ring of light.

"Here," he said, tossing a book to Lissa. It was stamped in gold on the front and side with the title she knew so well: *A High, Hard Land.* "You can read this tonight." He switched on a light that overwhelmed the intimate glow cast by the fire. Lissa quickly sat up, the sensuality of the moment brutally washed away in the flood of light. "We've got a lot of ground to cover in the next two days if we hope to accomplish anything."

The precipitous shift in mood was more than Lissa could adjust to. It left her feeling exposed, as if she had opened up too much of herself and what she had revealed had been rejected. She lashed back. "You mean if we hope to turn the Spritzi Soda Girl into a Jeannie that won't embarrass her all-knowing creator."

"You made that interpretation, not me," Matthew said, a note of warning chilling his words. "I'll light a fire in your room. Good night."

The book twitched in Lissa's hands as she fought the impulse to hurl the thick volume at the broad-shouldered figure sauntering away with such insouciance. "You toad," she hissed under her breath, determined not to let him know the extent of her agitation. From the back of the house came the sound of logs being set on a fireplace grate and of matches being struck, then the shuffle of footsteps, and a door slamming shut with eloquent finality.

Lissa continued to seethe for a few more minutes. The last thing in the world she was going to do was read the toad's book, she thought. She slammed it down on the couch beside her and got up to snoop around the living room a bit, looking for clues as to where the chinks in Matthew Briggs's armor might lie. His books, which ran heavily to historical treatises on the Old West and manuals on the care and feeding of quarter horses, were a distinct disappointment. She turned to the oddments displayed about the room. There were Indian pottery shards and arrowheads, bits of antique barbed wire, old-fashioned Spanish bridles and chunks of unpolished turquoise. But Lissa's attention could not be held by any of Matthew's treasures. She considered going back to the bedroom, but knew that sleep was still hours away. She riffled distractedly through a stack of magazines that appeared to be either literary journals or horse raising magazines.

A High, Hard Land

The book on the couch began to seem more inviting. As Lissa's temper cooled, she reminded herself that, for the sake of her role, she really should have a look at the novel. Just the briefest peek, though she doubted that such a maddeningly impossible man as Matthew Briggs would have any insights to offer her. Reluctantly, she sat down on the couch and picked up the novel again. Settling in with a thick book in front of a fire had always been Lissa's absolute favorite way to spend cherished leisure hours. Just picking up the book, even one by such an astonishingly infuriating author, soothed her. She began to read.

On a chilly spring day in 1939, when the melting snows had turned the roads to mud, Jeannie Duncan turned nine years old. Since no one, not even her mother, mentioned it at breakfast or during the morning chores, Jeannie figured that it would be forgotten like her last two birthdays had been. But then at lunch, between asking for the corn bread and for more syrup, Jeannie's stepfather told her that they were going to the rodeo that night. She was balancing a glass of milk in her hand and had to stop and make herself breathe slowly out of her mouth so that she wouldn't spill any in her excitement. But the excitement leaked out anyway. It squeaked out in a strange little strangled whimper of delight. Jeannie knew from the look on her mother's face, from the way she

89

worried the thin fabric of her pinafore apron, that she'd made a mistake. Another mistake.

"Gal," her stepfather said, squinting at her like she was one of the horse trader's wind-broke nags, "I hear one more a them mouse sounds outa you and I'll just leave you at home with a piece of cheese. Wouldn't you rather do that, Little Miss Mousy, 'stead a going to the rodeo?"

Jeannie didn't know how to answer. Didn't know if this was one of the mean jokes he was fond of or one of the tests of her respect that he was even more fond of. Jeannie looked to her mother, who slowly, almost imperceptibly, shook her head no.

"No, sir," Jeannie answered in a voice barely above the mouse squeak.

"No, sir, what?" her stepfather demanded. "Cain't you talk, gal? Your daddy raise you to be a dumb mute as well as a squeaky mouse?"

Jeannie hated it when he talked about her father. She wanted to run away from him. Run to the mountains where he would never find her. Where she could hide out like an Indian and live on berries and honey. But a rodeo. Jeannie had heard about rodeos. Read about them. She *had* to go.

"No, sir," she spoke right up the way her father had taught her. "I do not want to stay home with a piece of cheese. I would like to go to the rodeo." Because her real father had taught her to, she looked him straight in the eye, even though she hated seeing his face. And because she knew it was what her stepfather liked, she added, "Please, sir."

Jeannie got to go to the rodeo.

Lissa stopped. There had been no hint of a petty, tyrannical stepfather in the script. But now that she knew that Jeannie had had one, she understood why her character was so attached to the ranch that her real father had cherished. And why, at a very young age, she had fixated upon Quaid as a sort of sparkling savior, a fantasy figure who might one day rescue her. Lissa read on, completely ensnared by Jeannie's story.

In the next hundred pages, looking through Jeannie's eyes, she saw Quaid, the handsome trick roper, the way the love-deprived little girl had. She no longer thought of Quaid as Shaun Douglas, an actor with face-lift scars and bunions; he became a knight in shining armor who could make a lasso tremble in the air like a hummingbird and swoop like an eagle high over the heads of a spellbound crowd of ranchers and farmers. She was tugged so completely into the story that she became Jeannie Duncan and lost her heart to Quaid Dawson.

The next seven years of Jeannie's life were only sketched in roughly. Her mother and stepfather both died, and she assumed complete responsibility for running the ranch. Her hard, lonely life still had only one patch of light and warmth: her one-sided love for Quaid, the rodeo hero she saw only once a year on her birthday when the rodeo came to town. She had just turned seventeen and was at the rodeo alone for the first time when Quaid noticed her.

Lissa, reading the story of their courtship, was amazed at how perfectly Matthew had been able to capture Jeannie's sad longing as it turned to a woman's passion. A flutter of embarrassment passed through her as she read of Jeannie's desire. It was clear that Matthew knew his subject matter only too well. No doubt he had sensed her interest quickening earlier that evening and had sought to squelch it with a strategic retreat. But even the prickles of humiliation were easy for Lissa to ignore as she immersed herself in Jeannie Duncan's story.

A chill creeping through her several hours later was the first distraction that broke through the enchanted circle drawn around Lissa by Matthew's compelling narrative. She dragged her eyes away from the page and saw that the fire had died away to a few ashy embers. Tugging a Navajo blanket thrown over the back of the couch down onto her legs, she decided she would go to bed in a few minutes. Just a few more pages . . .

Chapter 5

Matthew was awake before his alarm sounded, and he switched it off so that it wouldn't disturb Lissa.

Lissa. He felt as if they'd spent the night together and, in the most significant of ways, they had. His thoughts had been with her all through a very long, but not terribly restful, night. Had he been too frank? Should he have tempered his honesty, denied the desire that pounded through his blood? Had he frightened her off?

Without finding answers to any of those questions, he wondered if she had started reading the book, and what she had thought of it. Hauling himself out of bed, he pulled on a pair of jeans and a flannel shirt. He never heated his room, preferring instead to pile quilts and comforters over himself at night in the winter, then to jump quickly into his clothes in the morning. He hoped Lissa's room had been warm enough.

Quietly, he moved down the hall, pausing outside of

her door. He planned to continue creeping down the hall and out the side door to where his livestock waited to be fed, but an out-of-place bundle on the couch halted his stealthy progress. Backtracking a few paces, he peeked again into the living room. It was Lissa, huddled on the couch, her knees drawn up for warmth beneath the gray and red Navajo blanket. Her hair was a sunburst of color fanning across the deep brown of the leather couch, as radiant as a lily on a forest floor. His book lay on the floor where it had tumbled to rest very early that morning.

Matthew considered not disturbing her, simply leaving her where she was to sleep to her heart's content. But then the chill in the air sent a slight shudder through her, and she pulled the blanket tighter. She couldn't be left there. Matthew went to the couch and, careful not to wake her, gently scooped her into his arms. Somehow, the contact seemed more intimate than even their kisses had. He was immediately overwhelmed by the rounded, womanly feel of her, her smell, the ivory sheen of her skin. Instead of holding her delicately, barely breathing for fear of waking her, Matthew ached to crush her to his chest, to bury his head in the thicket of her honey waves, to gorge himself on her smell, a delicately sexual scent that seemed to travel directly from his nostrils to his groin.

But then she moaned softly in her sleep and rolled over to tuck herself against the sheltering warmth of his chest, and all carnality went out of Matthew's response. She became Jeannie to him, the mistreated nine-year-old Jeannie, whom he'd ached to protect even as he was telling her story. He carried Lissa down the hall and tucked her into bed.

"Quaid. Quaid!" Lissa muttered urgently in her sleep, then mumbled something unintelligible.

She's playing Jeannie in her sleep, Matthew realized, watching Lissa's forehead rumple with vexation at the drama going on in her dreams. As she eased back into sleep, he noticed the soft bluish shadows beneath her eyes and the almost translucent delicacy of her skin. She suddenly seemed too frail and too young to be bearing all the responsibilities she had been carrying around for so many years. He pulled the curtains shut against the sunlight that was just beginning to slant through the window, then backed quietly out of the door.

The sun was high in the sky when Lissa woke up wondering how she had gotten to bed. Matthew must have carried her. She thought for a long, dreamy moment about that probability before she roused herself enough to take in her surroundings. Her room was just as stylishly homey as the living room. A round-bellied adobe fireplace swelled out from one wall. A couple of reproductions of paintings by artists whom she recognized and admired hung on the wall. An antique rocker graced one corner of the large, airy room.

It always took Lissa a fair amount of time to wake up fully and she usually enjoyed the dreamy time between sleep and waking. But today she was charged with an urgency that she couldn't pin down, feeling that something monumental had happened to her. She sat up to help her brain clear, then she remembered: Matthew's book. She slumped back onto the plump pillows and let memory bring back the magical experience that reading *A High, Hard Land* had been.

The book had moved her with its sweep and power, but most especially with the poignant accuracy of its emotional detail. She now felt a little in awe of Matthew, a little intimidated by the powers of perception he had demonstrated in the book. Perhaps someone with his depth of understanding might be justified in estimating her as a shallow and superficial Hollywood specimen. Lissa was marshaling an argument on her behalf when the door to her room opened the barest crack.

"Good, you're awake," Matthew boomed.

Her awe and intimidation vanished when he stepped in carrying a glass of orange juice in one hand and a spatula in the other.

"A little something to give you enough strength to make it out to the kitchen where I am now concocting my world-famous green chili and cheese omelet." Matthew handed her the glass of freshly squeezed orange juice. Smiling as she drank it, he noticed that the faint blue shadows that had lain beneath her eyes earlier were gone. He turned to leave and was at the door before Lissa could speak.

"Matthew," she blurted out. He paused. "Your book. I . . ."

"So that's what knocked you out," he said with a laugh. "Maybe I could bottle whatever's between those covers and put Ambien out of business."

For the first time since she'd known him, Matthew was uneasy and not the master of the situation. With a start, Lissa realized that he was nervous about her reaction to his work, that it really made a difference to him what she thought of *A High, Hard Land*. "No, Matthew, don't joke. It's hard for me to put into words how much I liked it. Even like doesn't begin to convey my reaction. It's a lot more than that. You put something truly special and rare in that book. In Jeannie." She swallowed and looked at him, determined not to falter now. "It's something I want to work very hard to try and capture. I'd like you to help me to do that."

Matthew nodded several times before words could make their way to his tongue. "That's what we're here for." He disguised the emotion Lissa's accolade had stirred in him by slapping the spatula against his palm as he walked away and calling out heartily, "Breakfast in ten minutes. Sleepyheads starve!"

It was noon by the time their late breakfast was finished. They had spent an hour over coffee talking about Jeannie, about who they each thought she was. Matthew had been impressed by some of Lissa's insights, and it was she who asked if they could ride around the valley, then up into the mountains to see all the places that Jeannie loved.

Matthew was happy to oblige and saddled up two of his more tractable horses. They roamed over the pasture-land and up into the foothills at the base of the mountain. Matthew led them to a trail that took them higher, until the valley unfolded at their feet. Then Matthew tethered the horses and on a sunny ledge they both sprawled out, side by side, on their stomachs.

The valley sparkled below them, green and un-touched. A large black bird wheeled through the blue sky overhead. Lissa thought she'd never looked into a sky so pure and apparently endless. "How can you ever leave all this?" Lissa wondered aloud.

Matthew smiled a wordless response.

"I mean," Lissa continued, "the world on the other side of this mountain is so remote to me now. Suddenly making movies seems like an incredibly trivial way to be spending a life."

"I suppose that's probably the healthiest attitude you could have about the whole thing," Matthew said, rolling up onto one elbow to face her.

"You know, you're right," Lissa agreed, a new per-spective suddenly opening up to her. "Everyone making a movie goes around acting like they're discovering a cure for cancer or something. They all rush around as if some terrible tragedy will befall the world if they don't get their movie made. Reporters fly in and ask the stars about everything from the color their hair is dyed to how world peace should be achieved. As if getting up in front of a camera and pretending to be someone you're not makes you an expert on anything besides which side of your face photographs best. It's ludicrous when you think about it."

"I love it!" Matthew rolled onto his back, laughing in delight. "You have just arrived at a conclusion that only the very wisest actors ever come to and then, usually, only after a few decades in the business."

Lissa glowed at being pronounced wise by Matthew. "Don't forget, though, that I've already put in close to two decades myself. My mother had me singing 'Tomorrow' with Little Orphan Annie curls by the time I was five. I didn't get my big dramatic breakthrough until I was eleven," Lissa joked. "When I played Anne in *The Anne Frank Story.*"

In a twinkling, sixteen years dissolved and Lissa felt herself back onstage in that production, a black wig hiding her blond hair and pale powder covering her pink cheeks, so that she looked like the tragic Jewish teenager hiding from the Nazis. She saw her father, home on one of his increasingly rare, increasingly brief visits, watching her from the front row. She had acted her heart out that night, thinking that if only she were good enough, he'd stay with them this time. That he wouldn't leave the way he always did. At the end of the play, he had leaped out of his seat to lead the applause, and Lissa thought her heart would burst with happiness. But, in the end, it hadn't made any difference and he had left to chase after the star that kept receding farther and farther into the distance.

"Yeah," Lissa went on somberly now, "I have sort of a head start on seeing how badly actors can mess up their lives when they take the whole thing too seriously."

Matthew watched her face, amazed by the range of emotions it mirrored. "You mean your parents?" he asked.

Lissa nodded. "Not my mom, really. I mean, she was definitely hooked on the roar of the crowd and the smell of the greasepaint." Lissa laughed. "But no, she didn't let it eat up her life."

"And your father did," Matthew guessed.

"Pretty much," Lissa answered, forcing her voice to stay light, casual.

Matthew rolled over onto his back, thinking about what she'd told him. He plucked a shoot of grama grass and plunged the white tip into his mouth. His lips and tongue worked over the tender shoot, extracting the burst of sweet juice stored at its center.

Watching the erotic marvels he could work with a simple blade of grass unsettled Lissa, luring her into dangerous territory. She tried to break the languidly hypnotic spell being woven by pointing to the bird cawing with a mechanical hoarseness overhead. "What sort of bird is that?"

"Quoth the blank, 'Nevermore,'" Matthew clued her.

"Raven," Lissa filled in, watching the black sheen of its wing turn to purple as it soared on the thermal currents.

A High, Hard Land

"You know," Matthew observed with an impish mischievousness Lissa hadn't thought him capable of, "this rock sure is hard."

Caught up by his lazy flirtatiousness, Lissa sat up. "Then, by all means, let me volunteer myself as a pillow."

Matthew smiled up at her, his eyes closed, as he settled his head on her thigh. Slowly, he opened his eyes. They weren't nearly as dark in the full sunlight. Lissa looked into them, fascinated to see layers of amber, flecks of green and an undertone of mahogany striating the iris.

"Your eyes look like some geological cross section," Lissa observed as she bent over him.

"I'm glad they give you something to look at," Matthew answered. "It's wonderful having you study me where you're close enough that I can feel your breath. It's warm and smells of clover."

"That's probably Crest, but thank you anyway." She tried to toss off his comment with a joke, but it wasn't easy. Not with the warm pressure of his head so close to the sensitized juncture of her thighs. Not when, if he only arched his neck, his lips would meet the aching tips of her breasts. With a jarring suddenness, Lissa announced, "Pillow duty is over."

Matthew sat up slowly. "All right, if I threaten you that much."

"Threaten?" Lissa said with a laugh. "I just want to see some more of this country that my character grew up on." She sprang up and smoothly mounted her horse.

Matthew hung back for a moment, watching as Lissa urged the horse into a gallop that lifted her hair up off her neck. She sat a horse well for a woman who hadn't ridden much, he noted, wondering all the while what she was running from and just how dangerous it might prove for him to become tangled up with the phantoms chasing her. In one fluid motion he mounted his horse and allowed it to amble slowly onto the trail. Then, when Lissa was almost out of sight around a bend in the trail, he expertly urged the animal into a gallop and effortlessly closed the gap between them.

By dinnertime that evening, Lissa was famished and not in the least bit unhappy to face another bowl of Teodora's posole. She lapsed into a sated stupor in front of the fire when they'd finished.

"All right," Matthew announced. "Enough lollygagging. We've got a movie to make and the fate of the Free World hangs on how well we do it." He tossed her a battered copy of the shooting script. "Let's run some lines."

A bolt of stage fright hit Lissa at Matthew's deliberately casual suggestion. In spite of the fact that she had been performing on cue for most of her life, she felt shy and uncertain in front of Matthew. He had already proved quite conclusively to her that he was an unerringly accurate judge of her performance. She couldn't skate by with technique or fool him with anything less than a wrenchingly authentic performance. She didn't know if she was up to it yet.

A High, Hard Land

"Might as well just take it from page one."

Matthew's suggestion was logical but threatening. The film opened with Jeannie's first conversation with Quaid. Her job as an actor in the scene was to portray the love, bordering on obsession, that Jeannie was hiding from Quaid behind a barricade of teenage sarcasm. Without waiting for her approval, Matthew started right in, acting the part of Quaid talking to a lovestruck Jeannie, who has followed him back to his trailer behind the rodeo arena.

"Does your mama know you're out this late?" Matthew asked, pretending to coil up the rope that his character, Quaid, had used in the rodeo arena. Lissa was astonished by how his accent, posture, even his facial features, had been transformed as he read Quaid's first line. He hadn't given the grandstanding performance that Shaun Douglas had when they'd played this scene for the cameras. Matthew was lost in the character he had created. Like a horse running with a fast herd, Lissa responded instinctively to the higher level of performance.

"Does your mama know that you'll be bedding down with a rope and your favorite horse tonight?" Lissa infected the false bravado of a scared teenager in her delivery.

"Well now," Quaid said, leaning back to take in his upstart visitor, "you got quite a mouth on you there, gal. Quite a mouth. Shame such a pretty mouth should be shooting off like that."

"It can do heaps of other stuff a lot better." Lissa felt

Jeannie's heart pound in her own chest at the false boldness she was using to prove to Quaid that she wasn't a little girl anymore.

"Is that so now? Like what?" Quaid's voice had lost some of its mocking quality and taken on the silky seductiveness of a rawhide Lothario. He moved closer to her.

"Like maybe you should find out for yourself," Lissa purred, only now it wasn't Jeannie's heart she felt pounding within her; it was her own. Matthew placed the roughened palms of his hands against her forearms and rubbed them exactly as the script called for. What wasn't in the script was Lissa's response to his warm, firm touch. Nowhere was it written that waves of liquefying pleasure should surge through her and that she would not be able to stop them, to will them away. The stage directions did not call for her to ache to surrender to the man in front of her, to tell him that there must be, there had to be, a second time. A shudder she could not stifle went through her.

Matthew felt it. His hands detected her arousal as unerringly as a Geiger counter. It was the response of a woman, not the scared teenager Lissa was playing. Suddenly, it seemed as if no time at all had passed since that velvet night in the truck. His lips moved to taste hers. Her lips parted as Lissa dragged in a panting breath, then Matthew's tongue eased between them. They feasted on each other.

In a remote corner of her mind, Lissa tried to remember when a man had ever so inflamed her with a single kiss. Never. Never had anyone taken such masterful control of her, undermining her will, making her ache to yield herself totally to oblivion, to do anything just so the unbearable sweetness would go on and on. Her hands fluttered over him like crazed doves, landing lightly on his shoulders, the columns of his back, his neck arched and curving down above her. Without her consent, they urged him on, just as the staccato harshness of her breath urged him on to the very edge of the precipice.

With an inhuman effort, Matthew dragged his lips from hers. "Say it," he gasped, feeling like a drowning man restraining himself from grabbing a piece of passing timber. He could not hold back much longer. He was seconds away from taking what he knew they both wanted.

Coy incomprehension was unthinkable, yet the enormousness of what he demanded frightened Lissa.

Matthew clung to the frayed end of patience, a position he was neither familiar with nor enjoyed. Lissa's torturing equivocation snapped the bonds of that patience. Roughly, his hands slid from her arms to cradle her buttocks. He pulled her to him so that there could be no mistake about his arousal, about what he was asking her. "Say it, Lissa, or send me away from you, now, while I have the tiniest shred of self-control left."

Lissa was frightened, alarmed by the way her breath seemed trapped beneath her heart when he held her to him, when she felt the evidence of his arousal and the quaking power behind it. It mesmerized and terrified her, all in the same instant. As strongly as she was drawn to Matthew by the vibrant intensity that hummed through him like a current through high-voltage wires, she was scared of it. Scared that it would overwhelm and obliterate her.

"No, Matthew." The edict was torn from Lissa's lips.

Her refusal seemed to Matthew the most arbitrary of cruelties. His hands fell from the warm, round places they had cradled. He felt dispensed with, dismissed, as if he had groveled and been turned away. He was unused to the rampage of emotion thundering through him. Unused to denial. He almost never made the first move with a woman, almost never had to. He looked at her. Her face was strangely passive, as if she were completely unaffected by the savage desire that clawed at him. His passion, denied in one area, quickly flared into anger at her passivity.

"What has this been?" he snarled. "Another one of your acting exercises?"

Lissa reeled from the accusation. She fought to cling to the tenuous hold she had on her self-control, to make sense of the whirling in her brain. But the injustice of Matthew's accusation ripped brutally through her.

Matthew waited for an answer, an explanation. With each second that passed without one, with Lissa's face a remote, impenetrable mask, his fury cooled into something even harder. Something that would, eventually, have frozen Lissa out altogether had he not noticed her hands. They were clamped into tight fists at her sides and trembled with a rigid tenseness. With a swiftness that baffled him, his anger drained instantly away, leaving behind only the pool of protectiveness that Lissa had undammed within him.

"Lissa, darling, what is it?"

Already anticipating an entirely different reaction, Lissa was prepared to lash out at him, to deflect the entire scene with an angry comeback. But that one endearment, that one tenderly spoken "darling," defused the fury she was on the verge of unleashing.

Then he saw that what he'd taken to be impassiveness was panic. She was scared out of her wits. Whatever drama was being played out at that moment between them, it had its roots somewhere else. Somewhere in a place that, he sensed, even Lissa could not understand.

"I'm not ready. I'm not . . ."

Matthew pulled her to him as she babbled on, rambling semihysterically. He held her close, stroking her fine hair with a gentle hand. She clung to him like a frightened kitten in a rainstorm.

"It's all right," Matthew said soothingly, tilting her head back in his large hands. "It's all right," he crooned, bending down to kiss away the tears coursing down her cheeks. He used his tongue to catch the crystalline drops. They were like salty dew on the petals of a rose, he marveled, not believing that human skin could be so soft.

"It's not, it may never be all right," Lissa protested with heartbreaking despair.

Matthew sat down and gently pulled her onto his lap, where she curled up just like the frightened kitten she had reminded him of earlier. He continued to stroke her hair, wanting nothing but to clear away the fear and sadness from her face, to see the radiance he so treasured beam forth once again.

Lissa slowly collected herself, then took several deep breaths before speaking. "I'm sorry. I really didn't plan for that to happen. It always surprises me when it does."

"So this is a regular occurrence?" Matthew asked, drawing away the tiniest bit.

"No, I mean, it's happened before. I don't know what's wrong with me. I do fine just sort of skimming along on the surface of things, but once I start—" Lissa stopped herself abruptly before she could blurt out the one word that would betray her: caring. Neither of them was ready for such a confession. But it was true; she knew it was. Her reaction had happened precisely once before, because she cared.

"Once you start what, Lissa?" Matthew probed.

"Let's not go into it."

"Let's do."

A slight chill tinged Matthew's command, just enough to remind Lissa that he could be a most driven and demanding man. So be it, she decided. I can be tough, too. Matthew Briggs is not going to force me onto a microscope slide so that he can dissect my emotions, then use the parts in his next novel.

A High, Hard Land

Matthew watched Lissa's expression change again from that of a heartbroken child to that of a steely, determined professional. And, he reminded himself, that profession is acting.

Both again remembering the other's occupation, they stared straight ahead into the fire as a gulf of suspicion and distrust opened up between them.

"It's been a long day," Matthew said, solemnly intoning the words as he rose. "I'll see you in the morning."

A suffocating feeling of abandonment crushed Lissa as he turned from her and started to walk away. The feeling was spiked with a horrifying sense of déjà vu, as if she'd known Matthew before and he'd left her before. Overwhelming all conscious thought, however, was something close to a survival imperative. She would truly drown beneath the waves of these suffocating feelings if Matthew left her. She had to stop him no matter what it might cost her pride.

"No. Matthew. Wait." She telegraphed the strange sense of emergency beating through her.

Matthew paused in the hall, Lissa's words touching some primal place in him that responded instinctively to their tone of desperation. For a second, he debated with himself. Was this an actor toying with her audience? If it was, Lissa was far better than either of them knew. If it wasn't, Matthew thought, the desperation in her words clawing again at him . . . He couldn't take the risk. He turned back to face her.

She looked as if the dark couch were about to swallow her up. Her skin was pale and her eyes large and dark in contrast. He waited. He would speak no more until she gave him some reason to believe he was anything but a foolish pawn.

"Matthew." Her voice was small and pleading. He did not move and still did not speak. Her chin quivered. Lissa bit her lip to stanch the flow of tears and made herself go on. She had to tell him. There was no choice but to expose herself, to take the risk that he was using her for character fodder. "It terrifies me to care. Matthew, it terrifies me to tell you. To have you know."

He came to her. "Oh, Lissa, you idiot. Why?" The shackles constricting Matthew's heart fell away and he breathed in happiness.

"Why am I the way I am?" she asked, light flooding the darkness that had engulfed her when Matthew had left. "I don't know. All I know is the panic, the fear, that overtakes me both when you get too close and when you leave."

"That doesn't leave me much room to move, does it?" Matthew asked, but the somber tone was gone.

"I know. It's not fair. It's certainly not normal."

"Normal is for body temperature; human emotions can't be calibrated that way."

Lissa laughed, a golden tinkling sound, as relief flooded through her at Matthew's acceptance. "No, I don't think there's a thermometer with a scale high enough to chart my emotions. Oh, Matthew, I want to respond to you in the right way, the way a woman should."

"There are no right ways, no shoulds for us, Lissa. Whatever way we choose is our right way." He opened his arms to her and she burrowed hungrily into them, glorying in his acceptance.

"Thank you," she whispered fervently into his chest. "Thank you for understanding."

"I may understand, Lissa," he said, his voice rumbling up from deep in his chest, a comforting growl against her ear. "But I'm damned if I'm happy. I told you before that I had a terrible habit of always telling the truth. It's about to get the better of me again."

"I want that, Matthew," Lissa said, her control returning as though she'd received a transfusion of strength from Matthew. "I want there to be truth between us."

"Even if there's nothing else?" he parried.

"I want there to be more," Lissa stated flatly, mastering the slight panic that feathered through her at the admission.

"I do, too," Matthew answered. "I want there to be as much as you'll allow. I told you before that I want to know you in every way possible. In all the miraculous ways that only a man can know a woman. But the more I'm around you, the more I want first and most crucially to know you as a person. We have time, Lissa, we have time."

Lissa framed his face in her hands. Firelight danced in the ebony depths of his eyes. She had never lost herself utterly and totally to a man before. Some instinct at the very heart of her being had always pulled her back from the brink of absolute commitment so that she'd never given herself completely. She would have been saved by that same instinct tonight if she hadn't called Matthew back. If he hadn't returned and sheltered her within his arms and his understanding. Now, looking into his eyes, which seemed to absorb the world whole and all its inhabitants and all their incredible complexity, Lissa felt as if she were standing on a sandbar. And the tide was going out. The very ground under her feet was slipping away. The face she beheld had become indescribably dear to her. She was falling in love. The simple, ineluctable realization caused a collision of great joy and mounting terror within Lissa.

All Matthew knew of the turmoil racking Lissa was the tremor that passed through her and the slight tremble he felt in her hands, cool against his face. "We'll take it slowly, Lissa," he promised her. "As slowly as you want. I won't rush you, and I pray to God that you're not the kind of woman that needs to be lured into bed, because I won't do that. When you're ready, come to me, Lissa. I won't ask again."

"Oh, Matthew, hold me, just for a moment, hold me."

Matthew held her to him but he wanted so much more. Wanted the feel of her naked body against him. The sound of her muted cries against his neck. Wanted the space between them to be gone. But he knew that that space could never be spanned by physical love, however much he ached now for its sweet release. He would wait. For Lissa he would wait.

"I have to go now, Lissa, or I'm going to break all my promises."

"Yes, Matthew, yes," Lissa mumbled, inwardly cursing whatever benighted quirk of her nature was keeping them apart tonight.

Without another word, Matthew stood. As Lissa watched him disappear down the long, dark hall, she muttered to herself over and over again, "We have time. We have time."

Chapter 6

H **ey, Snooze Queen!"**

The call, accompanied by a persistent rapping, invaded Lissa's dream, scattering the shadowy wraiths chasing her through a dark woods, where she had been wandering lost and alone.

"Lissa, you awake?"

"Yes. Just barely, though I can't think of any reason on earth why I should be at"—she rolled over to squint at the bedside alarm—"at six in the morning! Matthew, this is inhuman!"

He poked his head around the door to shout back, "This is ranch life."

"You are disgustingly chipper," Lissa observed, pretending a sourness she didn't feel. What she was feeling was exultant at the sight of him, the sharp angles of his face soft in the dawn light. She thought that never again would she mind waking up in the morning if Matthew could be the person to do the waking. Last night had been no dream, no trick of late hours and overwrought emotions. Every time she glanced at him, she felt herself slipping away just a bit further into love. Somehow, though, in the soft light of early dawn, the prospect of surrender was not quite as frightening.

"How would you like to ride over and meet the real Jeannie Duncan?" he asked.

"The real Jeannie Duncan," Lissa echoed tonelessly, though something twisted inside her at the way Matthew beamed at the mention of this person. "I didn't think there was an actual, real Jeannie Duncan. I thought she was more a composite of several women with liberal contributions from your imagination."

"Yes and no. Let's just say I was inspired by Vonda Kay. That's her name, Vonda Kay Monroe. Want to meet her?"

"Would she want to meet me?" Lissa answered non-committally. Jealousy. Lissa hated it. She'd rarely felt its awful sting because she had so rarely allowed herself to care. But it pricked undeniably at her now as she thought of the torrid passages in *A High, Hard Land* and concluded that it must have been Matthew himself who had played Quaid to his Jeannie. That was the only possible way for a man to understand with such thorough intimacy.

"Vonda'd be thrilled," he assured her.

Yes, but would I? Lissa shot back mentally. She was determined to keep the ugly green-eyed monster contained within a very small cage. It really was the most unbecoming of emotions.

"Breakfast'll be ready in fifteen minutes," Matthew alerted her, the discussion closed as far as he was concerned. "We'll head out as soon as we're through."

Matthew didn't notice how silent Lissa was during the ride to the Monroe ranch. He assumed that she was as dazzled as he by the beauty of nature waking up in the high country. But Lissa was oblivious to nature's charms as she lectured herself sternly about the folly of loving a man like Matthew. Then, when she'd finished berating herself on that score, she continued with a few choice thoughts on the futility of jealousy.

When she was through, she looked up. Matthew was tracking the flight of a hawk soaring on the air thermals rising from the valley. He looked so right in the saddle of a horse. He seemed so much a part of this land that Lissa felt her feelings for the awesome beauty of it becoming tangled up and inextricably bound to her deepening feelings for Matthew. Studying his profile, a singular line that was already carved into her heart, Lissa quietly began to loathe Vonda Kay Monroe.

In her mind's eye, she could already see the woman who was Jeannie's model. No doubt, Lissa thought, this Vonda person—Vonda? What a ridiculous name—was from a rich family who'd indulged her in a horse fixation that she'd never grown out of. The little rich girl playing cowgirl probably jetted into her ranch from Houston a couple of times a month, then went home to have her nails wrapped and her pores professionally cleaned. Lissa was certain that she was one of those impeccably cared for women that she detested because they'd had every advantage in life, took them for granted and expected more.

Lissa was so busy fuming as they approached the ranch that she barely noticed the stable hand who came out to take their horses. It wasn't until the "stable hand" took off her hat to reveal a long gray braid and Matthew made his introduction, "Lissa, I'd like you to meet Vonda Kay Monroe," that Lissa's attitude began to change.

Matthew's inspiration was no masquerading socialite. Vonda Kay Monroe was a true ranchwoman in her mid-forties. Her skin, tanned and wrinkled to a leathery brown by a high-altitude sun and drying winds, had clearly never been inside of a facial salon. Her nails were pared down to a bluntly functional length that fit with Vonda's strong, calloused hands. She wore a sage-green down vest over a checkered Western shirt tucked into jeans that bore no designer's stamp.

"I'm just tickled to death to meet you, Lissa." Vonda's twangy greeting had the warmth unique to certain rural people who, isolated from the constant, inescapable press of humanity, open their hearts immediately to new acquaintances.

"And I can't tell you how happy I am to meet you," Lissa responded with much more than rote politeness.

"Well, come on in. Coffee's hot. Hope you like it strong."

A High, Hard Land

"That's usually the only way I take mine," Lissa answered, feeling her jealousy melt away. "They make it so weak at the hotel."

"Ain't that the truth," Vonda chattered on as she led them into her home, a dwelling as unostentatiously comfortable as Matthew's. "Duane, that's my husband, took me there to eat for our twenty-fifth anniversary. This real prissylike waiter served us—"

"I know exactly who you mean," Lissa said, smiling as she thought of the determinedly haughty waiter who put on airs far too grand for a small mountain hotel.

"Well, anyway, we had a nice enough dinner until he brought what they're passing off as coffee down there. Duane takes one sip of it and he calls that waiter over and says, just as polite as can be, 'Son, might I trouble you for another cup of coffee? And on this one, could you possibly pass two coffee beans over the cup of hot water you bring me?'"

Matthew beamed as he relished Lissa's open enjoyment of Vonda's tale.

"What kind of lies are you letting this woman tell about me now?" A man pulling off leather work gloves and slipping a pair of wire cutters into the back pocket of his jeans stepped into the kitchen where they'd gathered. His face was as lined and leathery as Vonda's. Well before introductions were made, Lissa knew that the wiry man was Duane. She knew it immediately from the incandescent glow on Vonda's face when her husband walked in.

Life probably didn't offer too many pleasures greater than that, Lissa thought: being married to a man for twenty-five years and still lighting up with joy when he walked into the room.

The group took their coffee into the living room, where the easy flow of conversation continued. Vonda wanted to know all about Lissa, where she'd grown up, what her brothers were doing, what it was like doing what she did for a living. Vonda's curiosity and concern were insatiable. Lissa began to see how she had captured Matthew's admiration. The woman was as genuine, as unaffected and as emotionally nutritious as a bowl of stew.

Watching and listening to Vonda and Duane, Lissa began to realize just what Matthew had been trying to tell her about the people of the high plains. It was clear that Vonda had either inherited or cultivated a frame of mind that made the best of any situation. Certainly a dour, pessimistic type would never have survived the hardships of life that she had borne on a remote ranch. Lissa felt a sudden surge of gratitude to Matthew for not allowing her to play Jeannie the way she originally had. A woman of the high plains would never have let those narrow-minded churchwomen see her cry, would never have played out her emotions as dramatically as she had done in the early filming.

"You know, Vonda," Lissa said, smiling at the woman's warm curiosity and endless questions. "You missed your calling. I've never been interviewed so well by any reporter."

A High, Hard Land

"I love learning about people," Vonda said. "I'd meet my Waterloo, though, when it came time to write the thing up. My spelling would shame a chicken."

Lissa gradually turned the questions around to Vonda, who was as pleased to answer them as she'd been eager to ask. With a suitably muffled pride, she told Lissa about her and Duane's three children. The oldest one, their son Cody, was in veterinary college up in Colorado. Their daughter was just finishing her first year at a teacher's college. And Montana, a high school student, was off on some trip with the ranching club.

"Montana, he's the one not completely right in the head," Duane added, hiding his pride with a joke. "He actually wants to go into the ranching business with me. Now, a person's got to be a few bricks shy of a load to want to do a thing like that."

Lissa was moved by the simple love and bone-deep contentment that radiated from Vonda and Duane, from every detail of their lives together. The world waiting for her on the other side of the mountain seemed even more remote, even more shallow. What Vonda and Duane had together in this land of harsh beauty was built upon a quiet permanence that mocked the superficial, self-involved universe Lissa inhabited. She envied them.

Though Lissa could have happily spent the rest of the day absorbing the nuances of Vonda's outlook on life, Matthew knew that the Monroes' hospitality came with a price. "Well, Duane," he said, rising from the chair he'd settled into, "sitting around drinking coffee won't get that fence of yours mended, will it?"

"Don't I wish it would," Duane responded wearily, sorry to have the bright spot of companionship come to end.

"You'd surely better come on by again," Vonda warned Lissa.

"I'd love to," Lissa answered eagerly. "And if you have any interest in watching the filming, just let me know and I'll see to it you're allowed on the set."

"Now that might be fun."

"It is," Lissa agreed, "for about the first day. After that it's mostly just sitting around waiting while lights are moved and a powder puff is slapped in your face." She laughed, but the sound had a hollow ring to it.

They were halfway home when Matthew spoke, pulling Lissa out of her reverie. "I'm glad you saw what I did in the Monroes."

"It would be hard to miss."

"No, Lissa, I think probably most anyone else down there in Alta Mesa would have treated the Monroes as a couple of colorful country characters, quaintly crude but lovable. You saw their dignity, the significance of their lives. That's a talent that sets apart the great ones in your profession. You're going to be an actor, Lissa."

Lissa nodded in acknowledgement. It wasn't necessary to tell Matthew how much his simple prediction meant to her. She only hoped that she had the power to make it come true.

Back at Matthew's ranch, there was only time to pack up the few things she'd brought before they had to start the drive back over the mountains. As Matthew explained, "Human schedules are secondary concerns on a ranch. Here, everything is determined by the livestock. What they've determined for us is that I have to get you back to the hotel in time to turn right around and come home and feed them."

"Filthy beasts," Lissa said teasingly, tossing her bag into the bed of the pickup and sliding into the front seat with Matthew.

His hand on the ignition key of the truck, Matthew stopped and turned to Lissa. "Has it been worth it, Lissa?"

"Absolutely," she answered sprightly, trying to disguise the sadness that had rolled over her like a dark cloud. "I truly know Jeannie now." But she knew that wasn't what Matthew was talking about. As important as his character was to him, an even more vital concern had preempted it. As much as she might want to, she was powerless to hide anything from this man. "Yes, Matthew, it's been worth it."

His eyes seared into hers. He plunged into a welter of emotion more turmoiled than any he'd ever created for a fictional character. Impatience pricked along his hands, which ached to grab what he wanted. But he was certain that the instant he lunged for what he saw in Lissa's eyes

it would vanish. A groan of frustration slipped from between his clenched lips. "You tempt a man, Lissa, tempt
him sorely."

"Matthew, I—" But words were inadequate. She
wanted what he did with an equal ferocity. She leaned
toward him, her lips parting as her breathing accelerated.
That slight inclination was all the encouragement Matthew needed. His mouth found hers, brushing, teasing,
coaxing her into wanting more than the light flirtation of
his lips. It was she who parted her lips to him, who sought
out his tongue, stroked it with hers until his hunger could
not be restrained.

Lissa was swamped by the wanting that only Matthew
could stir in her. It spiraled out in a woozy warmth from
the pit of her stomach, spurred on by the furious accelera-
tion of Matthew's breathing, hot against her face.

With an anguished groan, he pulled her mouth from
his. Her chin captured in his hands, he held her but torturing inches from his swollen lips. He exhaled against her in
time with the violent thudding of his heart.

"Why do I torture myself like this?" he asked. His face
was alive with a fierce rapture. "Why does my resolve
not to touch you melt away every time you come close
to me?"

Lissa felt as if she'd stepped from sheltering darkness
into the brutal glare of a midday sun. Dazed, she could
find no answer.

Matthew turned the key in the ignition. The drive out

of his golden valley took an astonishingly short time, as short as the time it takes to wake from a dream.

But this is the dream, Lissa thought, as they passed the set on their way to the hotel. From the safety of the truck cab, she watched Jerome flitting madly about, brushing powder and blusher on Shaun Douglas, and Jack furiously pacing off a line, then marking it with a scratch of his heel on the dusty earth and yelling something to the cinematographer, Amado, who yelled right back. Just as Matthew had told her, she mused, it was all an illusion. An illusion that she would have to bring to life with her passion.

"You ready for all this?" Matthew asked, extending a hand to cover hers and give it a supportive squeeze.

"Yes, I'm ready," Lissa answered. As she turned her hand beneath Matthew's so that their palms met, she hoped with all her heart that she could make those words come true.

*C*hapter 7

Does *your mama know you're* out this late?"

It was odd hearing Shaun Douglas echo the words Matthew had spoken to her with so much more authority as they'd read lines together. But Lissa blanked out that distraction so completely that she heard only Quaid Dawson in the line and answered with the false bravado of a shy and lonely teenage girl.

"Does your mama know that you'll be bedding down with a rope and your favorite horse tonight?"

"Cut! Cut! Cut!" Jack Myers jumped out of his chair, waving his hands above his head and motioning his two stars to come to him. When he had them in a huddle, he said, "It's not working, people. I don't know why. It's just one of those things you can feel in your bones after you've been in this business as long as I have. Let's break while we noodle this out."

"Five minutes!" his assistant shouted.

Seconds later the set, constructed to look like the dilapidated dressing room backstage at a second-rate rodeo, was almost empty. Only Shaun, Jack and Lissa stayed behind.

Lissa took Shaun's seat at the dressing table, feeling a tiny surge of triumph as Jack pulled Shaun away for a private conference. She wished Matthew were there to confirm what she felt in her bones—she was blowing Shaun off the set with her acting. Or lack of it. She was Jeannie Duncan and Shaun was still Shaun, movie idol, trying to be a country rodeo hero half his age.

Off in their huddle, Shaun was nodding, his eyes cast meditatively toward the ground, while Jack drove each word he was speaking home with a balled fist. The director patted Shaun's back several times and the actor, still nodding toward the ground, left and came toward Lissa.

"So, you're raising the stakes on me," he said jovially.

"How's that?" Lissa asked.

"You're going to force me to really act if I want to keep you from stealing this picture out from under me. Your coach, Mr. Briggs, must have really done some, uh, intensive work with you these last two days. You've climbed right into Jeannie Duncan's skin."

"Thanks," Lissa said, choosing to ignore Shaun's snide innuendo in favor of the compliment he paid her.

"You know," he said, tilting his head and staring at Lissa through narrowed, appraising eyes, "I'm not sure I like this at all. You're making me work! I took this role mostly because I thought I could sort of sleepwalk through it. Skate along on charm and broad shoulders."

"You're too good an actor for that, Shaun," she said, remembering the times he'd genuinely moved her when she was a girl seeking to forget her troubles in a movie theater. "I grew up admiring your work. My mom, too. She's been in the business all her life."

"Hold it right there! Next thing you'll be telling me what a big fan of mine your great-grandmother was. I feel old and silly enough already trying to play a twenty-five-year-old. Ah, well, I guess I'll just have to reach way down in my aging actor's bag of tricks and pull out a performance."

"The talent's there," Lissa reassured him. "I've seen it enough times already."

"Yeah, well, it used to be there. We'll see, kid. Hop outta there."

Lissa relinquished his chair and moved away a few steps to give the actor some private room for him to collect his thoughts. She suddenly felt immeasurably better about the business at hand. As if, with that one exchange, she'd been promoted to a full partnership in the movie. She liked the feeling. Liked it a lot. She had one more thing to thank Matthew Briggs for.

When the crew reassembled and Jack called again for "Action!" Lissa faced a transformed Shaun Douglas. In the few minutes he had had to himself, he'd managed to drop two decades. Gone was his trademark bass voice, his manner, the way he carried himself. Lissa could have sworn he had even gotten rid of a few furrowed lines on his face. He was doing it, she thought, reaching for the performance he needed and pulling it out from somewhere. A bag of tricks. A dormant, but not yet dead, love of his craft. Wherever it had come from, the performance was undeniably there, and Lissa rose to it. The reality of his portrayal only added to the credence she was able to bring to hers. Like ballet dancers executing a pas de deux they each helped the other to ascend to heights they couldn't have reached alone.

When the scene was completed, Shaun collapsed into the chair. "Whew, that is hard work, kid."

"But good work when you get it right," Lissa countered. "And you did, Shaun, you got it just right."

"Couldn't have done it alone."

"None of us can," Lissa replied.

For the rest of the day's shooting, Lissa felt she was on a roll. She couldn't speak a word or make a gesture that was false. Everything she did and said was pure Jeannie Duncan, with a little Vonda Kay Monroe thrown in to keep her honest. She was elated. It felt like the time when she was six years old and her father had worked with her for what seemed like hours, running behind her, hanging on to her belt so that she wouldn't fall, until she'd finally gotten the feel of riding a bike without training wheels. Then her father had turned her loose, and she'd soared off down the street, flying, just the way she'd been flying all that day. Matthew had unlocked some genie within her and he was working pure magic.

That evening at the hotel, Lissa looked through her closet and couldn't bear putting on any of the trendy, neon-colored creations she'd brought with her. She had worn a clean pair of jeans and a checkered shirt to the hotel and simply slipped back into them after her bath. For as long as she could she tried to distract herself from the phone that suddenly seemed to dominate the room. She flipped through magazines and turned the television on and off, until she finally abandoned the effort and called Matthew.

"Hi," she blurted out the instant he answered. "I know I should play coy and give you a chance to miss me, but I held out as long as I could. I had to tell you about today. It was a revelation. I can act, Matthew. I can really and truly act. Even Shaun noticed the difference."

"I never had a moment's doubt. Not after the way you soaked Vonda up through your pores the other day."

"Did I? I thought I was being friendly but casual."

"I guess I spend so much time doing the same thing, figuring out what makes a person what they are, that I know all the signs. So shooting went well today?"

"Better than well. A new world opened up for me."

"Can't ask for too much more than that."

"Matthew, I've been thinking a lot . . . about us. Maybe it's presumptuous of me to even refer to an 'us,' but there's something there. Do you know what I mean?"

Matthew writhed inwardly at her blithe understate-ment. Had he misjudged her after all? Could what he thought might be possible between them just be some amorphous "something" to Lissa? "Yes," he dragged the answer out of himself, "I think I know what you mean." Before the hurt could overtake him, he added, "Look, Lissa, I've got a mare that's about to have her first foal. She might deliver any minute. I'd better get down to the barn."

"But when will I see you again?" She hated the needy note of desperation that warbled through her question.

"You'll have to decide that, Lissa. I've got to run." Mat-thew hung up the phone, but he didn't run. He sat for a long time, staring out the window and watching the moun-tains turn from a vivid rust in the glare of the setting sun to the dark burgundy of dusk. He had told the truth. There was a mare and she was about to foal. But he doubted that it would be tonight. No, he'd made his feelings clear to Lissa. If there was ever to be anything more than a vague "something" between them, it was up to her to make it happen. He couldn't force it, couldn't create it himself out of whole cloth. She had to want what he wanted. And what he wanted was a great deal more than "something."

Still, he wished he had been on the set. He had known when she left the night before that she would deliver. She had the depth, the passion, the insight. She had everything a great actor needed. Everything— Matthew stopped the thought before it formed. He got to his feet and stalked off to the front door where he jerked his jacket off a peg as he hurried out into the gathering dark to check on the mare he was almost positive wouldn't foal that night. He hurried to escape the thought that had formed in his mind. But the thought came anyway. After spending so many years chasing down the truth in his work, Matthew couldn't elude it now even when he wanted to. The fact of the matter was that all those qualities that would make Lissa a superb actor were exactly the ones he had always searched for in a woman. The woman he could love for the rest of his life.

"'Something' between us," Matthew hissed as he pulled open the door to the barn. The word sounded paltry and insignificant. It mocked what burned within him.

Lissa watched that same sunset burn the sky from rust to burgundy. Matthew had sounded so distant, so aloof. Maybe what she had felt had only been the warmth generated by a skillful coach urging a student along. No, it had been more, Lissa insisted to herself. It had to be.

Lissa clung to that forlorn hope throughout the evening. But her hold on it loosened as she drifted into sleep and again the dream came. She was in a dark woods, lost and alone. As she always did, she knew that a creature, evil and insatiable, was hunting her and that no one was coming to save her. Ever. Though her eyelids twitched as she slept and she mouthed silent cries of distress, the dream had receded by the time she awoke. All that was left was a residue of pessimism. She awoke with the sure knowledge that nothing was going to work out between her and Matthew. She wondered why she had ever imagined it could.

That certainty haunted Lissa for days. Subconsciously, it melded with the scene they were shooting. Jeannie had had her illegitimate baby prematurely that September and now, in a late-November scene with winter moving in and closing down even the rodeos to the far south, Quaid rode into her life again.

Shaun was magnificent playing Quaid as he saw his son for the first time. There was no doubt in his mind that the child was his. Jeannie had been a virgin when they first made love less than a year before and he was as certain of her fidelity as he was of his own lack of that same quality. But that would all change, Quaid had promised, now that he had a family. He volunteered to do right by Jeannie. He'd marry her.

As Quaid stepped back, waiting for Jeannie—the love-sick teenager who had adored him for as long as he could remember—to be bowled over by his truly magnanimous offer, something snapped inside Jeannie.

"Quaid Dawson," she spit at him. "I've loved you for as long as I've known what the word meant. I never tried to hide that. Maybe I'd have been better off if I had. But you came riding back in here too late this time."

"Jeannie," he answered, moving to her, his arms out, a coaxing smile on his face. The smile that had won her heart and had never failed to regain it since. "Jeannie, don't do me this way. I'm here now."

A High, Hard Land

"I can't deny that. But where will you be next spring when all those arenas start opening back up? When those bright lights switch back on? I can't have it, Quaid. I can't have it and neither can my boy. He's not yours, Quaid, so get that thought right out of your head. He's not yours and neither am I."

Lissa felt the fire of righteous anger burn through her as Jeannie declared her independence from a man who'd broken her heart with the regularity of the changing seasons for over a decade. She delivered the speech with a scorching strength that fit the power generated when closely held dreams finally die.

Shaun's reaction was perfect. He let everything that Quaid was experiencing play out on his face. The jovial forbearance he had first used turned gradually to disbelief as he saw that the girl he had always counted on for unconditional love had finally grown up and switched her allegiance to the child he was certain he'd fathered and she had borne in stubborn solitude.

"Jeannie, honey," he pleaded, seeing the rock-hard glitter in her eyes. "If you'd only have told me, I'd never have left last spring. I would have stayed by you, if I'd just known."

"You knew," Jeannie shot back with a finality that even Quaid could not deny. God curse him, he had known. He had known, when she'd placed his hand on her belly, that there was new life growing within her. Life that he had started and she would have to carry and bear alone.

What he hadn't known then was how much he would love the child she now held in her arms. How much he would finally realize that he had loved her all along. Now that he saw he was truly losing both of them, the high-stepping bravado that had carried him for most of his life began to collapse within him. His rodeo life suddenly seemed a pathetic sham, a foolish game that men played to convince themselves that youth and the freedom of youth could live on. It was long past time he finally grew up, he admitted to himself. He belonged with his son and the finest woman he'd ever known.

"What did you name him?" was the puny question that came out of a life falling apart.

"Named him after my father," Jeannie replied stiffly, forcing herself to remain rigid and strong just long enough to do what she had to do. Just until Quaid rode off. "Sherman's his name."

"Sherman," Quaid echoed. He put out a hand scarred from rope burns to touch the downy fluff on the boy's head, but Jeannie pulled back as if his touch might contaminate the child. Quaid looked up at her with eyes that no longer pleaded. She was a woman of the high plains and pleading did not work with those of her kind once their minds had been made up. He had given her far too much time to make up her mind. He was the one who'd fashioned the tragedy that he would now have to live with.

Members of the crew watched mesmerized as the actors metamorphosed into two people whose lives were cracking in half. Some of the old-timers out of range of the recorders whispered among themselves that they'd never seen Douglas act so well, not even in the early years before he'd succumbed to his own reputation. And that new girl, they marveled, searching for comparisons. For that level of intensity, they had to go way back. Bette Davis. Hepburn. They nodded and turned their attention back to the newcomer.

At precisely that moment, Lissa felt herself falter. She had prayed it wouldn't happen, though, when she'd rehearsed alone, she had feared it would. She had hoped that the energy of the scene would carry her along when she came to this part. But it was failing her even before she started speaking her last lines.

"I'd rather have no husband and no . . ." She stumbled and was sure that Jack would call for a cut. But he didn't. He thought it was deliberate. Lissa went on, but the intensity was gone. Her reading was flat. "No father for my child rather than one who's going to waste both our lives riding off after a fantasy."

A concerned, questioning look clouded Shaun's eyes. He'd felt the drop in intensity and asked Lissa about it with his eyes. The crew members who'd just been marveling over her performance raised their eyebrows and exchanged glances; they too had felt the heat drop. They sighed. No endurance. Not like the old-timers. These new ones just couldn't sustain an emotional pitch long enough.

Lissa had no choice but to go on. In a monotone that

clashed dramatically with the vividness of the scene's beginning, Lissa ended it by ordering Quaid to leave forever.

Shaun was still "on" and, as he mounted the horse his face told the camera what his character was too inarticulate to express. It told the story of a man who'd chased rainbows all his life. Then when he had finally stopped long enough to look, he discovered he had been carrying pots of gold in his saddlebags all the time. But the bags had been leaking, and by the time he finally got around to checking what he'd had from the start, the last gold coin was slipping out of his grasp. Priceless, irretrievable and gone forever.

Lissa tried but knew that nothing nearly as expressive was showing in her face. It wasn't mirroring any of the thousand and one emotions that her character would have been feeling. It was as if some vital nerve had been severed. Shaun rode out of her life and all Lissa felt or could portray was a deadened impassiveness.

After Shaun had ridden out of the frame, on a shot that opened up to take in Jeannie standing alone in the middle of her ranch, Jack called for a cut. Then he surprised Lissa by ordering the shot printed, which meant that he planned to use that take. She had been certain he was going to ask for another.

"That's a wrap for today, people," Jack called out.

A small "hurray" went up from the crew and they immediately began packing away lights and cables. Only the old-timers stood around for a moment, puzzled, unable to believe that there wouldn't be another take. Finally, an old lighting man shrugged and turned to his buddy. "Plastic emotions for a plastic age," he concluded and began unstringing the lights.

Lissa didn't join the exodus of actors away from the set. She knew she should halt the departure and call for another take. At least to redo the end of the scene from the point where she'd gone flat. She even got as far as calling out to Jack. He was walking away and froze at the sound of her voice, turning slowly with a look of intense exasperation on his face, anticipating her request.

But it wasn't the director's expression that stopped Lissa. She had made the decision that she wasn't ever going to sacrifice even the smallest increment of quality in her craft to win anyone's favor. Never again would she care that much about being a well-liked, easy to get along with "good girl." No, the force that stopped her had a root far deeper. It reached into a place that Lissa could neither see nor control.

"Yes?" Jack prodded her, peeved.

"I—" She couldn't go on. Lissa could not say that she wanted to do the scene again. Because the fact of the matter was, she didn't. For all the reasons why she had frozen before the cameras, she did not want to say those lines a second time. To think them. To feel them and all the terrifying emotions they called forth.

"I think it went well," she lied to the waiting director.

"Very well," Jack confirmed, his expression loosening.

"Maybe a little wooden there at the end," he added, watching her face for a reaction.

Lissa knew that he was testing her, knew that a true actor would not have found a portrayal that was "a little wooden" acceptable. For reasons that neither one of them understood, Lissa passed the test. "Maybe," she agreed.

When it was clear that she would say nothing more, Jack put his arm around her. "Your little confab with Briggs up there in the high boonies seems to have worked. We're on the same wavelength now, eh?"

Lissa nodded, but it wasn't enough for the director. He squeezed her as if trying to press an answer out of her. "Eh?"

"Yeah," she muttered. Anything. Anything just so she wouldn't have to repeat that awful scene.

The director released his hold on her and Lissa left. She fled to her room but found no sanctuary there. The scene kept threading through her mind, pestering her like a swarm of gnats she couldn't shoo away. She wanted badly to call Matthew, to talk the problem out with him. But the memory of his chilliness stopped her. Knowing she would find no peace with herself, Lissa forced herself to go downstairs to the dining room.

The moment she entered the crowded room, she was hailed from every side. Shaun flagged her over to his table and made a place for her between the two female crew members currently vying for his attention. After exchanging greetings and a few quips with those seated around the table, Lissa sat quietly. It was nice to be included in the group. There was often a wonderful feeling of camaraderie on films that were going well when cast and crew knit together to form a kind of family. Except that it wasn't a true family. Lissa had already discovered that on the other shoots she'd been on.

Oh sure, she reminded herself, everyone was close for the few months they were shooting. And there were always elaborate promises exchanged at the end that they would all stay in touch. And maybe there would even be a few dinner invitations. But the family feeling was always gone once the film was in the can. Back home, everyone's lives picked up tempo and they moved on to new projects that captured their minds and hearts. Or they didn't move on, and a special kind of anxiety, created for those who don't work in Hollywood, snared them. Whichever way it went, the bonds were broken, proving, Lissa thought bitterly as she listened distractedly to the bright, animated chatter, that there had never been a family to begin with. Not a real family.

She glanced over at Shaun, who rewarded her with one of the smiles that millions of women around the world paid to see on the screen and carry away with them in their fantasies. She had little doubt that Shaun would be only too happy to volunteer to keep her from being alone that night. Maybe even for all the nights they were together in Alta Mesa. But the thought of such an empty physical coupling depressed Lissa. Especially now that she yearned for an experience of total completion with someone who, she'd dreamed, might answer a need far, far deeper than a mere physical one.

Suddenly, as she thought of Matthew and recalled the serenity of her time with him at his ranch, she could no longer stand the empty charades being played out around her and excused herself, pleading a headache. The solitude of her room was more in keeping with the mood that had swallowed her up.

She was alone. She'd always been alone, she thought as she lay on her bed, fully clothed. Her career had always been number one in her mother's life. Her brothers had learned that lesson from her. They had been close growing up, but as their individual careers took center stage, they had seemed to have less and less in common. And her father? Lissa shrank from the pain that memory of him invariably brought with it. Her thoughts fled the hurt, instinctively clustering around one person, Matthew Briggs.

Lissa gave a snort of laughter. For a few minutes there, she'd managed to banish the basic fact of her loneliness in life with the illusion that she had found a soul mate in Matthew. How ridiculous, she told herself. She'd been as blind and as foolish as her character, Jeannie Duncan. But even as Lissa was telling herself that she was now, and always would be, alone, and that, in the end, everyone else was, too, she remembered the real Jeannie, Vonda Kay Monroe.

She remembered the radiant look on the woman's weather-beaten face when her husband had walked into the kitchen. She remembered something else then that had escaped her attention at the time: the look on Matthew's face as he beheld the couple. In a flash, that look connected with his novel to reveal a basic truth to Lissa—Matthew believed in together. He believed that love could conquer the bounds of solitude and, if she was reading his expression right, he yearned for that union in his life.

Great, Lissa answered her hopeful self caustically, but exactly what does the almighty Mr. Matthew's predisposition have to do with you? It was pretty clear from your last phone call that you are not to be the one to end his solitary state.

For several long minutes, Lissa slid into a lethargic, despairing state. It was not a state particularly compatible with her basic nature. Bit by bit, she rallied out of the uncharacteristic lethargy, finally reminding herself of Matthew's warning that he would not impose himself on her. That when she was ready, she would have to come to him. Why then had he been so distant, so brusque on the phone? she wondered, vaulting between hope and despair.

After she had batted the question about in her mind for half an hour, she clasped her hands over her ears as if she could shut out the natter of conflicting inner voices tearing at her.

"Enough!" she proclaimed out loud. If she had sat around courting doubt all her life, she'd probably still be in Minneapolis staging *Fiddler on the Roof* at the community theater. No, she told herself firmly, she was poised at the most crucial crossroads she had come to in her life. She could listen to the doubts that whispered Matthew didn't feel for her what burned in her heart for him. She could keep to the safe path she'd trod all her life. Or she could risk the terrifying prospect of eventual abandonment and venture down the path Matthew had opened up to her. Not knowing if she was ready or if Matthew was still willing, Lissa hurled herself out of bed. Nothing, she determined, could be worse than remaining huddled in her room haunted by phantoms she couldn't exorcise or even name.

She changed quickly, put on her boots and stepped out, bumping into Shaun in the hall. He had the pretty young desk clerk tucked under his arm and was listing just the slightest bit. He threw his arms open in drunken effusiveness when he spotted Lissa.

"Jeannie, my lover, mother of my child, why did you desert me?"

Lissa gave him a quick hug. "Shaun, I have a big favor to ask you. Could I borrow your Jeep?" With his star clout, Shaun had insisted in his contract that the studio provide him with a four-wheel-drive vehicle while he was on location.

"'Course," Shaun replied instantly, fishing in his pocket for the keys. "Nothing too good for the woman who's forcing me to act again." He dangled the keys in front of her. "Just tell me where you're rushing off to."

"Just want to get some fresh air." She smiled lamely. "You know, cabin fever can set in cooped up here."

A High, Hard Land

"I know, indeed," Shaun said, grinning lasciviously, dropping the keys into her outstretched hand. "I get that very same kind of fever." He winked at her as he pressed the desk clerk, who was looking goofy with adoration, against his chest.

"Thanks," Lissa said tersely, heading down the hall.

Shaun called after her. "Hey, I won that last round out there today, didn't I?"

"You did," Lissa admitted with a smile. "But don't expect it to happen tomorrow."

"That where you going? For a late-night drama lesson with your coach?" Before she had a chance to answer, Shaun held up his hands. "None of my business. Nobody's business what any of us does off the set. Is it, sugar dumpling?" he asked the desk clerk as he guided her back down the hall toward his room.

The vision of a drunken Shaun Douglas and his latest in an endless string of conquests haunted Lissa as she drove up the treacherous mountain road. She wished in a way that her motives were that simple. She prayed that Matthew's weren't. As it was, she thought, her grip on the steering wheel of the Jeep tightening, she had so much, everything really, to lose with the gamble of this trip.

For a second, her foot eased off the accelerator and the Jeep slowed in its ascent. Then the corollary to the risk she was taking clicked into place—she had everything to win. She pressed on the gas and the Jeep powered on up the mountain that separated her from Matthew.

Chapter 8

"**W**ell, this is a rare** and pleasant surprise."

Matthew's greeting was warmed by enough genuine pleasure to melt away a bit of the chilly layer of apprehension that had iced over Lissa's impetuosity on the long drive. Now that she was there, standing in front of Matthew as he was framed in the doorway, the golden light from the fire leaking out and haloing around him, Lissa faced an important truth—the reasons she'd come were many and complex. Something deep in Matthew called to her and made her dream of lives entwined. But all that was underpinned by the one response that made the myriad others possible. She ached to touch him, to have his arms around her, to know the feel of his weight upon her.

All those desires swarmed through her as she stood poised at Matthew's door, both of them waiting. Matthew waited for a sign, Lissa unable to make it. He ushered her into his home. Lissa entered, feeling as if she had let another precious moment, ripe with possibility, slip from her. She had come to him, chased by phantoms of loneliness, and knew it was up to her to explain that to Matthew. But now that she was there, facing him, his gaze studying her, still waiting, she couldn't do it. Couldn't risk exposing herself that nakedly.

"Shooting went pretty well today," she finally blurted out with a nervous chattiness. A flash of something close to pain appeared to shoot through Matthew's ebony eyes at the brittle, superficial comment. "We did the scene where Quaid comes back at the end of the rodeo season and Jeannie sends him away."

"Could have been a tough one to play," Matthew offered, managing to hide his growing disappointment behind a neutral tone. He had been stunned by the ferocity of his own joy when he'd opened his door and found her standing on his porch.

The past few days had been hard. He hadn't allowed himself to call her, denying himself the sound of her voice. But it had been clear to him that that was what he had to do. He wanted either all that this extraordinary woman was capable of giving or he wanted nothing. The polite, detached level they were at was unendurable for him, but Lissa had to be the one to end it.

"The scene was a bit hard," Lissa said, radically understating the hurt intensity of her reaction. Feeling as if she were ripping the cover off her emotions, she added, "I went sort of flat at the end."

"You mean where Jeannie tells Quaid that she'd rather not have any father for her child than one who's always running away after a fantasy?"

Lissa nodded, the inexplicable clot of emotions that that scene raised in her clutching at her throat.

"Why do you think that is?" Matthew asked, his instincts for the unexplored and unexplorable forces that drive human beings beginning to prickle. "Why was it so hard for you?"

Lissa shrugged off the question and turned away. The instant her face was hidden, she took several deep breaths to steady herself. She couldn't have spoken and let the tears she was blinking back fall in front of Matthew. Just as she had refused to give the mean girls who'd taunted her in high school the satisfaction of seeing her tears, she couldn't yet allow herself that vulnerability with Matthew.

To Matthew, the shrug looked like a casual dismissal of his question. The hope that had again been building within him was deflated. Had he been so wrong? Was Lissa really incapable of the depth he thought he'd seen in her?

The possibility loomed larger and larger when she turned back around, an odd glitter in her eyes, and began reciting trivial bits of gossip from the set. As she chattered on, Matthew felt his disappointment turn to stone within him. He had longed for her in a way that he'd never longed for any other woman in his life. Her brittle chatter mocked those longings.

"Did your mare foal?" Lissa asked brightly, scrambling frantically to steer the conversation into safe avenues. She had wanted to open her heart to Matthew, to share her hurt and exile her loneliness. But she couldn't, not with him studying her like a livestock judge trying to decide if she was a blue-medal winner or a fraud. She knew she was a fraud. She might be able to fake it for the cameras, but she couldn't bring to her own life the kind of passion Matthew had talked about. It was too frightening after all.

"My mare?" Matthew echoed, unprepared for the abrupt shift in conversation. "Yes. She had a little colt night before last." Not knowing what else to say, he asked lamely, "Want to see the baby?"

"I'd love to!" Lissa answered too enthusiastically.

They walked in silence through the darkness to the barn. Away from the lights, Lissa didn't feel she had to keep up the act of brittle congeniality she had used to cover up the terrible fiasco that her misguided expedition had turned into.

Matthew's tension uncoiled as they walked through the darkness. The silence bound them more closely than an embrace and it started to erase the brittle barrier Lissa had put between them.

Lissa breathed in the night air. It was coolly invigorating, alive with a piney seductiveness. In the distance an owl hooted. Farther off a coyote howled its plaintive wail.

A High, Hard Land

A full moon hung plump and silver in the sky, washing the mountains with an unreal light. They seemed to be the gilded towers of a high wall encircling the valley in a ring of enchantment that barred the world beyond.

At the barn, Matthew lit a lantern so that he wouldn't have to turn on the lights and wake up all the animals. The flickering kerosene flame cast a soft globe of light that didn't disturb the horses standing and sleeping in their stalls.

"Here they are," Matthew whispered.

Lissa glanced over at him. His expression, manner and voice had all softened when he presented the new mother and her child. The foal that had been nursing when they approached left his mother's side and came up to butt at the hand Matthew draped over the half-open Dutch door.

"This little guy's a lot friendlier than most babies," Matthew said, stroking the velvety muzzle the foal presented.

"He's lovely," she whispered. The small creature was so delicately put together, Lissa marveled, forgetting the anxieties that had been crowding in on her. His spindly legs were disproportionately long with knotty outsized knees. And his head seemed all wide, curious eyes and long, long eyelashes. He twisted his dexterous lips around to suck on Matthew's hand and take a few nibbles.

"Whoa, big fella," Matthew said, laughing as he gently pushed the foal away. "That's not a teething ring you're chomping into there."

Laughter bubbled spontaneously out of Lissa, cracking the icy veneer that had separated her from Matthew. They were joined in their delight at watching the scrappy colt discovering his world.

Lissa held her hand out for the foal to nuzzle, acutely aware of Matthew beside her. She barely felt the foal's whiskery mouth brush across her palm. All her senses seemed to have concentrated along her arm and back where Matthew's body pressed. As lightly as the passing of a bird's wings, she felt his lips on her hair.

Matthew had vowed he would not move a fraction of an inch closer to her. Would not touch her until she asked him to. *But this*, he thought as he closed his eyes and inhaled. The smell of her was pure witchcraft. In that same instant, he jerked his eyes open. He was already being lured along the road of wheedling and coaxing, and that was one journey he would not make, even for Lissa Bauer.

"Why did you come to me?" he growled, his lips near her ear, his hands moving to her shoulders to press her to him.

Lissa did not know that the anger in his voice was for himself. A dozen trivial replies flitted through her mind before she dismissed them all. "I came to see what there is, what might be, between us."

"Yes, this phantom 'something' you spoke of on the phone."

Once Lissa stopped shrinking from the anger in his voice, she realized with a start that there was hurt hiding

152

behind it. She had hurt him by downgrading the intensity of her feelings for him. "It's more than that, Matthew," she stated. "For me it is."

"How much more, Lissa?"

"I suppose that's what I want to find out."

He turned her in his arms so that she faced him. The kerosene lamp threw dramatic shadows across his face, a face born to cast dramatic shadows. His eyes were lighted clearly, however, and from them shone a naked need that told Lissa she could not possibly want Matthew any more than he wanted her. His mouth formed his next sentence slowly and deliberately. "How, Lissa, how do we find that out?"

Her eyes darted to his, seeking courage. His grip on her arms tightened, pulling her closer to his chest, where his heart throbbed with an urgent rhythm answered by her own thudding pulse. He gripped her as if he wanted to squeeze the words out of her, which would free them both.

His body shuddered against hers.

"By making love," she gasped.

"God, woman, you don't know how I've ached to hear you say those words."

It was as if the effort of self-denial they had both been making suddenly reversed itself and all that thwarted energy was released at once in a mindless delirium that consumed them both whole. Lissa's fingers twined desperately through Matthew's dark hair. His mouth, his kiss,

153

she had to have it, she thought feverishly. Now. The waiting and fear were over.

A bolt of sensation ran through her at the barest touch of his lips. His mouth hovered above hers for a second as he breathed in great, shaking breaths of air, while his eyes simultaneously seemed to drink her in.

A red mist seemed to obscure Lissa's vision as she looked back at Matthew. Her love and desire fused in that moment into an alloy of incalculable strength. Neither one nor the other could have been half as powerful alone. His lips crushing down on hers was a benediction. She tasted the same ferocious urgency that pounded through her. The same need, too overwhelming to deny any longer.

Matthew was a madman, fueled by insatiable need. He had held back for far too long. All he wanted was to feel, to smell, to hear. The silken thrust of his tongue plunging into her mouth. Her delicate, floral scent becoming denser, more sexual. The strangled moans that slipped from her throat.

Lissa heard her own moans with ears disconnected from her brain. Matthew's avid mouth dropped to her neck, to lick, to nibble at the source of such rapturously arousing sounds.

Her neck arched back to receive his attentions even more fully, her head lolling against the muscled support of his arm. Matthew had never known a woman who could arouse him to such heights of passion, much less one who could match him every step of the journey. His mouth plunged farther down her neck. He was astonished when her slender fingers slid to the buttons at her throat to open them.

Her blouse fell open as his breath warmed ever-widening circles of pleasure. His lips moved down farther, slowly. A faint, muffled groan tore from Lissa's lips as his mouth descended to the waiting swell of her breast. Then, at last, it was on the pebbled center, devouring, sucking from her all will, all thought, all strength. Her legs began to give way.

Matthew felt her list slightly against him. Without thinking, he scooped her into his arms. Sweeping a woman off her feet was a Hollywood gesture that he would never have dreamed himself capable of making. But with Lissa in his arms, staring up at him dazed and breathless, it was as if no man had ever before held a woman in just that way. Everything between them was fresh and new. Dazzling and devastating in its novelty.

"It's never been like this with anyone else, Lissa," he rasped. Ordering thoughts into words was an ordeal, but it was important for him to tell her, for her to know.

"I know, Matthew," Lissa murmured. "I know."

"There's so much I want to tell you," he murmured, overcome by the enormity of all he was feeling. "So much, I . . ." His words trailed off.

"You said it yourself, Matthew, there's time. For now, would you, please"—her voice became a whisper—"take me to your bed?"

Matthew's arms tightened about her and she felt his

great strides as they left the barn. Outside, the world was brilliant with light from the full moon. Gravel crunched beneath Matthew's feet as he stepped onto the path up to the house. The crunching slowed, then stopped. His eyes were bright and fixed upon her.

"I've never seen anything so beautiful in my life." His tone had an awed, hushed quality to it.

Lissa became conscious of how her blouse was hanging open, and how exposed she was in the moonlight. She moved to pull the blouse closed.

Matthew winced. "No, don't hide from me," he ordered, stopping her hand with his words. Reverently, he inclined his head to kiss the silver curve of her breast.

An electric thrill went through Lissa at the touch.

Then Matthew slowly removed his head and, crushing Lissa closer to him, resumed striding to the house. Once inside, he carried her to the living room, where the fire was still burning brightly, and gently set her down on the rug in front of it.

To Lissa he looked like some fiery god as he stripped off his cotton flannel shirt. His muscles were fuller, more generous than she had imagined they would be. His body pulsed with the same vibrant life as his spirit.

"Firelight suits you," Lissa whispered, surprised that she was speaking her thoughts out loud. "It fits a wildness in you that nothing else can capture."

"A wildness that only you bring out." He kneeled on the rug. "Come here." She edged forward until she was kneeling in front of him. He undid the few buttons still closed on her blouse and it slid off to pool at her knees. He stroked his fingers over her bare shoulders. "This is how I wanted to see you," he said exultantly. "Golden in the firelight." His fingers trailed down, gliding over her breasts. His eyes continued to hold hers as the teasing touch became more forceful, each of her high breasts covered by a hand that began to massage insistent patterns of mounting need into them.

"Radiant and unearthly." His last words were lost as his mouth claimed the golden prize his hand offered.

Lissa swayed against him, her own hands delighting in the smooth hardness and muscularity of Matthew's back and shoulders. Each touch put her further beyond the bounds of control.

As his lips slid down her flat stomach, Matthew's hands went to the snaps at her jeans and expertly unfastened them. He pushed away the denim, his lips caressing each newly exposed bit of silvery skin as he pulled away the last encumbering items of clothing.

Kneeling above her, Matthew hurriedly ripped free the fasteners on his jeans and shucked his clothing aside. As he stared down at her, a tremor passed through him. Lissa reached up to him and he tumbled to her side.

"I can't wait, Lissa. I want you. It's not human how badly I want you."

Her wordless answer was eloquent. She pulled him to her.

He lowered his body onto hers, Lissa gratefully taking the sweet weight. She felt him enter her body as smoothly as a bird soaring into the heavens. Without thought, her body arched to meet his. Already teetering at the brink, they joined swiftly in the same driving rhythm of release.

Lissa became a bow tautening beyond endurance. The golden world around her flamed scarlet, darker and deeper, until it burst apart in an explosion of color that was next replaced by the black of oblivion.

Lissa awoke to the sensation of being gently swayed as Matthew carried her upstairs.

"I fell asleep," she said, astonished.

"For hours." His smile was warm and happily fulfilled.

"I've never done that before."

"Maybe you've never been properly loved before."

"Possible," Lissa said demurely. "Quite possible."

"And you still haven't." Matthew stopped at the top of the staircase and stared into the depths of her eyes. "Not the way I want to love you. Not the way I can when I'm not out of my mind with desire."

"I like you out of your mind with desire," Lissa purred as they continued down the hall.

"You should," Matthew growled with mock anger. "You put me there."

She reached up to wind her arms around his neck. His kiss was different, flavored now by knowledge of her. She reveled in the taste, knowing that hers would be different as well. "I could definitely come to like this mode of conveyance," she said jokingly, a kind of lighthearted joy filling her.

"I don't mind it myself," Matthew replied teasingly, opening the door at the end of the hall. "As long as the destination is my bed."

His room was surprisingly bare, filled almost exclusively with rows of bookshelves built into the thick adobe walls. He plumped Lissa down squarely in the middle of the bed, then stepped back to look at her sprawled across the dark cover.

"You don't know how many times I've fantasized about this. About having you here in my bed."

"Probably about as often as I fantasized about being here."

"What took you such an excruciatingly long time?" he asked, sliding down next to her.

"Fear."

"Did I seem that much of a brute?" Matthew asked, with no sign of remorse in his voice.

Lissa was too happy now to think somber thoughts and make sad confessions. "Yes, you did!" she crowed, rolling over on top of him. "And you confirmed my worst fears. You are an animal." She leaned close to his ear to croon, "A total, untamed, savage, insatiable animal."

"Driven to desperation, my dear. The next time will not be so furious. The next time I want to love you gently and slowly, as slowly as you can endure."

His voice had become a honeyed seduction, melting

Lissa again. "I'm ready to take that challenge," she whispered, burying her face in his neck.

Matthew's hands were straying down the arch of her back when the click of the clock on the nightstand alerted him. He grabbed the alarm before it could ring. Lissa pulled the hand gripping the clock to her and read the dials. She sat bolt upright.

"Five-thirty?" she demanded, unable to believe the hour.

"Afraid so. That was quite a little nap you took out there, curled up against me."

"Oh, Matthew, I'm supposed to be on the set by seven."

He groaned and sat up. "Looks like that next time will have to wait then."

"You don't know how tempted I am to call Jack with some excuse for not coming in today," Lissa whimpered.

"Don't." Matthew's voice was sure and steady. "I want you more than I can say. But I don't want what we have together to ever, in any way, diminish you."

Lissa's heart swelled inside of her. Had anyone ever cared for her like this? More even than she cared for herself? "Oh, Matthew . . ." The words "I love you" were already springing from her tongue when she shut her mouth. It was too soon, what they had too fragile.

"Come back with me," she begged instead, feeling desolate at the thought of leaving him. "Please. I can't do these next scenes without you. Come on, you've got an investment to protect. You don't want the leading lady chewing up the scenery, making your work look bad. Come. Stay with me."

"They'll talk, Lissa, you know that much about a film crew. They're like a very small town with every one of the inhabitants on display."

"Let them talk. I don't care. I don't care about anything but having you near me for as long as I can kidnap you."

"Don't think the idea isn't tempting," Matthew said, his hand drifting down across her belly. "I feel exactly the same way right now. I want to tie you to this bed until we've tried out every depravity that appeals to us. But the livestock . . . the new foal . . ."

"Matthew, I'll just bet that son the Monroes have in high school would probably jump at the chance to make some extra money if all it involved was coming by here to feed."

Matthew grinned as he rolled over onto his back, pulling Lissa over on top of him. The curtain of her hair swung down on either side of her face to brush along Matthew's collarbone. "You know what? I believe you could win that bet." He lifted away her draping hair and leaned up to nuzzle her neck, growling like a hungry bear feeding at a honey tree.

Lissa felt the pull of his stomach muscles straining against her as he lifted himself. Then again, as he lay back down and threw his arms wide on the bed. "I surrender. I'm yours. Lord, I love women who know what they want and go after it."

"You'd better not be loving too many of them," Lissa warned with mock ferocity. "At least not in my immediate vicinity."

His arms came back up, his hands curving to fit the swell of her derriere. He pressed her to him so that she could feel the renewal of his desire.

"That next time can't come soon enough."

*C*hapter 9

Though she'd had only a few hours of sleep the night before, Lissa felt brighter and fresher than she had for weeks when she stepped onto the set. Driving back in the early morning, she'd watched the sun break over the mountain onto a glorious new day abundant with bright possibilities. Lissa had turned the radio up and sung along with every song, making up words when she didn't know the ones being broadcast.

Cast and crew members were just starting to drift in, most of them being led along by steaming foam cups of coffee. Lissa greeted each one of them with a smile that put a tiny bit more spring into their dragging, early-morning steps. She had happiness to spare that day. Matthew had promised to follow her down as soon as he had made arrangements with the Monroes' son, Montana, to look after his animals. Impatience pressed at Lissa as she tried to calculate just how long that chore would take.

How long it would be before she could see Matthew again. Before she could feel his naked skin against hers. In one short night, she thought, bemused, I've turned into an insatiable wanton.

"Goodness," Shaun's booming voice surprised her, "what mischievous little secrets are putting smiles like that one on your face at this ungodly hour?"

Lissa spread her fingers across her lips as if she could bottle up the grin blooming across her face.

"Must have been some kind of air you went out for last night. Seems to have cured your cabin fever and anything else that ailed you."

Lissa felt so radiantly alive and brimming with goodwill that she simply ignored Shaun's innuendoes. She handed him back the keys to his Jeep with a smile that made the actor yearn for an innocence that he'd lost too long ago. "Yes," she said beaming. "Nothing like some mountain air to put the roses back in your cheeks."

"Shaun! Lissa!" Jack's gofer, Stan Davisbury, barked out at them in the self-important, officious tone he adopted when doing his master's bidding. "Jack would like to see you in Sidney's trailer. ASAP."

Shaun quirked a conspiratorial smile at Lissa, mocking the assistant's officious tone.

In the producer's trailer, Jack had stationed himself behind the massive desk and had his feet propped up on it. His hands were steepled in front of his face, and he was tapping his index fingers against his nose. He pretended to be so absorbed in his ruminations that he didn't notice them enter. The obvious theatricality of his absorption would have annoyed Lissa on any other day. Today she was merely amused.

"Ah-hum." Davisbury cleared his throat as if the sound were necessary to alert the director that three people stood a couple of feet away from him.

Shaun rolled his eyes in exasperation. "Jack, you wanna come out of your trance and tell us why we're here?"

"Oh, Shaun, didn't notice you there. I was thinking through yesterday's scene. I screened the dailies last night. Tried to call both of you to come down and give them a look with me, but"—he paused to cast meaningful glances at both of his lead players—"neither of you were in your rooms."

"So give us each five demerits," Shaun shot back. "What's up?"

"What's up is, it doesn't play. It's not there. Something's wrong with the scene."

"You're right," Lissa spoke up after a moment's hesitation. "I lost the dramatic tension at the end."

"Maybe, maybe not," Jack quibbled.

One thing Lissa was learning about Jack Myers was that the only answers he valued were ones he personally came up with. She had just told him what anyone with the slightest degree of perception could have observed yesterday and he was denying it. She tried another tack.

"I can do that scene again and make it play." She wasn't entirely sure that she could make good on her offer, but at least she was willing to try. Or would be as soon as Matthew arrived.

"No, I've already called Briggs and he's coming in today to do a rewrite. We were going to do reaction shots from that scene today, but we'll skip ahead. Do the next scene five years later. Make sure you tell Jerome that, okay, Lissa? Those years have been hard on Jeannie up there alone, running a ranch and raising a kid. I want them to show on you. Got it?"

"Aye-aye, captain." Lissa, refusing to be dictated to, snapped off a joking salute and left the trailer. Things were really working out. Jack had just provided Matthew with the perfect excuse for being in town. She practically bounced into the trailer that was Jerome's tiny kingdom. As usual, the makeup man was in a snit. He waved his hands about at the bars of light installed above the mirrors he and his underlings worked in front of.

"I specifically told them to get me daylight bulbs and look at these . . . these . . . obscenities I have to work under! Floodlights," he sneered. "What do they think I'm doing in here? Making up Little Nell and Snideley Whiplash for a gaslight melodrama! Adversity. Why are the great ones always forced to work with adversity?" Jerome wondered aloud with a heavy sigh.

"Probably because you're the only ones who can meet the challenge," Lissa supplied.

A High, Hard Land

It was the correct answer. Mollified, Jerome directed Lissa to hop into the barber's chair he used. "Now, refresh my memory, what is Little Caesar shooting today?"

"There's been a schedule change. Jack wants to shoot the scenes five years after Quaid leaves. He told me to ask you to make the years show. Five hard years."

"Add five hard years, eh?" Jerome echoed, already smoothing a layer of matte foundation that wouldn't reflect the bright lights onto her skin. "This is going to be a feat considering you look five years younger today than you did yesterday. Child," he twittered, "tell Aunt Jerome what marvelously restorative activity you've been indulging in." He winked broadly and nudged her beneath the plastic cape he'd tied about her neck.

Lissa gave an enigmatic smile. She wasn't offended by Jerome's ribaldry and, any other time, might have bantered along with him. But today was like no other time in her life. What she and Matthew had together belonged to another world. A world that she wanted to keep safe from the slightest taint of tawdriness.

"Oh, all right," he fumed, pursing his lips and rolling his eyes skyward. "Keep your naughty little secrets to yourself. Deny this celibate even that vicarious pleasure."

As Jerome's skilled hands rubbed in slight hollows under her cheeks, smudged shadows under her eyes and drew in tiny wrinkles, Lissa began making the mental transformation to match the physical one being wrought upon her. She played out in her mind the hardships and sorrows that Jeannie had been forced to endure for five years.

She imagined herself as a young mother, isolated from civilization with a growing son, and aching for the man she'd banished from her life. She imagined how Jeannie would feel when the letters came from that man. How her hands would tremble at the very sight of his handwriting, at the return addresses growing ever more distant. She imagined the force of will it would have taken to do what Jeannie did with each and every one of those letters: she tore them into tiny pieces. Then, not trusting herself with even those scraps, she'd flung them into the fire.

None of that had been in the script, but it was all in Matthew's book and Lissa was grateful she had that kind of background to draw upon. It would add strength to her characterization.

By the time Jerome whipped the cape off her, Lissa emotionally felt and physically looked burdened by those five sad years. She was pleased to see how Jerome's skilled makeup job had aged her with shadows and wrinkles. She looked like what she was supposed to be—a woman who had endured.

Jack had the first shot already set up at the edge of town, near the abandoned ranch house that had been restored as Jeannie's place. The scene was to open with Jeannie repairing fences near the house. Lissa slipped on heavy leather work gloves and a prop man handed her a pair of wire cutters as Jack's assistants scurried about attending to the finishing touches. Then Jack was calling for everyone to take their places. Lissa made her mind a blank as she walked to the fence she was supposed to be fixing. With each step, her gait became a bit stiffer as she let the years of Jeannie's backbreaking toil seep into her.

By the time she reached the fence and began twisting strands of barbed wire together, she was Jeannie Duncan again. She was so immersed in the task at hand it took only a flicker of her eyes looking up from her chores to indicate that a distant sound had broken her concentration. She tracked the imaginary horse and rider that would be added in the editing room. But as Jeannie, Lissa saw the unmistakable way that Quaid reined a horse with his left shoulder dipping down. Noted the way the collar of his sheepskin jacket was up against the wind and how wispy tracks of frozen breath trailed from his horse's nostrils.

The wire cutters slipped from Jeannie's suddenly numb fingers to drop unnoticed to the dry earth. Quaid was back. Though a day had not passed in the past five years when her thoughts and heart had not turned to him, she had never expected to see him again. In one of those frozen moments when logical thought stops, Jeannie's head filled with random smells and sounds: the aromatic nip of juniper and pine; the raucously mechanical caw of a raven; the buzzing of a horsefly pestering the horse tied to a fence post.

"Ma, hey, Ma, there's someone coming."

It took a moment for her son's voice to pierce the

shocked numbness muffling her. "I see him, Sherman," she replied, forcing a measured evenness into her tone.

As the plume of dust raised by horse and rider drew nearer, Jeannie pulled her son to her. Her hand went from his sturdy little shoulder to the shock of sandy-blond hair that could have been taken from Quaid's own head. The boy was the image of his father. But, much as the way her son's hazel eyes, flickering with a certain spark that could only have come from Quaid, tore at her heart, she believed firmly that one night of love did not a father make. Quaid had not earned the privilege of being her son's father.

And he never would.

"Get on into the house," she ordered the boy, pushing him in that direction.

"No, Ma, I want to see who it is. We never get any company."

"This isn't company, son. Now get on into the house. I'll let you listen to *The Lone Ranger* on the radio tonight."

"Whoa, boy!" the boy whooped, scrambling into the house at the promise of the treat. Jeannie had heard about a new gadget, television, but they could barely receive radio signals up on their mountain and she rationed those.

"Hi-ho, Silver!" Sherman called out, breaking into a garbled but spirited rendition of the *William Tell* Overture.

Jeannie pulled off her gloves, held a hand out to shade her eyes and waited. In an unguarded moment, her hand went up to pat back the stray wisps of hair flying about her face. She jerked the hand away. There was absolutely no reason on earth for her to go and pretty herself up for the likes of Quaid Dawson, who should mean less than nothing to her.

Jeannie could stop her hand, but she was powerless to dictate to her heart. As Quaid drew near enough for her to make out his features, her pulse began to drum in her ears with a force that blocked out all other sound. As he came closer, she saw the evidence of five years on the road written on his face, just as she knew the time had been carved into hers.

But the few tiny wrinkles weren't what Quaid saw when he looked at the slender figure bravely guarding her tiny domain. He saw the treasure that he had dreamed of for five bitter years, ever since he was fool enough to have thrown it away. She had become a woman in those five years. It was there in her stance, in the set of her shoulders. She was no adoring teenager. She was a full-grown woman. His heart lurched violently within him, surprising even Quaid with the raw intensity of his reaction. Five years of longing coalesced into one heart-stopping certainty: he loved her and he'd die trying to win back what he'd thrown away.

Jeannie crossed her arms in front of her chest to keep them from trembling as Quaid reined to a stop some distance from her, then, leading his horse, came near on foot. He was, yes, as handsome as ever, but he'd changed. There was something in his face that hadn't been there when he'd left. Character? Jeannie batted the notion away. His guiles, no matter how they came disguised, were never going to work on her again.

"Jeannie, I—" Quaid started, then his voice failed him.

But the way he had spoken her name sent shivers she hadn't felt for half a decade running along Jeannie's spine. It was a danger signal that jolted Jeannie into a defensive wariness. "Why did you come?" she snapped.

"There's about half a million ways I could answer that question, but I guess I came because I had to. I couldn't stay away any longer, Jeannie. I should never have let you run me off in the first place."

"You didn't have much choice in the matter, just like you don't have much choice now. So you can just get back on that horse and ride on out of here."

"Jeannie. Don't."

For a second, Jeannie faltered, tripped up by the look and sound of utter desperation on Quaid's face, in his voice. But then she remembered her son back in the house and her obligation to raise him the best way she knew how. And that, she thought, included never letting him meet a father who'd left him once and might do the same thing tomorrow. Or a week from now. Or a year. It didn't matter, Jeannie was convinced, sooner or later Quaid would always leave.

"Leave. Now," she ordered him.

"Jeannie, listen, I heard in town that you're just barely hanging on to this place. That if you don't get some help, you'll lose it for sure. Now I wasn't expecting to come riding in here and have you take me in with open arms. I did wrong. Terrible wrong. But that was a different person. I don't expect you to accept that right off, either. I'll stay and work. Help you get the place back into the black. I want to make up for . . ."

He paused, snared by the sublime innocence he had first seen in her eyes fifteen years before. It peeked out at him like a shy child from behind the bitter wariness of her stare. He swallowed hard. That hint of soft vulnerability still hiding in her gaze was like the shimmer of an oasis to a man dying of thirst. "I want to make up for everything."

"You can't, Quaid," Jeannie stated with a wistful finality. "You can't erase all those times when I was alone and needed someone, anyone, to stand by me. When the ladies in town turned their noses up at me. When I had to take myself into town, alone, for the delivery. When Sherman got whooping cough last winter and I was snowed in up here and thought he'd die. You can't make up for that, Quaid, for any of it."

"My God, I'm sorry, Jeannie. I could go on saying that for the rest of my life and I know it wouldn't change anything. But you don't have to be alone anymore."

The tiny window of vulnerability, which had opened briefly for him, slammed shut. "You're mighty presumptuous, Quaid Dawson, just riding in here thinking that I'd prefer you to being alone anymore. I'm not that moony nine-year-old anymore. Not that lovesick teenager. I'll make it on my own, thank you."

"You won't and you know it," Quaid answered, unhesitatingly. "Without me you're going to lose this place, the place that your father homesteaded."

A sharp pang twisted through Jeannie at the mention of her father and at the unimpeachable truth in what Quaid said. She was on the verge of losing her father's ranch and the specter of that loss haunted her days and nights.

"Hey, mister," Sherman's voice piped up, clear and sweet, from the house. "My ma won't let me come out. You want to listen to *The Lone Ranger* with me? It's coming on pretty soon. Eleven minutes, probably."

"Be my honor to listen with you," Quaid replied in the man-to-man way that Jeannie knew delighted the little boy, who was starved for such male contact. Quaid was looking off at the house when Sherman poked his head around the screen door. Jeannie watched Quaid's face flood with joy at the sight of his son. The boy needed to have a man around, she reminded herself. As little else as she had been able to give her son, she could give him that. For a while. A very short while.

"Okay. You can stay and help me work the place." She bit off the words so that there would be no mistake about their intent. "But you will live in the bunkhouse. It's been abandoned for a good while now, but that's your lookout to see that it's fixed up. I'll pay you standard hired hand wages soon as the herd goes to market."

Quaid began to open his mouth to express his gratitude when Jeannie silenced him.

A High, Hard Land

"If you're so set on it, you can be a hired hand out here, Quaid Dawson, but nothing more. You can never be a father to my boy and you'll never again be a lover to me."

For half a second Quaid, chilled by the indomitable finality of Jeannie's tone, considered turning on his heels and leaving. But he couldn't. No more than he could stop breathing. His heart was here. He had walked away from it once and he had sworn that he'd never do that again. Never leave the woman he loved or the son she'd borne. His future was contained in the hope that someday Jeannie's heart would soften.

"Hey, mister." Sherman, a cheerful, outgoing little boy, could not resist the temptation of the rare visitor. "You got a 'Lone Ranger' mask? I'm saving up to get me one. Only thing is, my ma won't hardly ever get us store-bought cereal so I don't have very many boxtops. But I got some. You want to see 'em?"

"No, he doesn't, Sherman," Jeannie answered for Quaid. "This here's Mr. Dawson. He's going to do some work around here. I don't want you pestering him." She stared straight at Quaid, as if sealing their contract, and added, "He's here to work and that's all." With that, Jeannie turned and went into the house.

Quaid stood staring after her for a long moment, his face playing out the jumble of emotions churning inside him. Finally, his eyes narrowed the slightest bit as he came to a decision: he had a lot to prove and, by God, prove it he would.

The camera panned in for a close-up on Shaun's face, and he held Quaid's expression of dogged determination until Jack yelled, "Cut!"

Inside the refurbished ranch house, Lissa relaxed when she heard the director's call. She'd been answering questions from the young actor playing Sherman about who this Lone Ranger person was and why he had to wear a mask.

Though Lissa felt she had done a credible job, the scene had been exhausting. Not quite as threatening as yesterday's, perhaps, but close. She tensed up again when she heard Jack's assistant call for the scene to be set up again. Something wrong with the lighting. Lissa reminded herself that endless repetition was the very core of an actor's craft. Usually, she didn't mind, but the scenes they had been working on were different. They took more out of her than any others she'd ever played before.

As she stepped out to retake her place with the wire cutters at the fence, she spotted Matthew consulting Jack. Lissa restrained an urge to run up to him. She waited by the fence until he was through and walked over to her. Though it had only been five hours rather than five years since she'd last seen Matthew, Lissa felt what Jeannie had as the man she loved approached her. The buzz of activity whirling about her seemed to subside, then fade away altogether with Matthew's first words.

"The hours since you left have been the longest of my life. But I got Montana to agree to feed. So I'm all yours for the next couple of days."

"All mine?" Lissa echoed teasingly. "The mind reels at such bounty."

"Seems I would have been ordered down in any event. Jack wants some rewrites. Something about yesterday's scene not working. I won't be sure until I see the rushes after lunch. And speaking of lunch," Matthew went on, the gleam of desire sparkling in his eyes, "I pray that, if there's a merciful God in heaven, you do not have any absolutely unbreakable lunch plans."

"Your prayers are answered," Lissa gibed. "Just what did you have in mind?"

"Meet me at your hotel room and I'll show you in exquisite detail, Miss Bauer," Matthew promised.

"I suppose you'll need this then," Lissa said, fishing her room key out of her jeans and surreptitiously slipping it to him. "For this little demonstration you plan on conducting."

His cavalier grin faded as he looked into her eyes. The bantering mood was replaced by the building urgency of a need that confounded him with its power. "I felt like a virgin last night," he whispered hoarsely. "Do you understand what I mean?"

Lissa nodded, her throat having gone dry, burned by the flame of the same desire heating Matthew. She did know what he meant. She'd felt the same newness.

"It was all a discovery for me," he said, hungering now to share the rare emotions she evoked in him.

"For me, too," Lissa managed to squeak out before Jack ordered the set cleared.

"God, I ache for you," Matthew whispered, pulling away from her. "I'll be waiting."

Jack explained that all they had time for before lunch was her reaction shot watching Shaun ride up. Lissa nodded, only half hearing what Jack had said and barely noticing the camera pull in tight to her face. Her attention was riveted on the truck carrying Matthew off. Her imagination was already captured by the prospect of being alone again with him. She thought of Matthew in her room. In her bed. Naked. Waiting for her. The prospect was more voluptuous than any Lissa had ever before contemplated. Voluptuous. She'd never associated the word with any man other than Matthew.

"And, cut!" Jack yelled, startling Lissa, who'd been waiting for them to begin.

"Good shot," the director called to her. "Different from the one earlier. This one showed more of Jeannie's wanting, her need."

Lissa blushed to think that desire had been so nakedly written on her face. At least Jack had thought she was acting.

"Okay, people, lunch," the director ordered.

Lissa jumped into the first van that passed by, shuttling crew members between the set and the hotel. Most everyone else headed for the caterer's truck pulling up. Lissa was usually the first in line. The wisdom that an army traveled on its stomach applied doubly to a crew filming on location. Sidney had engaged a top-notch L.A.

outfit to keep his army fueled. The menu of the day was linguine with clam sauce, but eating was the last thing on Lissa's mind. The very last.

"I thought you might be heading back to the hotel," Jerome, the makeup man, chirped as he hopped into the van behind Lissa.

Lissa smiled enigmatically in return.

"Oh, I won't pry. Just let me warn you that if you're planning to do anything over your lunch hour that's going to leave you looking as young and fresh as you did this morning, don't come to me expecting my makeup wizardry to be able to make you look haggard again. It's beyond even my genius."

Lissa had to laugh.

"Look, dearie," he continued, "I know it's none of my business, but I've been staring at faces for most of my life and I can tell when one of them is attached to someone who is newly fallen in love."

"Jerome," Lissa scolded, not wanting to have her delicious secret aired in public.

But Jerome's face had softened and taken on a new look of understanding. "I just hope he deserves you is all I wanted to say. I also guess I'm a little jealous of all that lovestruck radiance. I mean, there just aren't that many men out there worth falling in love with, are there?"

"No," Lissa answered. "There really aren't."

At the hotel, Lissa flew up the steps. In her impatience, the hall seemed miles long and the walk to her door unendurably long. And then she was there. The door was slightly ajar. She pushed it open.

It was all just as she'd fantasized. Matthew in bed, waiting for her, the materialization of her most fevered imaginings. She stepped into the room and pressed the door quietly closed behind her.

"Hi," she whispered.

"Hi," Matthew answered. His smoldering gaze followed her into the room. "Was it my imagination?" he asked. "Or have I really been waiting here for half a year while you shot that scene?"

"Imagination, darling." Lissa pulled the heavy brocade drapes shut, creating an even more intimate, dusky atmosphere. "Shooting this morning only lasted three months." She began unfastening the buttons at her cuff. "I was counting."

"Come here, woman," Matthew growled. "Let me do that for you."

As Lissa walked toward him, arranged in her bed as masterful as a potentate of old, she wondered where all the air in the room had gone to. A dizzy, suffocating feeling stole over her so that she had to part her lips to breathe. Even then, it seemed that each breath was dense with Matthew's clean, masculine smell. The air seemed charged with the magnetic energy of his sheer physical presence.

Matthew noticed how very slightly her slender weight rocked the bed as she sat on the edge of it. Her expression, caught perfectly beneath a beam of sunshine peeking in through a crack in the drapes, touched him in places no other woman ever had. She was a singular heart-stopping mixture of a slightly frightened young girl and a woman ripe with wanting. His mouth went dry from the heat of needing her. "Give me your hand," he commanded. With painstaking skill, he dispatched the buttons.

Time seemed to slow, then to disappear for Lissa as his talented fingers moved up to the buttons at her neck, and then pushed aside her blouse. With great delibera-tion he uncoupled the snap at the front of her bra, and with an almost reverential languor, he parted the flimsy undergarment.

Though an aching spasm twisted within Lissa as the wisps of lace glanced across her full, high breasts, he did not touch her as he carefully slid the scrap of fabric off her shoulders. "I wouldn't have believed it possible," he breathed, marveling as the bolt of sun lapped across Lissa. "You're even more beautiful in sunshine than you are in firelight. I remember the first time I saw you like this, driving to my place at sunset. I was dying . . ." He leaned forward. The sheet, strikingly pale against the brown of his muscled torso, slipped down to his waist. ". . . to lick away . . ." He leaned forward a bit more and the sheet fell completely away to reveal the devastating extent of his arousal. ". . . all that buttery sunlight." Even as he spoke, his tongue was busily fulfilling that denied desire.

His mouth, ardent and skilled, sent a drenching wave

of warmth flooding through Lissa as it licked at the sunshine spilling down her neck, her throat, to stop finally at her breasts. She was lost again in that world of sensuality only Matthew had been able to show her. She teetered beneath the sensual assault. Matthew grabbed her to steady her and to press her even more fully to his voracious mouth.

Her hands wound through his hair, then down to rake lightly across his bowed back.

Frantic with desire, he tugged at her jeans, Lissa helping him in his efforts. He pulled her onto the bed on top of him, his hands roaming like uncaged creatures across her back, her bottom, her thighs. She fitted perfectly into the hard hollows of his body. Their mouths merged, lips and tongue fusing feverishly into one. She nipped at his lip. A shudder passed through Matthew, and he pulled his mouth from hers.

He paused, breathless, his eyes glittering as he stared into a face, softened with arousal, that grew more precious to him with every glance. A pounding need to have her, at that very second, knifed through him. He fought it and forced his labored breathing to return to normal.

"Slowly," he murmured, as much to himself as to Lissa. "Very, very slowly. So that our minds can keep track with what is happening to our bodies. Very"—he began pulling her lips back to his—"very slowly." His drawled words set a new tempo, heavy with an almost tropical languor. His kiss took time to explore and savor, his tongue making slow, dipping forays into her mouth as the tips of his nails brushed feathery caresses the length of her body.

Then his hands were gently tumbling her over onto the bed beside him where he could search out the passion-beaded tips of her breasts, stroking and fondling until he again heard the tiny gasps that signaled Lissa's pleasure. Guided only by that aim, he ventured further down the silken curve of her stomach and further still.

Lissa reeled from the devastating impact of his touch as it found the place where her need centered and, as gently as a man stroking the most delicate folds of a dewy rose, he brought her to a keening height of desire.

"This is a miracle to me." Matthew's whispered words seemed part of the delirium that burned through Lissa, part of the fire stroked by his hands. "That I can make you like this . . ."

"Love me, Matthew," Lissa answered. "Love me."

Matthew spread her legs and lowered his weight onto her, filling her, filling the ache that had grown unendurable. Lissa rose up to meet him, driven by the frenzied energy pounding through her. A groan of pleasure rasped from Matthew's throat as they joined.

"Oh, God," he muttered, "it's sweet, too sweet." With an effort, Matthew slowed the savage lash of his hips against Lissa's. "Be still," he commanded. "I can't control myself when you move like that. I want this slow, as slow as we can stand it. I want to feel you around me. I want you to feel me."

"Yes," Lissa gasped, drowning in a fathomless pool. "It's all I can feel." She pulled his mouth down to hers and felt Matthew swell within her as her tongue twined brazenly about his. His hips somehow found rhythms that alternately paralyzed Lissa, then drove her to the very brink of frenzy. Finally, neither one of them could forestall the inevitable crescendo.

For a long time they lay together, cradled by silence. It was Matthew who at last collected his wits enough to speak. "It's never been like that before for me. With anyone," he marveled.

Lissa, coiled up cozily against Matthew's chest, sighed her contentment and softly replied, "I know." What she and Matthew had shared seemed like an entirely different act from her few past involvements. She knew where the difference lay, too—love. She was saturated in love for Matthew. It beamed from her. She looked into Matthew's eyes and was certain she saw it reflected there. But she held her tongue. It was still too new, too fragile, to open up with words. She felt both exorbitantly cherished and terribly vulnerable. "I know," she murmured again, burying her face in the silken wiriness of the dark hair matting Matthew's chest.

Matthew liked the feeling of her curled in his arms, the tip of her nose burrowing against his heart. Liked it very much, indeed. Too much. Fighting the desire to pull her mouth up to his, he reached over to grab the pocket watch he'd laid on the nightstand. "Damn," he exploded. "The tyranny of time. Your lunch hour has more than vanished, my darling."

Lissa slumped back against the pillows. "At moments like these, I wish I could simply call and claim a sudden case of a twenty-four-hour virus that everyone understood meant I was taking a mental-health break. But you can't do that when you've got a hundred-odd other people waiting for you."

"Not if you're a professional you can't," Matthew agreed sadly. "And you are, my dear. Dammit all, you are. Dinner? La Fonda?"

"You've got yourself a date, amigo," Lissa answered, sliding out of bed and pulling on Jeannie's clothes and boots.

Matthew, enjoying the brief flashes of long, slender limbs, propped himself on an elbow. "I'll be watching you this afternoon."

"Oh, are you coming out to the set?"

"No, I'll be screening yesterday's film. Trying to figure out why Jack thinks it doesn't play."

Lissa, her back to Matthew as she perched on the edge of the bed pulling on her boots, stopped. She wished that the scene in which Jeannie banished Quaid from her and her child's lives would simply disappear. She winced, thinking of Matthew seeing her wooden performance yesterday. "*I* didn't play yesterday," she said, straightening.

"You'll see that soon enough. The scene is fine. I just can't play the ending. Maybe in your infinite cleverness you can write around it somehow."

Matthew narrowed his eyes slightly, then laughed as if choosing to believe that she had been joking.

Lissa smiled back but her heart wasn't in it. She wanted desperately not to have to play that scene again, rewritten or in its original version.

"You'd better run, babe," he coaxed. "Wouldn't want you cultivating a prima-donna reputation."

She stretched back over across the bed for a last kiss which almost convinced her that extending it would be worth any kind of reputation, but shook off the temptation. At the door, she paused to trill over her shoulder, "On with the show." In her last glimpse of Matthew, he was propped up in bed, regarding her with a wistful smile, as if he were already rewriting the problem scene in his mind. A sudden urge to rush back to him and banish with her kiss every thought from his mind surged over Lissa. She felt she was already losing him again to his work and it was too soon. Instead, she made herself walk out the door and shut it behind her. Made herself believe that it was all her imagination. She almost believed herself.

Chapter 10

The hours of waiting that usually seemed so end-
lessly tedious to Lissa while equipment, people and
even the sun moved to the right spot, drifted by effortlessly that afternoon. Since Matthew had entered her life,
she had gotten an entirely new perspective on the arduous, agonizingly slow process that was filmmaking. It was
as if another world had opened up to her beyond the one
where images were put on film. With most of her mind and
all of her heart still with Matthew, shooting that afternoon
became more of a diversion, an interesting, challenging
one to be sure, but not a life-or-death proposition. As tem-
pers around her frayed when some low-lying clouds scud-
ded across the sun and valuable filming time was wasted
as the entire crew had to wait until the sun appeared again,
Lissa felt only mildly concerned.

She no longer felt that her entire future hung in the balance with each word she spoke, each gesture she made.

Oddly enough, that new detachment helped her performance. Jeannie's character flowed even more naturally through Lissa without a barrier of anxiety to bottleneck it. As Jeannie, Lissa again played out the scene in which she had told Quaid that she wasn't a moony nine-year-old anymore and the little boy playing Sherman again called out to the visitor. Only this time the boy, raised on television, asked Quaid if he'd like to *watch The Lone Ranger.*

"Oops," the young, towheaded actor called out immediately, catching his gaffe. "You don't watch the radio, do you? Sorry."

Jack called impatiently for another take. The little boy, sensing Jack's exasperation, flubbed his line again. And a third time. Though Jack never scolded him, Lissa knew that the little boy was rattled by the director's strained patience. She asked for a two-minute break and Jack reluctantly granted it. Lissa hurried into the house where the little boy was waiting, alone, to say his line.

"I blew it, didn't I?" he said, his head drooping.

Lissa knelt beside him and recalled a conversation she'd had with her mom twenty years ago, backstage at a production of *Oliver Twist* when she, too, playing one of the orphans, had been blowing her lines and becoming more and more upset about it.

"Yeah, you did," Lissa whispered. "But you know what?"

He tilted his head up suspiciously at her. He was already a little pro and wasn't about to be conned by someone coming in and telling him that it didn't matter.

Respecting his skepticism, Lissa went on. "Film actors have a rare power that almost no one else in any other profession has."

"What's that?" he asked, still wary.

"The power to make mistakes vanish. You know when you make a mistake in real life, when you break a vase of your mom's or hit your sister, the vase stays broken and your sister stays mad at you, right?"

"Yeah, sure," the little boy agreed impatiently.

"Well, when film actors make a mistake they can make it vanish. Okay, you made a couple of mistakes."

He looked her full in the eye now, knowing that she wasn't going to deny that he had fluffed a few lines and wasn't going to tell him that it didn't matter.

"But you have the chance to make them vanish. If you just forget all about them and say those lines just like you did in the very first take, all the mistakes will go away. And when the movie comes out, no one will ever know that you didn't get it perfect the very first time."

"Yeah," the little boy agreed, the guarded look leaving his face. "Even Kyle Clayton at my school, who thinks he's so great just because he's been in some stupid Spritzi Soda commercial, will never know."

Lissa laughed at the irony of the little boy's choosing her former employer to disparage. "That's right, this movie's going to be a whole lot better than any soda commercial."

The next take went smoothly, the boy delivering his

line like the old pro he was. As they continued, though, a jet plane roared high overhead and the take was ruined. Shaun's nose started shining through the matte makeup halfway through the next attempt. A light burned out during the next. And so it went for the rest of the afternoon. One step forward and ten back. Lissa, her mood higher than even the passing jet, continued to be amused by it all and eager for it to end. Eager to be with Matthew again.

That time finally came. She spied Matthew, waiting in the lobby, the instant she rushed into the hotel. She stopped and studied him for a moment, experiencing the odd bit of gymnastics the mere sight of him put her heart through. He was seated at one of the banquettes, bent over a tablet of yellow legal paper, scribbling away with his left hand.

He's left-handed, Lissa thought, watching his curled-up hand push the pen across the page. The knowledge seemed monumental to her. How much more was there to learn about Matthew Briggs? To love?

He was utterly absorbed in his work. Oblivious to the crew members swarming in around him, he went on writing. His eyebrows jerked and his mouth moved ever so slightly as he copied down the words he was hearing in his mind. So this is how he works, Lissa thought, feeling that she had stumbled onto something that was rare and precious. As if they had drawn that much closer together physically, Matthew looked up. His face lightened the instant he saw her. The look of brooding concentration dissolved as he rose to his full height and strode toward her.

"Ah, Lissa, my darling," he said softly, whisking her into his arms and whirling her around the expansive marble floor. The production crew, long inured to dramatic outbursts by show people, merely parted to give the twirling couple room. Still, a few eyebrows were lifted at the public display of a new bond among two of their rank, two of the more stellar members: the leading lady and the world-renowned novelist turned screenwriter.

A mad suffusion of color was brightening Lissa's cheeks by the time Matthew released her. She straightened out her shirt, which Matthew had twisted about in his bearish exuberance, and when the twirling finally stopped in her head, she greeted him. "Well, hello to you, too, Mr. Briggs."

"You're a cool one, Lissa Bauer," he said, beaming at her. "All those years in the frozen north have chilled any warmth right out of you," he teased.

She leaned close to whisper to him, "That's not what I remember you saying at lunch."

"If I said what I'm really feeling now," Matthew whispered back, his breath warm and sweet against her ear, "I'd have us both arrested and guarantee you the front page of the *National Enquirer*."

"Now what are you two gettin' all giddy about here?" Shaun Douglas strode up and asked the question in his best tall-in-the-saddle-type accent.

"Shaun," Matthew said, sticking his hand out. "I have to congratulate you."

Shaun warily eyed the man who had taken him to task for sloppy acting.

"I saw yesterday's dailies," Matthew continued, "and you were magnificent. You're putting some real high-voltage stuff on film."

Shaun's wariness disappeared in a flash, the compliment opening him up like a daisy in the sun. "Mighty nice of you to say so, pardner." The actor continued with his mock Western motif. "Have to give some of the credit to Lissa. She sort of dragged me up by the scruff of my neck."

"However it happened, you came across great."

Lissa silenced the question—"What about me?"—which surfaced in her mind as Matthew went on to point out the subtle perfection of Shaun's performance. But she put aside the petty inquiry. Shaun was an old trouper who'd gotten back into form and deserved some recognition for making an effort that he really didn't have to make at this point in an established career.

Praise, coming from someone who'd been such a harsh, but perceptive, critic as Matthew warmed Shaun Douglas immensely, and he insisted that Matthew and Lissa both join him for dinner.

"What do you think, Lissa?" Matthew asked.

Even as Lissa accepted the invitation brightly, she inwardly rejected it. She wanted Matthew all to herself. She had dreamed of them hiding away and eating a room-service supper in bed. That impulse was new to her. Never before had she felt the urge to hide herself away with anyone. Always before, such exclusivity had seemed unbearably claustrophobic to her. But with Matthew, it was as if there were unexplored continents waiting for her within the man. Continents that she yearned to discover, that she would never have enough time to know. She forced herself to overcome the disappointment that nipped at her as Shaun rounded up a dinner party. It wouldn't do for her to suffocate Matthew with her love.

Once Lissa set her mind to it, she genuinely succeeded in reversing her mood. She enjoyed the warm conviviality that enclosed their group, the bond between them, all craftspeople working together to produce something none of them could have achieved alone. She liked the way Matthew was able to meld with the others. His sincere curiosity about people came out as he questioned Amado de la Cruz, the Venezuelan cinematographer, about his work. Listening in, Lissa learned more about the self-effacing man in one conversation with Matthew than she had the whole time they had been working together.

"We are the same, my friend," de la Cruz said, lifting his glass to Matthew. "We spend our lives trying to bring what is up here"—he tapped his bald head—"out here, into the world." The Venezuelan held his hand out, the fingers wrapped around the imaginary bundle of visions that both he and Matthew tried to share with the world.

"We all do," Matthew concurred, holding his glass

aloft to the actors and technicians who sat around the table. There was hearty agreement and much clinking of glasses. Lissa was pleased that Matthew had included everyone and brought them all together with his toast.

"So, Briggs," Shaun said, putting down the wineglass he'd just drained. "Word is that Jack got you back down here for a rewrite on that scene yesterday when Jeannie sends Quaid away. What are you planning?"

Lissa leaned in closer to hear the answer to the question she herself had wanted to ask.

Matthew shrugged. "I've got a few ideas for playing the scene slightly different. Nothing that would affect you much."

That leaves only one other person to be affected in that scene, Lissa thought. Me.

"Good," Shaun said with bumptious joviality. "Nothing I hate more than learning lines."

Lissa looked over at Matthew, but he glanced away before her questioning gaze could capture his. His reluctance to meet her gaze chilled her. What did Matthew have in mind? she wondered. Fervently, she wished that the whole scene would simply vanish. The unpleasant prospect of having to reshoot it had come to loom increasingly large in her mind.

Sensing her growing unease, Matthew reached out a hand under the heavy damask tablecloth and found hers. It was icy to his touch. He wrapped it in the warmth of his own hand and pulled it onto his thigh. There, like a tiny wounded animal he sought to heal, it nestled, and Lissa thought no more about the painful illusion Matthew might be creating for her to portray. She joined in the conviviality, letting its warmth swirl her away.

Only when Matthew's hand let hers go, to spread possessively on her thigh, did Lissa again yearn to be alone with the troubling man beside her. Heat seemed to pour from the fingers that began to massage the inside of her thigh. It was as if the sheer barrier of the jersey dress she wore had been burned away, leaving her exposed to the plundering hand. Though wrenched by the sensual battering, Lissa had to maintain the facade of the congenial dinner companion, laughing along at the jokes and contributing her share to the general banter.

She stifled a gasp when, with a torturing leisureliness, Matthew began to shift the sheer jersey, sliding it with a sensual caress up her smooth thigh. As the dress inched higher and higher beneath the table, Lissa's color rose accordingly.

"Lissa, sweetheart, are you too warm?" Jerome asked solicitously. "Your cheeks are flaming."

It was the severest test of Lissa's skill as an actor to have to reply with the utmost casualness, "Why, no, though I do think I might have gotten the tiniest bit sunburned today."

"Good," Jerome said approvingly. "That fits with Jeannie's look." Fortunately, at just that moment, the waiter arrived to describe the delights available for dessert, and everyone's attention turned to Chocolate Decadence and Amaretto Cheesecake. Lissa took the opportunity to shoot Matthew a warning glance. It was a glance that melted as his talented fingers found the elastic at the leg of her panties and tugged it open just enough to slip the barest of touches in under the silken fabric. Seeing that her control was faltering dangerously, Matthew stopped the mesmerizing massage.

"And for the lady?" the waiter asked, pencil poised over his order pad.

"Nothing for us," Matthew answered for her. "I'm afraid I have a long drive home ahead of me." He stood and began pulling Lissa's chair out for her. She quickly brushed her dress back into place before rising on legs that had gone wobbly. "So, I'll just see Lissa to her room, then I have to call it a night."

Lissa whispered a prayer of thanks for Matthew's fiction. She was quite content to let people speculate, but, in the end, what happened between her and Matthew was nobody's business but their own. With her arm secure in the crook of his, they glided out of the dining room.

*C*hapter 11

But why won't you tell me about this top secret scene you're creating for me?" Lissa asked, rolling over in bed and propping herself on an elbow so that she could look down at Matthew lying beside her. There was no edge on her demand. All sharp edges had been blunted by their lovemaking. Lazy with love, Lissa traced a fingernail through the miniature whorls of dark hair on Matthew's chest, delighting in the way the flesh tautened beneath her touch, the nipples tightening into puckered nubs.

"I never said I wouldn't tell you," Matthew replied, his fingers trailing with an easy familiarity over Lissa's neck. "I just said I'd rather wait until tomorrow when I've had a chance to polish what I've written. The changes aren't substantial. I just added a few lines that might help you get to the heart of the scene better."

Lissa felt the goose bumps that Matthew's feathery

touch was raising shiver along her neck, down to the sensitized tips of her breasts, and almost forgot what she was asking, why it was so important. But the scene haunted her like a shadow, and the moments of forgetfulness were brief. "So, you don't think I got to the heart of the scene yesterday."

"Do you?" Matthew boomeranged her question.

"Why do I have to penetrate to the heart of every scene?" Lissa, too, deflected the question. "I thought that scene could be played more effectively with a little detachment. I still do," she maintained stoutly.

"Detachment is one thing," Matthew reminded her gently. "Flat and wooden are entirely different matters."

"All right," Lissa said, laughing, so comfortable with Matthew that she could dare to turn the whole thing into a joke. "So I didn't make film history. For two minutes, I didn't hit the emotional nail on the head. I don't know why, Matthew, but something in me just bounced off that scene like rubber. I *couldn't*, didn't even *want*, to get to the heart. Do you understand?"

"A little. I'm starting to, at any rate. Tell me about it."

Lissa shrugged. "What's to tell? Some scenes you play and some scenes play you."

"There's more to it than that, Lissa."

"I suppose. I mean, there always is, isn't there? But if I started psychoanalyzing every facet of my life, there wouldn't be much time to just go ahead and live it." She wanted badly to dismiss the whole affair. "Listen, would it hurt for you to just write around that scene? Maybe Jeannie could just leave a note for Quaid?" Lissa offered.

A deep laugh rumbled in Matthew's chest. "You are an original, Lissa. I've never before heard of an actor actually asking for fewer lines. You're supposed to be battling for ever larger chunks of screen time."

His laughter was an improvident bounty. There was nothing stingy or measured about it. Its lightheartedness flowed around Lissa, buoying her and bearing her away from the pestering phantoms haunting her. Floating, cradled by the sea of Matthew's understanding, Lissa felt the grip of anxiety loosen its hold on her, freeing her.

Matthew marveled at the expressiveness of Lissa's face. While they had made love, it had been a mirror reflecting back to him the exquisite depth of his own passion. Then a dark, hunted look had shadowed her features as they had talked about the scene he was rewriting. But, with one laugh, the shadows had disappeared and her face was illuminated by an incandescent radiance that made her more beautiful to him than she'd ever been before. Looking at her at that moment, he was overcome by an outpouring of emotion from the deepest wellspring of his being.

He ached to reveal to her what was in his heart, but feared she wasn't ready to hear it. There were still barriers that had to come down. He was certain that any love that grew within their bounds would be a puny and stunted thing. He wanted more for Lissa, for himself. He wanted to live within the fullest flowering of the love that was unfolding within him. There was so much he couldn't yet put into words. He knew instinctively that Lissa was still holding back. And before their love could become complete, the walls she had built around her hurt had to be scaled. He reached out and pulled her to him, aching to say with words what his arms would have to express for the time being.

"Hey, King Kong," Lissa said with a laugh, "that's some grip you've got there." But Matthew didn't answer with his own laugh. Lissa felt a powerful emotion vibrating through him as he hugged her with a kind of mute desperation. Instinctively, her arms went up to wrap around him. He needed her, needed something from her. "Matthew? Are you all right?"

He didn't answer. He couldn't, not yet. He could only press her to him even closer, until she too felt the power of the feelings pounding through him. Much that could never be put into words flowed between them in that embrace. Matthew prayed that it was enough, that he was doing the right thing. "Trust me," he finally whispered. "That's all I ask for now, your trust."

Lissa nodded, though she had so much more she yearned to give. More than she had ever dared to dream of giving anyone again. Not since . . . From her past, a blurred and distant image swirled together and flitted through her memory, an image of her father teaching her to ride a bike and then, nothing, nothing except a puzzled annoyance. Why should such an image intrude upon her thoughts now? At that point she recoiled from the half-formed question and snuggled deeper into Matthew's arms. The only safety she knew was in them. Safety and the worst danger. She clung tighter but could not force out the dawning realization. She had already given more than trust. Matthew had all that was most essential to her. He had taken it all with her full consent and avid cooperation. She had to trust him; she had no other choice now.

"Tell me," he asked, seeing the change in her expression. "What were you thinking about just then?"

For some reason, a chill went through Lissa and the thought of lying flitted through her mind. But she trusted Matthew. He had asked for that and she had given it to him. "It's stupid," she answered, trying to defuse with a weak laugh the odd tension pulling at her. "But for some reason I was thinking of my father. It's one of my few memories of him. Him teaching me to ride a bike. Funny, isn't it, how the mind wanders?" she asked.

He nodded gravely, staring into her eyes almost as if he could see the image that had troubled her so. "Funny, too," he finally answered, "how the mind always homes in on the truth."

There was no answer to his observation nor did he expect one. Sensing that, Lissa snuggled back down against his chest. But, for some reason, she could no longer find the comfort that had been there just moments earlier. The night grew dark and still beneath the mountains ringing Alta Mesa, but for a long time neither of them slept.

Matthew was gone when she woke up after a few brief hours of restless sleep. On the pillow next to hers was a note saying that he had gone to Jack's office to polish the scene revision and would have to leave immediately after that to check on his animals back at the ranch. He promised to meet her that night for dinner and wished her luck on the day's shooting, saying he knew she could pull off any scene he could write.

Fueled by the dark pessimism that had been building during the sleepless hours of the night, Lissa had her doubts about that proposition. She was on the verge of crumpling the note in her hand when her scanning gaze dead-ended on the four short words that ended it: "I love you, Matthew."

Incredulous, she smoothed out the scrap of paper, afraid that, because she wanted to believe those exact words so badly, she'd forged them out of her imagination. But no. They were there. Written with far more precision than the rest of the note done in Matthew's headlong scrawl. Like dawn breaking on a dark night, her spirit was flooded with radiant light. Buoyed by Matthew's love, she could act any scene ever written. She wished he were with her. She wanted to watch his lips say the cherished words. She wanted him to tell her a million times that they were true and to tell him that her heart resonated with the same love.

She floated down to the hotel lobby, still clutching the precious note, unable to suppress the smile that broke out across her face.

"It should be illegal for anyone to be as blissful as you obviously are before noon," Jerome sniped playfully as she joined him at the bulletin board where the day's shooting schedule was usually posted. There was nothing on it besides a cryptic order to meet out at the ranch house set on the edge of town. The crew trundled off to catch a van headed that way.

By the time Lissa had snagged a cup of coffee, Jack was calling the gathering together. "Stan," Jack barked out, calling for his assistant, who came running immediately, pushing his way through the crowd.

"The sound of his master's voice," Lissa overheard one gaffer whisper to another at the sight of Davisbury so eagerly and obsequiously doing his master's bidding.

"Pass out the script changes, Stan," Jack ordered. "We'll be shooting this scene as soon as it's set up."

"Why all the big mystery?" the gaffer, a beefy man in his late thirties, asked his buddy, a younger but equally beefy man, who just shrugged with early-morning indifference. As the two men waited for the assistant to reach them, the older man turned to his friend. "Hey, you hear the one about the Polish starlet?"

"Naw, what about her?"

"She was so dumb she slept with the screenwriter."

"I don't get it," the younger man responded.

The older man looked away in disgust. "That's the problem with you young guys: you ain't been in the industry long enough to know squat. Got to have everything spelled out. Okay, I'll spell it out. Starlets are supposed to sleep with the director. That way they get cast. Get more lines. Get better treatment. Everyone knows the screenwriter is low man on the totem pole."

"Oh, yeah, so the starlet would have to be real stupid to sleep with the screenwriter," the younger man said slowly.

Lissa was still staring at the backs of the two men's heads when Stan stuck a copy of the script changes into her hands.

The two gaffers read the changes at the same time that Lissa, standing silently behind them, read over her copy. She was stunned. She had hoped and even hinted that the scene she feared would be shortened, maybe even eliminated. But no, Matthew had done the exact opposite: he'd doubled her lines. The two gaffers noted the same expansion of her role.

"Hey," the younger one guffawed to his chum, "maybe it isn't always stupid to sleep with the screenwriter. Looks like our leading lady bought herself some lines that way."

Lissa slid away from the crowd, feeling as if she'd been punched twice in the stomach. First by a couple of jerks whose names she didn't even know, and a second time by Matthew. With a mounting sense of unreality, Lissa looked around her. She'd been up and down the emotional roller coaster one too many times and the gears were beginning to get a little stripped.

The crew bustled about her, preparing for the scene they would be shooting. In the distance, Jack shouted directions but his words didn't reach her. The words on the page she held echoed too loudly for her to hear anything. She looked again at the scene Matthew had rewritten, but the words hadn't changed. Nor had their import: Matthew had betrayed her. She had given him her trust and he'd returned it with betrayal. The note she'd been cradling fell from her hand into the dust at her feet. Words. The four that had been so precious minutes before were now meaningless. They'd been drowned out and washed of all substance by Matthew's other words.

"Lissa. Lissa!" Stan's voice rose on a note of annoyance as he attempted to catch her attention.

Looking into his face caused Lissa actual physical pain, as did concentrating on what he was saying and what was happening around her. She wanted nothing more in the world than to turn away from them all and to escape.

"You learning the new lines?" Stan asked.

She wanted to swat him away like a pesky fly.

"Jack says he'll be ready in a few minutes. Get those lines down. He wants to shoot them fresh. And get into makeup."

Lissa nodded and walked dumbly into makeup, where Jerome threw a cape around her and started in, carping as he slathered on the cosmetics about how difficult it was for an artist like himself to work under conditions where no one told him anything until the last minute. As he nattered on, Lissa wondered how long it would take her to hitchhike from Alta Mesa to Albuquerque. And if her career would be ruined if she walked off the set. For a few minutes, her professional future hung in the balance as Lissa considered sacrificing it and anything else she had just to be able to run from the pain confronting her. She couldn't go on.

Then, in a blaze of unbidden insight, Lissa thought of her mother, Amanda Bauer. Of the countless nights she'd gone onstage in nightclubs, dinner theaters, cabarets and community productions because she'd had to. Because she had no other way of supporting herself and her children. Lissa thought of all the nights when she'd gone on to sing happy songs and act carefree roles when the burden of raising four children alone and loving a man who'd left her must have weighed her down beyond endurance.

She would have to do the same. She couldn't lose everything at once. Not Matthew and her career. With the greatest effort of her life, she made the decision not break down. Not to allow herself that luxury. With a strength inherited from her mother and nurtured through her years of struggle against everyone and everything that sought to hold her down, she steeled herself against feeling. Against the thousand and one barbs that Matthew had pointed at her heart. Against his betrayal. Psychically braced and buttressed, she began to memorize the lines, refusing to feel the pain they brought. By the time Jerome had finished applying the mask to her face, Lissa had constructed another one that concealed the raw edges of her wounded emotions.

When Stan stuck his head in the trailer to yell, "Jack's ready for you," Lissa was ready as well.

Jack, waiting with Shaun outside the ranch house, motioned impatiently for her to come to him. "Okay, you know the lines?"

Lissa nodded.

"Hate to spring a rewrite on you like this," the director apologized. "But it's a good technique. Helps actors to connect intuitively with the power of a scene if they don't have too much time to overanalyze it. It'll play fresher this way."

Lissa knew that Matthew had persuaded Jack to spring the revision on her. He'd written it for maximum emotional impact and then enlisted Jack to make sure that none of its surprise attack power would be wasted. And she had responded just as Matthew had anticipated. He had pulled exactly the right strings and she'd jerked just the way he'd thought she would. A cold core of anger opened up in Lissa as she contemplated the magnitude of Matthew's manipulation.

An admonition she'd heard from her mother right on through to her most recent drama coach rang through her head: "Use it in your work." No matter what the grief or joy, it was all grist for the actor's mill. Every experience and emotion was raw material. Well, Lissa thought, she had an ample supply of hurt and anger to use in her performance today. And use it she would. With that determination, she huddled about the flame of her pain, warmed herself on it and stored its heat.

"You okay, kid?" Shaun asked as they took their places on the set, noticing how his costar's clenched jaw contrasted with her teary eyes.

Lissa didn't answer. She barely nodded. Nothing would take her from the source she would draw power from for this scene. She focused entirely on it, only gradually transferring that power to Jeannie to bring her, sputtering at first, to full crackling fire. The prop mistress handed Lissa a doll wrapped in a receiving blanket and, for Lissa, now Jeannie, it became her newborn son. It was late November and the winter storms were already arriving when Quaid rode back into her life. With Shaun standing in front of her when Jack yelled "Action!" they picked up his return midway through the scene.

He'd already offered to do the right thing and marry her, and she had refused his offer.

"Jeannie, don't do me this way," Quaid pleaded. "I'm here now. I'm willing to do right by you."

"It's too late, Quaid," Jeannie answered.

"Think about what you're saying, woman," Quaid ordered.

"You think I haven't?" Jeannie spat out with a contained fury that Lissa would never have been capable of before today. "You think I don't know what it's going to be like to raise this boy alone?" Lissa took a deep breath. Her concentration teetered the tiniest bit as she gathered herself at the edge of the new lines Matthew had stolen from the most wounded region of her heart. She funneled her new knowledge of betrayal into Jeannie as she asked, "Do you think I don't know what it's going to be like for my boy to grow up without a father?"

Quaid had no answer in the face of the suffering he'd inflicted.

"I know that you won't be there to put him on his first horse and hold him there until he can ride on his own. I know that you won't be there when kids are mean to him at school and he needs a father to dry his tears and make it all right. I know that every step in his life is going to be just that much harder without a father. But that's the flat truth of it, Quaid. My son has no father. You lost the right to call yourself that when you rode out of here last spring."

"But Jeannie," he pleaded, "if you'd only have told me. I'd never have left. I would have stayed by you if I'd just known."

"You knew," Jeannie answered with a cold finality.

"But Jeannie," he said, all the bluster drained from his voice as he spoke her name, "the boy needs a father. And you . . . you need a husband."

This time there was no faltering over the line that had tripped Lissa up the last time. Her delivery shot unerringly to the pierced and bleeding heart of the moment between a man and the woman who must banish him from her life in order to protect what is most precious to her.

"I'd rather have no husband and no father for my child than one who's going to waste both our lives chasing after a fantasy. So get on down whatever road you have to follow, Quaid. Just make sure it never brings you this way again."

The conviction with which Jeannie ordered Quaid away was rock solid. Everyone's attention was riveted. No one doubted that Quaid Dawson had no choice but to mount and ride off. The spectators didn't start breathing again until Quaid had ridden off camera and Jack had yelled, "Cut! That's a take. Print it!"

A spontaneous round of applause burst out. Lissa knew she deserved every clap, and any other moment in her life she would have been elated. But not now. Once the cameras stopped rolling, she'd stopped feeling. All she could manage were a couple of wan smiles in response to congratulations.

Sensing her detachment, the crew turned its adulation on Jack, who was only too happy to receive it.

"Well," he admitted, faking modesty, "shooting raw like that was just a little experiment I thought I'd try. So I had Matthew fiddle around with the lines a little just to give my actors something slightly fresh to work with. I thought that an element of surprise might be crucial. I'm only glad that it worked out."

Jack's duplicity in claiming credit for Matthew's idea left Lissa unaffected. She found Stan and asked when she'd be up next.

"Let's see here," the assistant said, pulling half glasses down off the top of his head and fitting them on his nose to read. "The rest of the day we're doing Quaid's wandering scenes. Doesn't look like you've got a scene until tomorrow morning."

Lissa mentally gave a prayer of thanks for small favors. If she'd had to, she would have somehow managed to get through a day of shooting. She was grateful she wouldn't have to summon up the strength. One thought was still uppermost in her mind: escape. She knew that the hotel, which was constantly buzzing with crew members and reporters, offered no sanctuary. She glanced about, feeling trapped and desperate without a car or even a destination. The company's wrangler was set up not far from the set. Making a quick decision, Lissa made her way over to where he had his string of horses corralled.

"Hi, Jake." She tossed off a bright greeting to the gnarled cowboy in charge of the stock used during shooting. "I'm not up for the rest of the day, so Jack told me to take some practice time. Said I sat on a horse like a greenhorn." She manufactured a chuckle to go along with the lie.

"Hellfire, you don't do so bad," Jake argued chivalrously. "But it's a beaut of a day for ride. Wouldn't mind putting the spurs to one of these nags myself today. Get up there into the mountains away from all that." He nodded his unshaven chin toward the beehive of activity buzzing just beyond them.

Lissa studied the frenzy. From her vantage point, it looked like a hundred adults playing an elaborate game of make-believe.

"Well, here you are, Miss Bauer," Jake said, handing her the reins of a chestnut gelding he'd culled out of the herd. "Name's Scout. He's gentle and knows the best trails through the mountains if you want to head off that way."

"Good suggestion," Lissa agreed.

She swung easily up into the saddle and let Scout follow his own lead. He headed immediately for the foothills. For as long as she was within view of the crew behind her, Lissa made herself sit up straight and hold her head high. The instant that they reached the sheltering pines of the foothills, she sagged in the saddle, grateful that Scout knew the mountains better than she. Once she let her facade crumble, she couldn't have even summoned up the strength to control the old horse's careful, plodding movements. She certainly couldn't have turned back the bitter tears that flowed without measure.

Lissa couldn't remember having wept so copiously, with such lack of control, since she was a girl. Since . . . But the cruel memories that Matthew had callously unearthed were still too painful. That's why she'd buried them. Why she had intended never to bring them to light again. But Matthew had forced her to do just that. In front of a hundred people, some of whom were convinced that she'd bought the despised lines with her body.

She grabbed the saddle horn as sobs two decades old wracked her body. Tears splashed down over her hands and rolled onto the horse's back, darkening his brown coat. Scout trod on, his slow, steady swaying almost like the rocking of a cradle as a tired mother sat through the night comforting a fitful child.

Lissa let the animal carry her higher and higher into the mountains, not seeing or even caring where they went. The awe-inspiring sweep of the land spread out below her was completely lost on Lissa. Her thoughts revolved with obsessive passion around Matthew's betrayal, and she didn't even notice the chill that settled into the air as the sun lowered, until the shivers started. A combination of her frayed emotional state, the thin cotton blouse she wore and not having eaten all day laid her bare to the cold that now seeped into her bones.

It was only that, and the realization that Scout was probably more than ready for his dinner, that finally drove Lissa back down. As she drew closer and closer to the small town below, she decreed that, with each tear that fell from her eyes, she was forcing a tiny bit more of Matthew Briggs from her system. By the time the last one trickled down her cheek, she would be done with him forever. Another man had betrayed her before him, just as cruelly, and she'd learned to close her heart to him. She could do it a second time. Only this time her heart, once locked, would never again be opened.

Chapter 12

B ack at the hotel, the desk clerk stopped Lissa's headlong flight upstairs.

"Mr. Briggs called with a message for you," she informed Lissa cheerfully, imagining herself the bearer of treasured tidings. "He said to tell you he won't be able to make it back to town tonight," the clerk chirped. "Some kind of trouble with a new colt. He'll call you in the morning."

Lissa nodded, a thin smile of thanks tight on her face, and trudged upstairs. Mentally, she scoffed at the flimsy excuse. She wouldn't have believed it a day ago, but it was not surprising now to learn that Matthew didn't even have the courage to show his face. If she hadn't already closed the door on him, this latest evidence of his emotional cowardice and duplicity would have slammed it shut. Lissa knew that she would grieve excessively someday for a love she'd thought might be hers, but not tonight. Not until she was safely back in the privacy of her apartment, where she could fall apart without jeopardizing her career.

Halfway down the hall she ran into Jerome. "There you are," he called out to her.

She could barely manage a tight-lipped smile.

"You look thoroughly done in. Planning an early evening? A full night's sleep? Wouldn't want any bags that my talented brushes hadn't artificially created under those scrumptious eyes."

"I'll rest," Lissa said, knowing that, as upset as she was, sleep would be a long time in coming, if it came at all.

"You'll have to do more than rest." He dug into his pocket and fished out an antique cloisonné pillbox. "Here." He handed her a capsule. "Listen to Uncle Jerome and take this. You'll sleep like a baby."

Lissa nodded and went into her room. After a bath and a few bites of supper brought up by room service, Lissa took the pill. If sleep was the only escape available to her, she would take it gratefully. She didn't want to think anymore. Not tonight, she thought, not for a long time. Unused to medication, Lissa, not even pausing to lock her door, barely made it to her bed before she was steamrolled by sleep. Neither dreams nor her own cries in the night pierced the heavy veil she pulled around herself. So deeply did she slip under that she would have slept and woken without knowing anything about the sobs that wracked her slender body or about the tears she shed had it not been for the strong, sure voice of her father comforting her.

"Lissa," he crooned softly in her ear. "It's all right, baby. I'm here now. It's all right. It was just a dream, just a bad dream."

At last, he'd come back to speak the words that set her free from twenty years of loneliness. Of waiting. It had all been nothing but a bad dream. He'd never left. Still without waking, Lissa curled into the comforting arms that hadn't been there so many other times when she'd cried in the night. And, wonder of wonders, it was all right. The sorrow that had been clouding her sleep dispersed like an early-morning fog burning off in the sunshine. In her half-dreaming state, she reentered the glorious world in which she and Matthew were together and everything was all right. Had always been all right and would continue to be all right, as long as his arms were wrapped around her the way they were at that moment.

Then the comforting embrace turned to something far more demanding. It was a demand that Lissa, her dream melding with reality, responded to hungrily. As Matthew pulled her closer, Lissa's sleeping brain instantly filled in with a background that drew bits and pieces from their own histories, as well as the histories of the characters in the film and their real-life models. In the dream Lissa was at Matthew's ranch. It was winter, and she was curled up on the chair in front of a fire reading a book that turned out to be her own biography, a biography that Matthew had written.

She couldn't make out any of the words in the book.

All Lissa knew for certain was that all the darkest crevices of her life were brought to light on the pages Matthew had penned. As she read the secrets he had uncovered, she felt increasingly exposed and ashamed that Matthew knew all her hidden fears and inadequacies. That sense of vulnerability was translated in her dream to the discovery, as she sat before the fire reading, that she was actually, physically, naked. In the same way that she'd known the book was all about her without reading any words, Lissa knew that Matthew was coming. She scrambled about frantically, searching for something to cover herself with. She remembered the Indian blanket that had been in the living room and ran to hide herself within its folds. It was gone.

Her heart beat faster as she felt Matthew drawing nearer, on the brink of discovering her. And still she couldn't find the smallest scrap to cover herself with, to hide herself behind. An awful sense of doom invaded the dream as she accepted the inevitability that Matthew would see her, see her for exactly what she was, and leave her forever. That he would abandon her to rope and ride in Broadway musicals starring singing cowboys. If only she could hide. With the skewed logic that prevails in dreams, Lissa began tearing pages out of Matthew's biography of her and trying to paste them to herself.

Then, with the suddenness and unconscious insight of dreams, Matthew was beside her, his hands on hers, stilling her frantic efforts at concealment. Though no words were spoken, she understood immediately that there was no further need to hide. That Matthew had seen all that she sought to conceal and that he not only accepted her unconditionally but also loved her, flaws and all. The pages she'd torn from the book fluttered down around her like a shower of autumn leaves. She turned and Matthew was holding her, loving her.

In the twilight between sleep and waking, Lissa met Matthew and responded to him, her mouth softening beneath his kiss just as her body softened and yielded beneath his silken touch.

Matthew felt his heart lurch as Lissa curled her sleep-warmed body next to his. In his arms he held all he wanted most in the world. "I love you, Lissa," he whispered into the soft strands of hair that made him think of curled sunlight. "I love you." It felt so damned good to say the words, even if Lissa couldn't hear them.

Still asleep, Lissa soared along the magic cusp where fantasy intersected with reality, where Matthew had never betrayed her and their love lived on. The dreaming fantasy turned to a waking one as Matthew gently roused her and came into her body. That most compelling of sensations drove all thought from her mind. She listened only to the urgent demands of her body, straining with a will of its own to take all that Matthew offered.

In the aftermath of their loving, Lissa drew comfort from the promises Matthew had made with his hands, his lips. That he could not have betrayed her, then loved her so completely, was the first conscious thought that appeared in Lissa's love-dazed mind. There must be an explanation for everything, she assured herself as she curled her back into the sheltering warmth of Matthew's chest.

"Tell me about your nightmare." Matthew's voice was as soft as the dove-gray dawn beginning to creep in.

"It was one of those silly, disjointed ones," Lissa answered, "that mean nothing to anyone other than the dreamer. And even at that, I'm not entirely sure I understood it." It was a lie. The nightmare had been a graphically accurate depiction of all her most immediate fears. Fears she was working hard to banish, to prove to herself they were groundless.

"How did the scene go?" Matthew changed the subject.

Lissa paused, her eyes searching the predawn dark. "Jack was pleased," she equivocated. "I got a hand from the crew." Matthew's arms tightened around her in a congratulatory squeeze.

"I knew I could pull it out of you," he whispered.

"What?" she asked, forcing herself to try to believe she hadn't heard what she had, and Matthew's words didn't mean what she feared they did.

"I knew that you knew exactly how to play Jeannie's hurt if I could only get you to connect with it."

"And how did you accomplish that?" Lissa had to hear him say it, to admit specifically to what he had done.

"Why, by using key incidents from your past, from your experience with your father."

"I never told you about my father."

"Well, no, not in so many words. You didn't have to. It was more what you didn't say about him anyway. You babble on happily about everyone else in your family, except him. And your photo album. It's packed with pictures of you, your mother, your brothers. But there's what? One, maybe two shots of him. And you're a baby in both of them."

"So what? My father wasn't around," Lissa lashed out. "Big deal."

Matthew reared up on an elbow and turned Lissa in his arms until he forced her to face him. "What are you doing? I feel as if I've had a door slammed in my face."

"That can happen when you poke into places that should be left private."

"Lissa, I don't believe this is happening. Please, baby, talk to me."

"Talk to you?" Lissa threw back. "Why? Do you need to write a few more gut-wrenching scenes?"

"Lissa, don't do this. Don't hang on to your pain."

"Pain, what pain? When did you get a degree in psychology that allows you to pry into people's lives?"

"Honey, a person doesn't have to have a degree in psychology to feel your pain and to know that it will cripple you if you don't get it out."

"Well, then, tell me, what does a person have to be to use that pain to get what they want? Because you used it, Matthew. Just like the old directors used to tell child actors that their dog had been killed to get the poor kids to cry. You took my secrets and used them against me in exactly the same manipulative way."

"Lissa, I can't believe you feel that way."

"I trusted you, Matthew. Can you honestly say that you honored my trust?"

"Yes, yes, I can say it!" Matthew insisted passionately. "Don't you understand, if you hadn't gotten past the barrier that your father's leaving represents for you, it would have stood in the way of your work and, more importantly, it would have stood forever between us. Oh, I'm sure we could have glided over it if we'd wanted to have that kind of superficial relationship. But that isn't what I want for us, Lissa. We can have something together, something that I never thought I'd find with a woman. We can have it all. I want that for us. Desperately."

"So you tried to get it by having me rip open my soul in front of a hundred strangers?"

"Lissa, you had to confront those demons. If you hadn't they would have stunted you in your work and caused what we have together to eventually shrivel and die."

"And what do we have?" Lissa hurled at him. "We have you constantly baiting me, goading me on to be better. When will it stop? When will I ever become good enough? Passionate enough? Perceptive enough for the all-seeing, all-knowing Matthew Briggs? I may never be enough and I'm tired of trying. Tired of twisting myself into new shapes for the almighty Matthew Briggs."

"I never wanted new shapes," Matthew responded, his voice as flat and drained of emotion as his expression. "All I ever wanted was the real woman behind them."

"Well, maybe there's no real woman back here," Lissa taunted. "Or not one real enough for you. Maybe I'll never be another Vonda Kay Monroe. Maybe you haven't found the heroine for your next bestseller."

"Lissa, stop," Matthew commanded, his voice tight with restrained anger. "What you're saying is wrong and destructive."

"Wrong? Destructive?" Lissa echoed, her voice going shrill with a strangely manic energy. "And I suppose planting my deepest hurts in a movie script so they could blow up in my face isn't? You got what you were after this time. But how many more horrendous memories will I have to dredge up for you? Now it's for the movie. Later on would it be for the next novel? Would I be the one required to bring your heroine to life with my pain? Well, I don't think I care much for the position."

Matthew slowly rose from her side, too shaken to reply. A sense of having careened into the boundary that separates the ordered world from chaos overpowered him. Everything he had hoped for and dreamed of had been destroyed in a few sentences. He fumbled his clothes on, and jerkily moved to the door, frozen by the shock of having his world overturned. At the door, he paused and looked back. He beheld the vision of a pearlized dawn streaming its pink radiance around Lissa, like a man dying of thirst looking back on an oasis where he had tried to drink sand. They had brought passion to the illusion but had failed to infuse it with reality.

"I'm sorry."

Lissa barely heard the words Matthew choked out as he opened the door.

"I asked for too much."

And then he was gone. Lissa sat in bed, unmoving, barely breathing, her eyes darting from the door to each corner of the room, then back to the door. *What had she done?* The question howled through her mind, leaving ripples of indecision in its wake.

"Matthew!" she called out, flying off the bed. She yanked the door open and was halfway down the empty hall, running to catch him, when she remembered that all she had on was her underwear. At the sound of voices—Jack in an early-morning conference with the producer, Sidney, coming from the lobby—Lissa retreated.

Back inside her room, she was swamped by the panicked certainty that she had committed a grave error. All she had wanted was for the pain to stop, to protest the public humiliation she had endured. Now that it had happened, she realized how desperately she had not wanted Matthew to walk out of her life.

He couldn't really be gone, Lissa told herself. If he felt for her a fraction of what she felt for him, he would have to come back. Have to. Clinging to that wobbly belief, Lissa managed to prepare herself for the day ahead.

"Glum thoughts cause wrinkles," Jerome chided as he whipped the makeup cape around her.

Lissa forced a small smile. "That means I should be a crone by nightfall."

"That glum, eh?" Jerome arched an eyebrow. "Trouble with our firebrand writer?"

Lissa nodded. During the hours they'd spent together, Lissa had grown to trust Jerome. Though he made a great show of cattiness, she'd seen that, unlike some other crew members, he didn't trade on the confidences bestowed upon him.

"The volatile ones are the hardest to love," he said, his voice heavy with experience. "But, in the end, the only ones worth loving."

"He asks for so much." Only after she'd said them did Lissa realize she had echoed Matthew's last words to her. "There's probably no point, though, in even discussing him anymore."

"It's over?" Jerome guessed.

"I suppose I'll find that out soon enough."

"I hope this isn't one of those prideful standoffs," Jerome said with a sigh. "You waiting for him to call. Him waiting for you to call. Both determined not to be the first to give in. Until, somewhere in the middle of all this fierce pride, the love just kind of withers away." Jerome whipped the cape off her and crowed, kiddingly, "Okay, Jeannie for a Day!"

Lissa appraised his work in the mirror. Though her thoughts were tugged in Matthew's direction, she forced them back. Makeup was the first step she took toward getting into character. She studied the changes Jerome had created, the painted-on effects of years out in the sun and wind. What she had to add now came from within. She had to add the burden of five years, the time from when Jeannie banished Quaid from her life until the scene they would be shooting that day, when he works on the ranch.

As Lissa walked to the set of Jeannie's ranch house, she thought more about her mother. She remembered the time when she and all her brothers had come down with chicken pox. Her mother had finally gotten a shot at doing her cabaret show at the best-paying club in town. She'd had to open after skimping on rehearsal time, stolen to stay home and take care of her sick brood. For the first time, Lissa wondered how often her mother must have cried herself to sleep at night, overwhelmed by exhaustion, loneliness and desperation. Had Amanda Bauer been like her character, Jeannie, and bravely hidden her own unhappiness from her children just the way Jeannie sheltered her son, Sherman?

Lissa slowed her tread as she approached the ranch house, the bare glimmering of realization taking shape in her mind—she was doing exactly what Matthew had predicted she would. She was using the hurt of losing her father to understand her character in a way she hadn't fully explored before.

"Lissa, Lissa." Jack, conferring with the lighting director, spotted her as she passed and trotted to catch up with her. He draped a fatherly arm over her shoulders. "Do we need to go over this scene? Have you checked out the motivation and all that stuff with Matthew?"

Jack entirely missed Lissa's ironic look as the director dismissed what was at the heart of her craft with "and all that stuff."

"I think I'm okay with it."

"So, let's talk it through," Jack suggested.

Lissa wondered if he'd been reading interviews with famous directors and had finally figured out that this was the kind of thing he was supposed to be doing. She decided to humor him. "Quaid's back now after five years, but Jeannie is continuing to freeze him out. He's living in the old bunkhouse and they work side by side all day long getting the ranch in shape, but she won't allow him to get one inch closer to her emotionally."

"Good, good." Jack stroked his chin. "That's pretty much the way I read it, too."

Jeannie gave him a tight smile as he clasped her to him in what was meant to be an encouraging hug, then he darted off, yelling at a grip who was setting up the wrong camera angle. With Jack's total ineffectuality to compare Matthew to, Lissa began to see how much Matthew had given her. Slowly, she was working her way to the conclusion that, perhaps, just perhaps, he had not actually betrayed her. Maybe he'd only done what any competent director would have.

"Shi—" Lissa started to hiss out the curse word in her frustration at the snarl that had been created by tangling her personal and professional life.

"Cursing Quaid, I hope," Shaun said jovially, joining her beside the ranch's windmill. "Should help you to get into character to think dark thoughts about the cad."

She had time only to flash Shaun a brief smile in response before Jack's assistant appeared to point out their markers to them and set them up for the scene. Shaun had to climb up into the windmill, while she stood on the ground surrounded by tools. In the few minutes' delay, while the lighting and sound people made their last-minute adjustments, Lissa fought to clear her mind of pestering thoughts about Matthew. Seeing that that was impossible, she stumbled upon an even better solution; she transferred the flurry of conflicting emotions to Quaid. They all fit. She now intimately knew Jeannie's hurt pride and the protective mechanism that she was employing to save herself and her son from further hurt. She added all that to Jeannie's high plains upbringing and felt it settle into her bones.

Her jaw stiffened as she looked up at Shaun, fast becoming Quaid for her. She felt Jeannie's struggle to keep her emotions clamped in, to keep locked within her the love that she had never stopped feeling for Quaid. By the time that Jack called for the set to be cleared and for the action to begin, Lissa had once again become Jeannie Duncan.

Jeannie shielded her eyes from the harsh sun as she gazed up at the windmill to where Quaid stood straddling its metal legs. For a few tender seconds, when there was no danger that Quaid could ever see it, the love she worked so hard to smother flashed across her face. Jeannie squashed it with an impatient call. "I told you I could fix that rod. Been fixin' it regular every year for five years now."

"Fix it right once and we won't have to fix it next year. Send up the spanner wrench." He lowered the basket tied on a rope next to him.

Jeannie put the large wrench in it and hauled the basket back up. " 'We' won't be fixing anything next year," she corrected him.

"Pardon me for being so presumptuous. I keep making that mistake, don't I?" He jerked angrily on a frozen bolt, straining against it and the limits of his own patience until the rusted bit of metal squeaked loose. A shower of rust particles rained down on Jeannie as Quaid worked on in a quiet rage. He replaced the bolt and checked to see that the rod was working smoothly again, then he scrambled down the metal structure. Jeannie felt the weight of his dark mood descending with him and turned to escape from it. But Quaid was quicker than she. He jumped down and took three giant strides after her. Reaching out, he caught her wrist and pulled her to a stop.

"Turn around here and look at me, Jeannie Duncan!" he thundered.

"I will not."

"You will if you don't want your wrist broken." The threat was empty, they both knew that, but the anger behind it was real. Jeannie stopped and faced him. The impassive expression he had worn since the day he'd ridden back into her life and she'd banished him to the bunkhouse was gone. In its place was the face she remembered, a face crackling with life and fierce pride.

"Yes," she replied coolly, desperately trying to stanch the tide of emotion that rose up in her at Quaid's touch. "What do you wish to discuss?"

"Don't you high-hand me," he warned. "I've put up with it for nearly half a year now and I've had my fill. I've worked the hide off my hands fixing fences, doctoring cattle, branding, feeding and generally playing your hired hand. And I'd do it all again. I'd keep doing it for the next ten years if I thought it would get me anywhere, but it's not. It never will, will it, Jeannie?"

"I never made you any promises, Quaid Dawson."

"And I never asked for any. But I have to have some hope, and you surely haven't given me any of that. I can't go on working by your side day in, day out pretending to be nothing more than your hired hand. Not when I feel what I do for you, Jeannie. Not when I want to take you in my arms and hold you again, love you again. I want to be a husband to you and a father to our son."

"*My* son," Jeannie stated, her protective instinct roused at the mention of her child.

"You won't forgive, will you, woman?" Quaid demanded. "Even though you're hurting for me as badly as I am for you, you won't forgive. I was wrong. God knows I've cursed myself enough for that, and I've tried to show you how sorry I am. But I can't spend the rest of my days out here doing penance. Maybe the hurt just runs too deep for you to ever come back to me. Or maybe it's something else. Pride maybe. I don't know. I know I'll go to my grave wishing I could have changed it, but I can't. I've tried, Jeannie, but you haven't given me the tiniest shred of hope to keep on going."

Quaid let Jeannie's wrist fall, but she didn't turn from him, or from what he had to say to her.

"You're not the only one who's hurting, Jeannie. I can't stand being so close to you and my son with no hope of being anything more to either one of you than a hired hand. So, unless you say something, right here, right now, to give me that hope, I'm leaving. Tomorrow at sunup." His gaze was steady and unwavering as he waited for a word, a sign from Jeannie.

Though her heart was pounding with five years of unspoken love and the words rose to her sealed lips, she could say nothing. She knew that the rest of her life hung in the balance, but she could not speak, could not give voice to the love that filled her.

Quaid watched her, waited and hoped. But she said nothing. Unable to endure another moment, he turned from her toward the bunkhouse.

As he slowly walked away, Jeannie, panicked by the sight of his departing figure, forced her mouth to open. All the bottled-up words of half a decade teemed in her mind. Which ones did she dare speak? She called out Quaid's name. He stopped but did not turn. He couldn't. Couldn't allow Jeannie to see the tears coursing silently down his weathered cheeks like the rarest of trickles across the face of a desert mountain. His breathing stopped as he waited to hear the words that would release him from the empty life Jeannie had condemned him to with her silence.

With great difficulty, Jeannie forced her mouth to start working. But she could not cull out the words she wanted to say, the words that would stop Quaid from leaving. Instead, she fastened on to the first safe thoughts she could grab. "What about the stragglers?" she asked in a choked voice, referring to the few cattle they hadn't rounded up yet, the ones that had drifted higher up into the mountains than the rest of the herd.

Quaid had trouble adjusting what he actually heard to what he'd desperately wanted to hear. When he finally accepted what Jeannie had said, his head drooped the tiniest bit. It was the only indication he gave of his immense and bitter disappointment. With difficulty he collected himself and answered. "I'll stay around tomorrow, long enough to go with you to gather them up. After that, I'm gone." Without waiting for any further reply, Quaid strode off to his lonely resting place, where he would spend his last night near the woman he could no longer bear loving.

Chapter 13

For the next several days, the cast and crew nibbled away at Quaid and Jeannie's farewell scene, shooting and reshooting it. The master scene Lissa played out so smoothly had to be broken down into tiny chunks as close-ups and reactions shots were filmed and filmed again so that there would be a wealth of material available when it came time to edit the film. Like most actors, Lissa felt that some of her best work in prior films had been left on the cutting-room floor, but she didn't see any way that that would happen with *A High, Hard Land.*

From the moment that she admitted to herself the truth about her performance, she was able to concede that maybe, just maybe, what Matthew had done might not have been a betrayal. After all, hadn't she used her personal experiences just as Matthew had predicted, to build increasingly powerful performances on? She was able to utilize all the emotional energy she had stored up during the years when she had harbored her father's rejection as a dark secret like an enormous battery. It fueled her throughout endless takes and retakes, each one even more unerringly accurate than the last.

Lissa began to feel as if she were finally beginning to learn to use all the complicated machinery that drove her emotions. Each night she would go to her room, drained but satisfied, sit by the phone waiting for Matthew to call, and try to build up the courage to call him. Each night she would stop one digit short of dialing his number and convince herself that he would be on the set the next day. It would be so much better to talk everything out in person, she reasoned. There was so much she wanted to tell him, to show him. She wished he had been on the set to watch her. If he had, there would have been no need to tell him anything. He could have seen it all in her work.

Finally, they wrapped up the delicate farewell scene, and Jack called everyone together. "Okay, people, I want everyone to get a good night's sleep. Tomorrow we're doing the fire sequence and I want everybody, and that includes cast, crew, everyone, to be on their toes. I'm going to try to get it in one take, so give me all the help you can, all right?"

There were shouts of hearty assent and the group broke up. Lissa went straight back to the hotel. But that night she didn't conduct her usual debate about whether she should call Matthew. There was no doubt in her mind that he would come for the fire sequence. She would see Matthew and straighten everything out. Instead of going over her lines for the next day, Lissa rehearsed what she would say when she finally saw Matthew again. The rehearsals never got too far, however, as they kept dissolving into the sweetest of scenes, with Matthew kissing away her words of explanation, of apology. For the first night in a long time, she slept a sound sleep, unmolested by nightmares of abandonment.

The next morning, Lissa was on the first shuttle up into the mountains. The fire scenes were going to be shot on the Monroes' property, high up in the piney peaks, which was used for summer grazing when the grass in the valley withered. Lissa's spirits, buoyant with hope and happy expectation, rose even higher as the crew van carried her into the country she'd fallen in love with even as she was falling in love with Matthew.

The mountain air was cool and sweet. They passed a meadow, golden in morning sunlight; a magpie, a flying domino of black and white, skimmed above it chasing insects. A stream, less full than it should have been at that time of the year, meandered through the meadow. As the van lumbered up the road, they traced the course of the stream back to where it began as a mountain creek. An early-morning fisherman stood in its icy foam, his legs protected by heavy green rubber waders. A floppy canvas hat, decorated with a dozen fuzzy lures, was perched on his head as he patiently cast his line into a promising pool, angling for a bite. Lissa watched the scenery slip past her window, happy in the certainty that she would soon see Matthew.

She was the first cast member to arrive at the set. The Alta Mesa Volunteer Fire Department was already there with several large water trucks parked around the site. She searched the faces that were clustered around the catering van accepting cups of coffee and pastries.

"Looking for anyone in particular or just looking?"

So intent was she upon scrutinizing that the voice startled Lissa. She whirled around to find Vonda Kay Monroe smiling at her. A pang of guilt shot through Lissa as she remembered how she had thrown Vonda's name up to Matthew, accusing him of wanting her to be like the ranchwoman.

"Just trying to see if Matthew had gotten here yet," Lissa answered, forcing herself to sound casual and not overly concerned. "You haven't seen him, have you?"

"Not this morning. Come to think of it, I haven't seen him in over a week. I know he's been at the ranch, though. I've seen the woodsmoke. But he must get up awful early to feed his livestock, then stay inside the rest of the day, because I haven't seen him out and about for a good long while now."

"He's not sick, is he?" Lissa couldn't keep the concern from her voice.

"That was the very next question I was going to ask you. But you don't know, do you?"

A High, Hard Land

Lissa shook her head no.

"Trouble in paradise," Vonda Kay guessed. "Well, he's probably feeling pretty low then, but it's usually not anything anyone dies from. You only wish you would."

Lissa was cheered by Vonda Kay's lighthearted assessment of the situation. It was just the way Jeannie would have looked at it. "He'll come today, won't he?" she asked, infected by the woman's warmhearted candor.

"If there's any danger to you, and I expect there will be today, he'll be here."

Seized by impulse, Lissa hugged Vonda Kay.

"Hey, got one of those for me?" Shaun ambled up and Lissa included him in her exuberant embrace.

"I've never seen a woman so excited about the prospect of getting charred to death," Shaun joked when she'd released him.

"Oh, Shaun, look around," Lissa directed.

The actor glanced about at the teams of fire fighters and pumper trucks.

"The only fire fighter not out here today is Smokey the Bear," Lissa teased. "And besides, almost all he wants of us are close-up shots. You know the doubles will do the dangerous stuff."

"Still, if I were you, I'd be griping. You're going to carry most of this towering inferno nonsense."

"Jeannie can handle it," Lissa smiled.

"Well, we already know what a fainthearted wretch old Quaid is," Shaun bantered back. His gaze glanced away to somewhere behind Lissa. "Looks like Fearless Leader wants us."

Lissa turned around to see the director gesturing for them to come to him. The wrangler, Jake, stood beside him grasping the reins of half a dozen horses.

"Okay, guys," Jack began, "pick your mounts and saddle up. We'll get the stunt doubles in for the tricky stuff, the falls and all that. What I need from you two is some footage of Quaid and Jeannie heading into the mountains to pick up those stragglers. Then we'll do your close-ups during the fire. Shouldn't be any danger if we all watch what we're doing. Got it?"

Lissa and Shaun nodded in acknowledgement.

"Great. Listen," Jack continued, "I'm going to try to sync the sound on this, so the sound guys will be making with the rolling thunder." He gestured off to where a couple of sound men held a sheet of metal. Seeing the director looking their way, the man cracked the sheet. It produced a resounding thunderlike boom. "Should help you with your reactions, if nothing else. It's just something I want to try. If we don't get the effect, we'll sweeten it in editing. Everyone ready?"

"I was born ready, boss," Shaun answered.

"Okay, Jake." The director turned to the wrangler. "Get my stars up on a couple of cream puffs."

The wrangler helped them pick out two of the most tractable animals in his string, along with the spare horse they would be leading. "It'd take dynamite to spook these nags," Jake promised. Lissa mounted her old friend, Scout, comforted by the horse's familiarity and by the wrangler's promise. If there was one quality that would be needed that day, it was calmness in the face of chaos.

As the cameras began rolling, Lissa and Shaun let the horses pick their way uphill as they both slid further and further back into their characters. It required no great leap of imagination for Lissa to submerge herself into Jeannie's state of mind. She completely understood the quiet desperation that would have engulfed her as she followed Quaid up the mountains, knowing that as soon as they came back down she would lose him forever.

After only a few seconds, it was Jeannie Dawson who watched Quaid's broad back as he led them ever higher up into the mountains where the last few cattle had strayed. Lissa let herself think the thoughts that Jeannie would have been thinking. By ignoring the long delays between takes and the crew of technicians hovering about, she was able to bring Jeannie's story to full life in her own mind. Letting her imagination fill in the gaps in the action that the stunt doubles would attend to later, the entire scene played out as smoothly in Lissa's mind as it eventually would on the movie screen.

Though bereft of hope with the certain knowledge that Quaid would ride out of her life forever, Jeannie's thoughts still occasionally flew to her son, Sherman. Usually she brought him with her when she had to be away from the house for a long stretch of time. But he had awakened that morning with a sore throat. Jeannie had been forced to make the tough decision whether it would do him more harm to stay unattended at home or to be dragged into the mountains and exposed to the possibility of coming down with something really serious. She had finally left him in bed with a full day's stock of snacks. Then, just as she was stepping off the front porch, she'd turned and locked the front door. A ranch could be a dangerous place for a five-year-old boy on his own. She imagined, though, that Sherman would probably sleep most of the time she was gone.

Jeannie leaned forward in her saddle, urging her horse and the extra mount she had tied to her saddle up a steep slope. Her horse stumbled and a spray of rocks clattered down the mountain. In the next instant, the horse regained its footing and lunged upward. Quaid looked back, assured himself that Jeannie was out of danger and pushed on. He wanted to be back at the ranch in time to head out before sundown.

Jeannie wondered if her expression was as inscrutable as Quaid's. Could he possibly be hiding as much hurt behind his stony visage as she was behind hers? She resigned herself to the fact that she would go to her grave wondering about the questions she could not risk asking. The steady crunching of crisp pine needles beneath the horse's hooves was broken occasionally by the sharp snap of a dry branch cracking away as they brushed against it. The dust they raised bit Jeannie's nostrils. The snowfall the past winter had been sparse, then the spring rains had never come, leaving the mountains dry as tinder.

But Jeannie had no time to reflect upon weather conditions. A rangy steer darted out of the underbrush on the ridge above them.

"Head off that way!" Quaid commanded, gesturing with the loop of rope he held. "Drive him back toward me!"

Jeannie spurred her horse into action, bursting out after the renegade steer. The animal, however, was wilier than most and didn't run directly from either Jeannie or Quaid. Instead, it broke free and headed uphill. They tore out after it. Quaid shot a lasso that flew as straight as a spear through the air. It hovered for a second above the steer's wide curving horns before the animal dropped its head and shook the rope free.

"Damn!" Jeannie heard Quaid's curse as he reeled in the rope and looped it again, all the while still charging after the errant steer.

The chase brought them to a high ridgeline where they broke free of the pine forest and into a wide clearing. The steer was nowhere to be seen. Instead, Jeannie beheld an ominous sight that ranchers of the high plains dread seeing during dry spells: billowing, gray thunderheads churning overhead with not a drop of humidity or the merest whisper of a breeze to promise rain.

Quaid reined his horse to a stop and stared at the angry clouds as he said, "We'd better gather up those beeves. Sherman doesn't like thunder."

Jeannie followed him, wondering when he had learned of her son's fear. What else about Quaid Dawson had she hardened her heart and mind to? The pestering doubts were scattered as she plunged back down below the timberline. It was all she could do to simply hang on as Quaid careened after the half-wild steer as it led them on a hair-raising chase.

As the sun crept higher and higher overhead, the summer's heat began to pound away at Jeannie. Though she risked having her arms flayed by twigs, she shed her denim jacket. The air, hot and still as it was, felt cool for a moment on her sweat-dampened back.

"Quaid," she called, surprised by how her voice cracked with dryness. "Quaid!" This time he stopped and looked her way. "I've got to catch my breath."

He nodded and reined his horse around as Jeannie unlooped the canteen from her saddle horn. Without the sound of her own blood pounding in her ears, Jeannie could hear the dark rumblings from above. Like a prima donna who waits for the audience to be still before performing, the sky loosed its first bolt of lightning into the silence. Jeannie counted the seconds until it was followed by a colossal clap of thunder. There were too few of them. From the brief interval, Jeannie calculated that the lightning was dangerously close.

At the next boom of thunder Jeannie's horse reared, knocking the canteen from her hands. Quaid jumped from his horse to the ground to retrieve the precious water spilling into the dry earth.

"Quaid, don't—" Jeannie screamed even as the heavens detonated what sounded and looked like an arsenal of high explosives. The next shard of lightning illuminated the day that had gone gray around them. The boom of thunder followed almost instantaneously.

The eyes of Quaid's horse grew huge with terror. It reared up, yanking mightily against the reins Quaid held in his hand.

"Whoa! Whoa, boy, whoa!" Quaid yelled, trying to calm the panic-stricken horse. But the lightning was too near, the danger too real. The next crack of lightning drove the animal into a mindless, frenzied state. It reared back to paw and snort at the attack from above. Blinded by terror, the animal lashed out at any obstacle standing between itself and escape.

Jeannie heard the snap of Quaid's leg as the horse knocked Quaid to the ground, then landed a hoof just below Quaid's knee before it bolted down the mountainside.

Quaid's face was a mask of controlled pain when Jeannie reached him. "Blindfold the other horses and stuff something in their ears." He gritted out the words. Jeannie rushed to obey, all the while watching Quaid's face go whiter and whiter as the waves of pain washed away his color. She feared he would go into shock before she could get him down off the mountain. How on earth, she wondered frantically, was she going to get him onto the saddle of the extra horse?

The first few times Quaid tried to stand on his good leg, he passed out. Watching Quaid lose strength with each effort, Jeannie knew that it wouldn't be long before he lost consciousness completely. All the while, the few seconds between flashes of lightning and the boom of thunder grew shorter. There was no more time for gentleness or half measures. Jeannie played out her rope and wrapped it around Quaid's waist, then pulled it up and over the spare horse's back and looped it around her saddle horn. With this improvised pulley system, she backed her horse up and hauled Quaid to a standing position, then, finally, up and onto the horse's back.

But there was no time to celebrate her ingenuity, for the next splinter of lightning shattered the sky at almost the same time its accompanying thunder cannonaded over the mountain.

"Hang on, Quaid," she whispered, as she secured the rope tied around his waist and to the horse. "We'll get you down, just hang on."

"Jeannie, I—"

But Quaid's words were lost as a renegade bolt of lightning sizzled out of the sky. It struck the tall pine that Jeannie had roped her horse to and turned it into a resin-soaked torch. All around them, other trees exploded into flame with a horrible roar.

"Leave!" Quaid ordered.

Jeannie wouldn't have believed that there was enough strength in Quaid to issue such a forceful command. She fought down the panic that battled to take control of her mind as she mounted and grabbed for the reins of the horse that Quaid was lashed to.

"No!" he yelled above the ravening blaze. "Leave me here! You'll never make it down in time. The fire. Save Sherman."

His strength was fading, but not his instinct to protect his son.

"I can't!" Jeannie screamed above the boom of thunder and the sound of trees exploding as they were ripped apart by the intense heat of the flames engulfing them.

"Save Sherman!" Quaid's voice was a harsh bellow.

Jeannie tugged at her reins but couldn't make herself leave. The truth was finally ripped from her. "I can't leave you here, Quaid! I love you! I never stopped loving you!"

"Then save our son," he commanded.

One thing on earth could have torn her from Quaid's side, and it was the vision that came to her of Sherman, alone and locked in the house, watching the fire race down the mountain toward him, driven by the thunder that terrified him so.

"Go!" Quaid yelled. "Go, Jeannie. I never stopped loving you, either. I never will." Quaid collapsed.

In that instant, Jeannie was ready to risk her son's life to try to save Quaid, but the moment she relaxed her hold on the reins, her horse burst away from the inferno that was raging in the branches above it. Smoke seared Jeannie's eyes and heat tore at her lungs as the animal bore her away from the one man she had ever loved in her life. Her one last backward glance showed her only a rippling hell of orange closing in around a wounded man strapped to the back of a horse. The frightened horse she was on lunged forward with a piercing whinny, jerking the reins from Jeannie's hands. She grabbed the horse's neck and clung to it. She had to survive for her son. Her own life was over, but she would save his.

"Cut!" Jack yelled, and a couple of dozen technicians swarmed onto the set, grabbing the horse's reins and pulling them to safety. Three trucks began pumping water onto the blaze, which was, in fact, quite a minor fire contained within a wide firebreak.

Lissa slid from the back of her horse, patting the animal and telling it that it had done a good job. She waited for Matthew to emerge from the crowd gathered behind the director's chair. But she saw no sign of him. Soot had rained down upon her and melded with the trickles of sweat running from her temples to leave her face streaked with gray. She wiped at the trickle with the back of her hand. Still searching for Matthew, she caught sight of Shaun. He was as immaculate as he had been at the beginning of shooting, since a stunt double had stood in for him.

Lissa was still looking when she heard Jack's voice explode in anger.

A High, Hard Land

"You idiot! I can't believe this!" She turned to see him berating a camera operator who was balancing a hand-held camera on his shoulder. "How could you have used the wrong settings?"

The man stuttered out a reply that only fed Jack's rage.

"Don't blame the equipment," the director bellowed. "Listen, I don't know what it will take, but I'm going to have your union card, fellow."

Lissa approached the shouting match. "Jack, what is it?"

"This . . . this . . . incompetent jackass shot your last reaction shot on a wide setting. If we move in close, we'll lose too much resolution." The enraged director turned back to the camera operator, who appeared to be on the verge of tears. "Didn't I tell everyone yesterday that I wanted to get this in one take? Don't you think checking your settings might have helped us accomplish that goal?"

"I—I did," the operator stammered.

"I'm sure you did," Jack cooed with blistering sarcasm.

Unable to stand seeing the operator being flayed in public, Lissa stepped in to try to avert Jack's sarcastic wrath. "If it's just my last reaction shot he missed, we can stage that again without too much trouble."

"Are you sure?" Jack swiftly transferred all of his attention to Lissa.

"Well, I'm not exactly thrilled at the prospect, but if it's only one reaction shot."

The camera operator looked at her with such an expression of pure gratitude that Lissa had no choice but to follow through on her offer. She wasn't eager to breathe smoke and be half-charred again, but it was a slight discomfort compared to the destruction of a man's career.

"Stop those trucks!" Jack yelled the order at his assistant, Stan, who scampered away to halt the flow of water being pumped on the still-burning pine trees.

Vonda Kay Monroe was in the crowd watching the fire fighters. As soon as she heard the director's orders she stormed over. "What in the blue blazes is this about you reshooting that blamed scene?" she demanded.

A tight smile creased Jack's thin lips. "Certainly not the whole scene, my dear," he answered condescendingly. "Just a very brief portion at the end. Nothing for you to worry about. You'll be more than compensated."

"It's not compensation I'm worried about. I want you to come out from behind that camera and take a good look out here."

"My dear, we're wasting time—"

"Don't you 'my dear' me," Vonda Kay snapped back at the supercilious director. "Now get down here before I chase the whole bunch of you off my property."

With a look of peevish annoyance, Jack obeyed.

Vonda Kay bent down and picked up a handful of pine needles and crushed them next to the director's ear. "Hear that? That's what a forest sounds like when it's dry, and this one's dry as a bone. This isn't just movie magic you're playing with. This is the real thing. Now, because you met all my safety requirements, I allowed you to set my forest on fire, but playtime is over. We're sitting in the middle of a tinderbox here."

"I absolutely agree, my duh"—Jack caught himself—"Mrs. Monroe. All we're going to do is put Lissa back in the fire ring for one extremely brief shot, then we'll extinguish the fire. If we can get started, it won't take more than thirty seconds."

"Thirty seconds?" Vonda Kay questioned. "I have your word on that?"

"You have my word," Jack promised.

"I'm warning you, any longer and you'll have yourselves a serious situation on your hands."

"Great, no problem," Jack finished, already walking back to the camera operator who was preparing to reshoot the last few moments of the scene. "Lissa, mount up," he barked.

Lissa looked at the fire. As soon as the trucks had stopped pumping water, it seemed to have burst into a great orange blossom. She was comforted by the pumper trucks and the wide firebreak containing the blaze. Surely, she convinced herself, the fire marshal in attendance wouldn't allow anything dangerous to happen. Lissa swung back into the saddle and Jack grabbed the reins.

"Okay, what I need from you is to get into position so that we can pick up fire all around you. Then you give us one tear-filled glance back at Quaid and we wrap. Got it?"

Lissa nodded. Jack handed the reins to the wrangler. There was no way that the horse would willingly go back into the firebreak. It had to be led.

"This horse has more sense than I do," she tried to joke with Jake.

"Don't expect an argument from me," the grizzled wrangler replied, clearly displeased. "This is going to be a tight shot," he told her, "so I plan on staying right by your side holding these reins."

"Good." Jake's sure, steady presence reassured Lissa a bit. Still, she felt her throat go dry and her stomach tighten as they approached the ring of fire. She thought it must be her imagination, but the fire seemed brighter and felt hotter. Sweat poured off her as waves of heat rippled across her line of vision. The wrangler backed the horse into position.

"Get that old coot out of the frame!" Jack screamed.

"Just make the goddamn picture!" Jake screamed back.

"You're in it! Get out or we can't shoot!"

The wrangler hesitated for a moment, handed Lissa the reins, then backed away. Lissa was left alone in the heart of the inferno.

"Lissa!" Jack screamed, his voice sounding farther and farther away. "Look heartbroken, not terrified!"

But Lissa *was* terrified now. Her moment in the ring of fire had gone on too long. If Jack wouldn't, she was going to end it. She pressed her heels into her horse's flanks. At that same instant, the fire reached the critical point where the flame's heat and the pine's dryness combined to create the fire fighter's nightmare—crowning out. All around her a dozen different tall pines exploded into flames with a bang that scared Lissa's horse witless.

The deranged animal lunged forward with no warning. Lissa was thrown to the ground, her screams lost in the fire's roar. Utter, mindless terror swamped her as the world dissolved into a shimmering orange haze that could have been Dante's vision of the inferno. There was no way out of the wall of flames, dancing ever closer. No escape from the smoke that was clogging her lungs and blacking out her thoughts. In an odd millisecond of serenity that overtook Lissa before she passed out, she thought of how much better she understood Jeannie now, of how it took the extremity of death to make her wish fervently that she'd told Matthew how much she loved him.

Chapter 14

What's it say in her contract about accidents?"

The question insistently wormed its way past the sedatives and Lissa's jumbled dreams. It forced itself into a particularly lovely dream in which Lissa found herself floating effortlessly above Matthew's golden valley. Suddenly, Sidney Feldman's face superimposed itself over the pastoral vision. Lissa was puzzled. What was her producer doing in Matthew's valley?

"We've got our legal guys going over it now."

Stan Davisbury, who answered the producer's questions, was even more out of place in the rugged country that she'd come to love. The steady pricking of anxious questions and answers kept on until Lissa slowly dragged herself from sleep. Judging from the painfully mundane nature of the conversation being hissed near her bed, she concluded that she must be alive. Surely, more respect would have been shown for the dead. Lissa had no choice but to listen.

"You think she'll sue?" Sidney asked.

"Wouldn't you?" Davisbury replied.

"Jack." The producer spit his director's name out. "You know what I think his last name should be, don't you?"

"Donkey, but not so nice?" the assistant director guessed, delighted by Jack's colossal foul-up because it was causing the producer to take him more seriously.

"He should be so smart as a donkey," the producer moaned. "What was he doing letting that fire burn so long? What do the insurance people say? Are we covered if she sues?"

"I'm not going to sue." Lissa's voice was weak, and it took a moment for the producer and his flunky to believe that they had actually heard it.

"Lissa, darling, you're awake." The producer hurried to her side. "Now is not the time to discuss legal nastinesses like suing. Now is the time to rest. Recover. Be well. You really aren't going to sue?"

Morning sun streamed through her hospital room. Lissa thought about lawyers, depositions, suits, countersuits. She closed her eyes, which were still swollen and raw from the smoke, against the brightness, and shook her head in a weary negative.

"You are an angel!" Sidney whooped. "If I wasn't already in love with your acting, your beauty, your charisma, I would be now."

A High, Hard Land

"What are you gentlemen doing in here?" A tiny nurse with an imperious manner stepped into the room and chased the two men out just as exhaustion again overtook Lissa. The last thought that flickered through her mind before she succumbed was: who saved me?

It was late in the afternoon when Lissa came around again. She was much happier this time to open her eyes and see Vonda Kay's face.

"Well, glory be, am I happy to see you open those gorgeous peepers," Vonda Kay exclaimed. "How are you feeling?"

"Groggy," Lissa answered slowly. "Very groggy."

"'Magine so with all that smoke you inhaled and everything they pumped into you here."

The question that had been bothering Lissa surfaced immediately. "Who saved me?"

Vonda Kay's bright expression clouded. Unused to subterfuge, she could only look away to avoid the question.

"Who pulled me out of the flames?" Lissa repeated. "Was it one of the fire marshals? The wrangler? I want to thank whoever it was. Do something for them."

Vonda Kay's lips twitched as if she were physically trying to hold back the answer.

Lissa couldn't understand what was causing Vonda's reticence. "Who was it?" she persisted with a light laugh, trying to defuse a situation that had become inexplicably tense. When the ranchwoman still refused to answer,

Lissa abandoned any pretense of lightness. "Vonda, I want to know who saved my life."

"I'm not supposed to tell," she answered edgily, uncomfortable with anything other than the plain, unvarnished truth.

"Vonda Kay, please tell me. I have to know. I have to thank them. Imagine how you'd feel if you were in my place."

Vonda Kay did just that for a few seconds and knew that it was one secret she couldn't keep. Owing someone your life was too great a debt to keep secret. "It was Matthew. Matthew rode in and plucked you out of that fire while everyone else was just standing around blithering about what to do and who should do it."

"But Matthew wasn't even on the set," Lissa said, dumbfounded.

"He was in the hills right above it. He was watching the whole thing."

"Matthew? Saved my life?" Lissa said with wonder. A bit of the haze burned off her memory and she vaguely recalled Matthew lifting her into his arms before she passed out. "I thought it was a dream," she whispered, the implications of the act of courage beginning to form in Lissa's mind. "But it really was him," she exulted.

Vonda Kay gave a smiling confirmation.

"He saved my life," Lissa marveled. "He was watching the whole time." A strange, manic surge of energy shot through her and she raised herself up off the pillows. "He risked his life for me. Vonda Kay, he loves me, he must. I have to see him. Please tell him to come to me. Please." Lissa sank back down against the pillows.

"I can't, Lissa," Vonda Kay answered sadly. "I can't send him to you because he's gone. He left last night just as soon as he heard that you'd pull through all right."

"Where did he go?" Lissa demanded, frantic to bridge the gulf of misunderstanding and distrust that had separated her from Matthew. "We can call."

Vonda Kay shook her head. "No, Lissa, there's no place to call. He went to start researching a book he's setting in the Navajo nation. He's going to be following the sheepherders. He'll be living like a nomad, just the way they do. Even if we knew where it was he'd gone to, we couldn't reach him. Cell phone reception is even worse out there than it is here."

Lissa's emotional defenses, already undermined by her roller-coaster ride from life to death, from hope to despair, couldn't withstand this latest assault. She barely tried to stanch the flow of tears that sprang to her eyes.

Vonda Kay said nothing. She didn't make silly comments, insisting that Lissa cheer up or try to forget about Matthew, or that he obviously wasn't right for her. She didn't lie to Lissa, and she didn't try to put a happy face on Matthew's departure. Her response was simply to take Lissa's hand and hold it. To let Lissa cry until weariness overtook her again, and she slid back into sleep's welcoming arms.

Over the next couple of days, as Lissa's strength gradually returned, Vonda Kay became her most constant and most welcome visitor. Hers was a comforting presence that made no demands. Most of the time she simply sat with Lissa and worked on some bit of handicraft to keep her hands occupied. Occasionally, they would exchange a few innocuous comments. Bit by bit, Lissa worked back up to the topic that possessed her every waking thought.

"Do you think there's any chance of Matthew coming back before shooting's over?"

Vonda Kay looked up from the horse bridle she was braiding and let it drop onto her lap. "Do you?" she turned the question back on Lissa.

"No," Lissa had to answer. "I don't think there are many grays for Matthew. He lives in a world of black and white, doesn't he? At least as far as his emotions are concerned."

Vonda Kay nodded noncommittally, letting Lissa continue to put into words the turmoil that had been churning through her for days.

"I misjudged him, Vonda. I think he was ready to commit himself to me, to us, entirely."

"I think you're right," Vonda Kay affirmed, remembering the talks she and Matthew had had. "When he first moved into this valley, he lived like a hermit. Folks around here pretty much let each other do what they want, so no one bothered him much. It was my youngest, Montana, who first got to know him. He used to ride across

Matthew's property a lot. He'd stop by to ask for a drink of water or to see if Matthew had any chores he wanted to hire out. I think, more as a favor than anything else, he started letting Montana come around. They got to talking, one thing led to another, and pretty soon Matthew was stopping by our place for dinner fairly regular or having us out for a barbecue."

Lissa watched Vonda Kay's tanned face beam with the memories of good times.

"It was funny," she continued. "At first I think Matthew thought Duane and I were putting on some kind of a show for him. He honestly didn't believe that two people could be as happy together for as long as we've been happy together. Once he was convinced that we were just what we appeared to be, he couldn't ask enough questions: how we'd met, what we'd been doing, why'd we split up, how'd we get back together."

"And that became *A High, Hard Land*," Lissa interjected.

"Combined with a lot of Matthew's imagination it did. Anyway, once he started believing that the kind of life Duane and I had together was possible, he started working on trying to find someone to share his life with that same way."

A mischievous smile crept over Vonda's face. "There sure were enough candidates eager for the position. He was always flying off to deliver lectures, meet with film producers, do TV interviews. There was always something pulling him away from this valley, and there always seemed to be a woman waiting when he got wherever it was he was going. And they all wanted to help him fill that gap in his life. But no one ever could. He never found what he was looking for. 'A woman for the long haul,' was how he put it. Not very romantic, but the thought behind it was. He was looking for a woman he could spend the rest of his life with and nothing less would do. He'd about given up, then he met you, Lissa."

Lissa realized she'd all but stopped breathing as Vonda Kay recited her tale. "Me?" she whispered.

Vonda Kay laughed. "You. Of course, you. If you didn't know that, you were the only one who didn't. It was no surprise to me when Matthew came over one night and made the announcement. 'I've found her,' he told me. 'The woman I want to spend my life with.'"

Lissa pressed her eyes shut to block out the pain that assailed her. "Why didn't he tell me?"

Vonda Kay squeezed her hand, knowing that Lissa already knew the answer to that question. Matthew hadn't told her because he was too busy breaking down the walls she had constructed to block out the hurt of her father's desertion. Lissa winced as she thought of Matthew trying as best he knew how to release her from the emotional prison she'd locked herself in. And of how she'd thanked him for his effort—by accusing him of betraying her, of using her sad memories as grist for his story mill.

"Vonda," Lissa whispered, "I was so wrong. So very, very wrong."

"There now," Vonda answered, not digging for details, just letting Lissa talk. "Don't be too hard on yourself. Takes two to tango, as my mother always used to say."

Lissa could draw scant comfort from the platitude. In the end, it didn't really matter what she had or had not done or who was at fault. The fact still remained— Matthew was gone. Even as her body mended, her few remaining hopes that he might still come bursting in through her door withered and died.

"You're a very lucky lady," the doctor, a Mexican-American man in his mid-fifties with steel-gray hair, announced early the next day, after making his final examination. "The damage from smoke inhalation was minimal. Just a few seconds more, however, and it would have been a completely different story."

"But she's perfectly okay now, right, doc?" Jack asked nervously. "I mean, we're three days behind the shooting schedule, but I don't mind at all about that. The important thing is that our leading lady feels up to coming back to work."

"I feel up to it, Jack."

"You're sure now?" the director quizzed her. "You sound a little tired."

"I feel a little tired," Lissa answered, not caring to play the director's game of false concern. She knew that Jack's head was on the block. He had screwed up by risking her life and, what was infinitely worse, the profit margin of the picture. Now he was desperately trying to make amends, to rescue his reputation, by playing up the fatherly concern, although he was desperate to get back on schedule.

Still, it was true, she did feel tired. When the last flicker of hope that Matthew might still come back to her had been extinguished, Lissa had felt something of the boundless energy which had always carried her along through a difficult past, dwindle away from her. She was glad that they'd already filmed all the lighthearted scenes. She could play an older, wiser and considerably sadder Jeannie, but not a peppy, happy young one. Not now, not the way she felt.

With Jack looking eagerly over the doctor's shoulder, she finally concluded, "I'm ready to come back to work."

For the first few days back on the set, everyone treated Lissa as if she were a china doll. They mostly did pickup shots, filling in small gaps they'd missed earlier. Gradually, the crew became caught up in its work again and stopped taking special notice of Lissa. She was grateful when the suffocating solicitude ended. All she wanted was to do her work and leave. To go somewhere as far from Alta Mesa and its cruel memories as possible.

Only a few major scenes remained to be shot, and Lissa began mentally preparing to submerge herself into Jeannie's character once more. Though she felt now that she could play Jeannie better than she ever had before, it had become painful to reenter Matthew's creation, to become part of his world again, knowing that it would end. Lissa was grateful for the large store of professionalism she had built up from her earliest years as she leaned on it and let it carry her over the rough spots and into the climactic final scene.

Luckily, the scene called for Jeannie to look ravaged. Lissa, who had had no interest in food since learning of Matthew's departure, was able to pull that look off with little cosmetic help from Jerome.

"Your cheekbones are divine," the makeup man trilled brightly at her the morning of the final scene. "But too much dieting can cause a certain lack of luster around the eyes."

"I haven't been dieting," Lissa answered simply.

"Don't pay any attention to me," he went on, leaning close to her ear, the trill gone from his voice. "I can see the difference between dieting and a broken heart. It shows on the skin."

Lissa jerked an anxious gaze around to meet his.

"Don't worry," Jerome said soothingly. "No one else has guessed. They just think you're still recovering from the accident."

He stepped back, resuming his role and the twittering tones that went with it. "The only thing anyone around here worries about is why you didn't sue Sidney and Company. I mean, talk about negligence."

Lissa caught Jerome's eyes in the mirror. For a brief

second, the makeup man was still as he gave Lissa's shoulder an encouraging squeeze and answered her smile with one that was kind and genuinely concerned. Then he returned to daubing soot over Lissa's face. "Oh, the ravages of fire. Nothing I like better," he chirped. "Unless, of course, it's a good earthquake."

On the set, crew members with fire hoses were sprinkling the area around the ranch house to simulate the rainstorm that had come in time to save the house. The yard, however, was nothing but charred and smoldering lumps of charcoal.

Lissa stared at the desolation of the scene, letting it sink into her psyche. She was dressed in clothes that had been torn during Jeannie's headlong flight down the mountain to save her son. Without forcing it, Lissa felt Jeannie's character, her thoughts and her sadness settle over her. When Jack ordered her to take her position in front of the house, huddled with her son, Lissa felt that it was with Jeannie's eyes that she looked out at the fire-blackened fields that once were pastures.

But Jeannie did not mourn the loss of the grazing land as the cameras started to roll; the silent tears mixing with rain on her face were for Quaid.

"Ma," Sherman asked, twisting in her arms to face her. "Where's Quaid? Is he still getting the strays? Will he be back soon?"

"No, son. No, he won't be coming back."

The boy stared for a moment into the ravished

emptiness in his mother's eyes, then burrowed closer against her. She wrapped him in her arms, sheltering him from the truth in just the way she wished she could be sheltered from it. But life in the high plains was too harsh, too uncompromising, for such luxuries. Quaid Dawson was gone.

"I like Quaid," the boy whispered. "I like him a lot."

Jeannie brushed her son's white-blond hair out of his eyes. "I know," she answered, her body beginning to sway a bit as she rocked them both. All around her, wisps of gray smoke rose through the drizzle in the hazy dawn.

Neither mother nor son moved for a long while, which would have been much longer had the snort of a horse not disturbed them.

"Hey, Ma, it's Blaze."

Blaze! The name echoed through Jeannie's mind. It couldn't be. That was the extra horse they'd taken up onto the mountain. But there she was, Blaze, a bone-tired chestnut mare with a patch of white on her face, dragging into the yard. The surge of hope that shot through Jeannie was cruelly quashed the same instant it swelled within her. Quaid wasn't on the horse's back. All Jeannie could see through the haze and drizzle was the rope she'd tied around the horse's middle. Quaid must have slipped off.

"Get Blaze some feed and water," Jeannie directed, her voice a mechanical drone.

The boy got up to obey. "Ma!" he hollered as he reached the tired horse. "Ma, come quick!"

A spark of life flickered in Jeannie's eyes, ignited by the joyous urgency in her son's voice. Every bone aching, she rose to her feet. Fighting back the hope beginning to surge through her, she forced herself to walk slowly. But her feet seemed to gather speed all on their own until she was running across the smoldering yard. Running to the rebirth of hope in her life.

A limp body, unconscious and covered in black ash, was lashed to the side of the horse. Though barely alive, it was Quaid. Quaid Dawson. Jeannie felt her heart lurch back to life again.

"Hold on to Blaze," she ordered her son as she began untangling the rope. Once it was loosened, Quaid slumped to the ground. Somehow, she and Sherman managed to drag him into the house, where she bathed and bandaged his burns and got him into her bed.

For days he was lost in a coma of fever and pain. Jeannie sent her son down to the lower unburned meadows to collect willow branches, which she soaked and made into a poultice that relieved the pain a bit. She dripped sugar water into his mouth so that his strength wouldn't wane any further, and he swallowed it without regaining consciousness. When his fevered sweat had turned the bedclothes into a sodden and rumpled mess, Jeannie would take fresh sheets from the cupboard and tenderly work them beneath his burned body so that he always lay on fresh, clean linen.

She stayed by his side, night and day, fearing that if

she left long enough to make the arduous trip into town to fetch the doctor she would lose him once and for all. She couldn't take that risk. Two lives were at stake: Quaid's and hers. For days he teetered on the thin edge between life and death, moaning in pain and calling out her name. Always when he called her name, he was imploring her, begging her to change her mind. To forgive.

It was then that she would lean close to him and quiet his feverish pleas. "I'm here, Quaid. Everything's forgiven. I love you." Over and over, she whispered the words she'd withheld from him for so long. Somehow, they seemed to soothe Quaid, and he would grow quiet and sleep again.

After five days of wandering through a limbo populated by gray phantoms and black regrets, Quaid opened his eyes at his usual waking time, four-thirty in the morning. He found himself lying on snowy white sheets that smelled of laundry soap and sunshine. Next, he saw Jeannie curled up in the rocking chair next to the bed, an afghan pulled around her. Quaid was forced to conclude that he hadn't made it down off the mountain. He'd died and gone to heaven. He was pleased to discover that his dearest hope had materialized and that Jeannie was there with him. He figured an eternity was just about long enough to make everything up to her and to love her to his heart's content.

With a reverent hand, he reached out to stroke her cheek. It was real. They hadn't passed into the Great Beyond quite yet. His memory had betrayed him. Her skin was even softer than he had remembered it. It was softer than any other thing his rough hands had felt. Her lashes fluttered a bit, then opened.

"Quaid," she whispered, taking the hand that stroked her cheek.

"Jeannie," his voice was deep and gravelly, still dry from smoke and dehydration.

"Don't try to talk now, Quaid."

Quaid ignored the advice. "There's one thing I have to know right now, woman. I've been through hell for you. I want to know if you're going to send me back."

Jeannie shook her head, unable to speak. Quaid opened his arms and, very carefully, Jeannie entered his embrace.

"Jeannie, Jeannie." Her name was an insensate rumble that Quaid repeated like a litany of thanksgiving for his deliverance from the long, empty years. "Jeannie Duncan, I'll love you till the day I die and probably then some."

"Quaid. I can barely remember a time I didn't love you."

Her heart was so filled that it took Jeannie a moment to remember what was missing. With infinite care, she raised herself from Quaid's chest and left the room. When she returned, she led a sleepy Sherman by the hand. With a formality that somehow befitted the momentous occasion, she directed her son, "Go shake your father's hand, Sherman."

With one small fist still rubbing a sleepy eye, the boy

cocked his head to look up at his mother. It was clear from her expression that she was not teasing him. Even with a white bandage swathing his forehead, Quaid was a welcome person in Sherman's life. The little boy thought the whole matter over for a few seconds and, in the end, was quite satisfied with having Quaid as his father. He approached the man he'd grown to love and gravely stuck his small hand out.

Jeannie watched Quaid clasp her son's hand with a genuine solemnity that showed his respect for the boy and for the dignity of the ceremony that joined them into a family more surely than any marriage ever could. Family. That was the word that loosed Jeannie's tears, tears of joy that the long years of loneliness were finally ending.

When Quaid looked up at her, his eyes were glistening, too. "Reckon we could get a preacher out here to perform a wedding?"

"I imagine we could," Jeannie answered. There was nothing more to be said.

When Jack called for a cut, Lissa found herself unable to oblige. She couldn't yank herself from the emotional clutches of the scene. Unable to speak a word of explanation, Lissa ran from the set, tears streaming down her face. They weren't Jeannie's tears of joy for the end of loneliness and longing; Lissa's tears were for herself. For the empty years that had only just begun.

Chapter 15

Lissa stood on the terrace of the small house of whitewashed stucco that the studio had rented for her, and looked down the long hill to the Nile River, jade green and sluggish in the pummeling heat. A line of pure white egrets flew across the river like a string of clean sheets drying in the hot wind. Lissa thought of the pine-scented cool breezes and cobalt-blue vistas of Alta Mesa and ached with a homesickness no other spot on earth had ever stirred in her. Egypt was so exotic and lovely in its way. Lissa knew she'd probably even have enjoyed her time on location if . . . if Matthew were with her. She brutally stopped that train of her thought, just as she'd derailed any thoughts in the past three months that appeared to have Matthew Briggs as their destination.

A rap at her door startled Lissa out of her reverie. A servant in the ubiquitous flowing white cotton tunic, trousers and turban thrust a familiar suitcase into her arms. Lissa recognized it as her own, though it was now battered. She handed the delivery boy a tip and he melted away.

She stared at the suitcase and, in a rush, the final days of filming in Alta Mesa all came back to Lissa. After her emotional collapse at the end of the final scene, she had barely managed to pull herself together for the last few days of shooting. When her agent called to say that, on the basis of insider gossip about the brilliance of her performance in *A High, Hard Land*, she'd been offered a part in *The Hieroglyphic Heist*, an Agatha Christie–like caper with an international cast, Lissa had had only one question. While her agent babbled on about how a light comedy role would be a good switch after the heavy drama of *Hard Land*, all Lissa had asked was where the filming would take place. When she had heard "Egypt," she'd accepted immediately.

All Lissa had wanted then was to get as far from all the crippling memories of Matthew as she could. In her headlong flight to do just that, she'd forgotten one of her suitcases. The studio had forwarded it, apparently by camel train, Lissa thought disparagingly as she opened the suitcase.

She knew why she hadn't missed the enclosed items. Most of them seemed to be the bohemian items her wardrobe used to consist of: the jeweled beret, the bandolero belt, the many-zippered pants. Sometime in between meeting Matthew and losing him, she had abandoned that style of dressing in favor of one less concertedly trendy. Lissa was getting ready to stow the whole mess under her bed when she caught sight of the sheer jersey of the one dress she'd worn in Alta Mesa. Her hand moved to touch it. Once she'd made that contact, no force on earth could turn aside the memories it evoked.

As if it had all happened the night before, she recalled the night she'd worn the dress, when she and Matthew had gone out to dinner with the rest of the crew. She again felt Matthew's hand on her, brazenly inching the soft fabric higher and higher up on her thigh. She trembled at the memory of his intimate daring, all the while keeping up a conversation with their unsuspecting fellow diners. She remembered how they had barely closed the door of her room behind them before Matthew was stripping the jersey dress away. It had fallen to the floor at their feet. Matthew, galvanized by her uncovered beauty, had been unable to move from that spot. They had crumpled to the floor and made mad, desperate love on top of the fallen dress.

Lissa brought the wrinkled dress to her face. It smelled of him. She had no defense against that, against his smell. Lissa sagged against the open suitcase. Her face buried in the traitorous dress, she wept violently. She cried the tears she'd stifled until she couldn't see, then dragged herself to her bed and escaped into sleep.

She awoke to darkness more bereft than ever, certain that he'd been in the room, that he had touched her. Then the ache of not having him sliced through her again. In the alien darkness that was too hot and too still, Lissa felt she would sell her soul to have Matthew's arms about her again, to have his mouth on hers, to hold him inside her body once more.

Seeing what little difference three months had made, Lissa wondered dully when, if ever, she would heal. When she would stop feeling so utterly adrift. When life would again become anything other than a mechanical charade.

Shooting ended three weeks later. Lissa had formed no friendships because the cast, other than herself, had consisted almost entirely of big-name stars who had jetted in to give cameo performances, then fled from Egypt's shimmering heat as soon as possible.

Before she packed away her laptop, she checked her e-mail and found a message from Jack. The director was inviting her to attend the premiere of *A High, Hard Land*, to be held in Alta Mesa. An instinctive answer of "no" rose up in Lissa. She couldn't go back there. It would destroy any progress she might have made toward getting over Matthew. As she read on, however, she saw that Jack wasn't inviting her to the premiere. He was pleading with her.

"Lissa," the second paragraph read, "you know how people can be in this business. Rumors fly, fueled by nothing but jealousy and ambition. Anyway, the ones flying around now say that you were permanently disfigured in the fire and that it's all my fault. I can trace said rumors to a certain assistant director." Lissa thought of Stan Davisbury, secretly yearning to displace the master he served so obsequiously. "But in the end that doesn't matter. The only thing that will quash them is for you to show up whole and lovely as you always were. I'd regard it as a personal favor if you came. Best, Jack."

Lissa's immediate reaction was that she owed no favors to Jack Myers. But such pettiness could not take root in Lissa's nature. She found holding a grudge too great an effort to bother with. The note of desperation in Jack's message hadn't escaped her, and she knew that the Hollywood rumor mill was probably eating him and his career alive. If putting in an appearance was all it took to disengage the director from the jaws of the mill, Lissa figured she could do that much.

Once she reached the decision to return to Alta Mesa, she couldn't stanch the flow of optimistic fantasies that attended it. Matthew, having suffered as direly as she, would have forgiven everything. He would come to the premiere ready to open his arms to her. The final fantasies always closed out on hazy scenes of her and Matthew together at his ranch, surrounded by the children she would bear him.

Try as she might to chase these visions from her mind, they kept a tenacious hold on Lissa's deepest dreams. They came fully to life when, after an exhausting journey through too much land held in the grip of a hot, dusty summer, she stepped back into Alta Mesa's fresh mountain coolness. The town was alive with critics, flown in by the studio to view a film they had great confidence in. From all sides Lissa was hailed by old friends. With each happy greeting, her spirits rose higher until she could no longer deny her fantasies. They overwhelmed her as she walked back into the hotel where she'd known such exquisite happiness. The desk clerk issued a sincere welcome back and put Lissa in the very room she'd stayed in before.

As Lissa reentered the room, a feeling of destiny swept through her. Everything felt so right to Lissa, so bound to happen. She sank onto the bed and smoothed her hands lovingly over the spot where Matthew had taught her all the sweet mysteries their bodies knew. He *had* to come to her. She could not be alone in the feeling that overpowered her.

The premiere was that night. Lissa knew she had no choice in what she would wear. Of course, it would be the jersey dress. Though cleaned and pressed, she still detected the scent of lovemaking, dense and compelling, as she slipped it over her head. She walked downstairs, certain that Matthew's eyes were on her. That he would poke his head around one of the shadowed columns at the back of the lobby and that, with no words exchanged, he would open his arms to her. But, when she came to the end of the staircase, the only person lurking in the shadows turned out to be Jerome.

"Lissa, you've gone all coppery," he called to her, commenting on her tan. Rushing up, he peppered the air around her ears with kisses. Caught up in his excitement, Jerome didn't notice how Lissa's eyes darted about, searching. "That Egyptian sun must have magic in it. Either that or it's pyramid power. Whichever, you look radiant. And that's coming from a professional."

"Thanks, Jerome." Lissa beamed, having collected herself. "You look pretty terrific yourself."

Jerome grabbed her arm. "Come on, I'm escorting you to this movie."

"It'll have to be a double date minus one then." The booming voice that accompanied a grab for Lissa's other arm could only have belonged to one person: Shaun Douglas. "Old Home Week, eh, babe?" he quipped, returning greetings from other cast and crew members.

"All in all, *Hard Land* was a pretty happy shoot," Lissa answered, comforted by the feel of being flanked by two genuine, if wildly divergent, friends.

Shaun stopped the trio and examined Lissa. "Well, I see that the rumors of your disfigurement are wildly exaggerated."

"Nothing more than what I was born with," Lissa gibed.

"Lissa!" Jack Myers burst upon them. "Lissa, you angel, you came. Thank God. How about mingling a bit with the members of the Fourth Estate?" he asked eagerly, cocking an eyebrow in the direction of a cluster of reporters and critics.

"Maybe after the screening," Lissa answered.

"Right, right," Jack agreed anxiously. "Shall we head on over?" he asked, wedging himself in between Jerome and Lissa, careful to present a picture of beaming solidarity to waiting photographers.

The theater represented the one claim to extravagance that Alta Mesa had made since her glory days as a goldmining boomtown. It had been constructed in the thirties and was a true palace of the illusions Hollywood had nourished during the grim days of the Depression. Though it had fallen on hard times, it had since been renovated to all its former opulence.

Lissa walked down the aisle slowly, trying not to be too obvious as she searched the rows of spectators in evening gowns and tuxedos. Matthew wasn't among them. It would be like him, she decided as they settled into their reserved seats, to sneak in late. He would be at the party. She was certain of it.

Only when the lights began to dim and the first chords of the sound track swelled through the theater, did Lissa turn her attention to the film. Her thoughts had been so fixed on Matthew that she hadn't even had time to become nervous about her performance. She winced and sank down in her seat the instant her first close-up filled the screen. She always hated seeing herself so magnified, and could concentrate only on her flaws. But unlike her other films, the feeling of self-consciousness did not last long.

As if she had never heard Jeannie Duncan's story

before, Lissa became caught up in its telling. She totally lost any sense of herself, as the person on the screen who resembled Lissa Bauer became Jeannie Duncan. There was no barrier, no wall of actor's tricks or techniques, separating her from the character she portrayed. That she owed to Matthew. The feeling of her indebtedness to him grew as the film continued. When the scene came where Jeannie sent Quaid away, Lissa was stunned by the raw power of the emotion she projected. All around her she heard a chorus of sniffles come from the audience. They were feeling the honest pain that Matthew had helped her unleash.

Matthew. Though his face wasn't on the screen, he was in every frame of the film, breathing life into it, injecting it with his passion, the passion that made the illusion real. Lissa felt his presence all around her. He was there, she knew it. Only through a force of will did she make herself remain in her seat until the lights came on. Then she was up, searching the crowd for Matthew's face.

Matthew paused at the back of the theater only long enough to steal one glimpse of her. The sight of her, more radiant than ever, knifed through him with a pain that took his breath cleanly away. The hurt was as new and brutal as it had been that morning when she'd unmoored every new anchor he'd sunk, ripping apart the foundation of his new life. The one he'd planned to share with her. God, he thought, she was even wearing the jersey dress she'd worn that night at dinner. The pain twisted within him as he wondered who would take it off her at the end of the night. Probably whoever it was she seemed to be searching for so avidly. He hadn't expected the anguish to be quite so intense. When he'd accepted the invitation, he thought he could stand seeing her again. He couldn't. Before her gaze could reach the back of the theater, Matthew withdrew.

Escorted by Shaun, Lissa walked to the party like a woman in a trance, sustained only by the fading hope that Matthew might still appear.

The party was being held in the hotel's ballroom. The corps of caterers flown in from Hollywood for the event had decided, since the movie was set in the West, upon a barn-dance motif. Bales of hay were scattered about for studio executives and their elegant dates to perch upon while a band sawed away at country and western favorites. In contrast to the corny ambience, the food was strictly haute cuisine, with chefs in high white toques stirring sauces heavy with wine and cream.

In the light cast by lanterns, Lissa visually sorted through the human maelstrom swirling about the ballroom. It was a typical Hollywood party in that nearly everyone there was working harder at this nominally social event than he ever did in his plush office. Studio executives approached one another with hands outstretched, paused for a brief clasp, a few words, a quick assessment of what each of them could or was willing to do for the other, then they each do-si-doed on to the next partner.

A High, Hard Land

No one seemed to be going about the business of partying Hollywood-style with more fervor than Jack Myers, who was desperately trying to reinstate himself. Lissa watched him go from one studio executive to the next. Each time, he directed their attention to her, to point out what fine shape she was in and how ridiculous the notion was that he'd ever jeopardize a picture by being careless with its stars. Lissa waved obligingly.

"Uh oh," Shaun whispered into her ear as a pack of reporters approached, "looks like they've picked up our scent." He straightened up to beam at the journalists and greet each of them warmly by name. As part of the crowd split off to interview Lissa, Shaun turned to her and winked broadly behind their backs. Lissa had to smile. It was all a game to him.

"Lissa." A thin woman with hair a vivid henna purple-red poked her face in front of Lissa's. "You were marvelous as Jeannie. How did you prepare for the role?"

At that moment, Jack swooped in between them. "Lissa, with your kind indulgence," he asked, giving her a broad smile. "We did a lot of work together getting into character. We spent time with the locals. We roamed this beautiful country soaking up atmosphere. We really just tuned in to the land and its people."

The reporter dutifully scribbled down Jack's answer. Lissa quirked an eyebrow at the director, and he answered with a look that pleaded for her not to blow the whistle on him. He needed every scrap of credibility he could get. Lissa sighed and drifted away as Jack went on taking credit for all of Matthew's work.

As Lissa made her way to an obscure corner, where she planned to study the crowd unobtrusively, snippets of conversation floated past her. "American classic" and "rural masterpiece" seemed popular pronouncements among the critics. Lissa knew she should be jubilant, but it seemed as if all her emotions were frozen in suspended animation while she waited for a glimpse of Matthew to return them fully to life.

She was quietly nursing a drink, feeling remote and detached from the festivities, when Jack Myers made his way to a group of critics nearby. Though none of them could see her hidden behind one of the ballroom's tall columns, Lissa could hear every word of their exchange.

"Hail, hail," a critic called to Jack, by now the unofficially crowned conquering hero.

"Boys, how'd you like our little picture?" Jack asked with a calculated show of modesty.

Again the terms "American classic" and "rural masterpiece" rang through the air, with one critic finally asking, "What I want to know is, how did you get that performance out of Lissa Bauer?"

"That was no small challenge, gentlemen," Jack answered, in a tone of man-to-man confidentiality. "I mean, what did they give me to work with? The Spritzi Soda Girl, for God's sake. I mean, come on. But I sensed some depth there and just worked like a dog to bring it to the surface."

A High, Hard Land

An icy rage welled up in Lissa as she listened to the director's self-serving lies. She could no longer bear hearing him take credit for what Matthew had done. Sweeping out from behind the column, she took great delight in watching Jack's face fall.

"Uh, uh, Lissa." He fumbled with the words. "There you are. Been there long?" he asked nervously.

"Long enough, Jack," she answered with a gleaming smile. Turning to the critics, she asked in a tone of utter innocence. "Has anyone seen Matthew Briggs?"

"Let me know if you find him," one of the critics said. "I'd love an interview. Jack says he hasn't been anywhere near Alta Mesa since shooting began."

"Jack, you're kidding, right?" Lissa asked the director. Then turning toward the critics, she went on, "Why, Matthew was here from the beginning. He was the one who introduced me to the real Jeannie Duncan. Without him you would have seen the Spritzi Soda Girl up there tonight." She gave a charmingly self-deprecating chuckle, and the critics clustered a bit more tightly about Lissa, turning their backs on Jack, to inundate her with questions that she kept subtly bringing back to Matthew's contribution. She knew that he wouldn't care whether he got credit, but she did, and she was determined that he would have it.

As she broke away from the ring of critics, Lissa felt someone grab her by the elbow. It was Jack. "Thanks, kid," he hissed angrily at her. "Really showed a lot of gratitude there, making me look like a liar."

"I've repaid any debt I owe to you," Lissa answered icily. "And you don't need any help from me to look like a liar."

Anger flashed in the director's face. "You'll never make another picture with me as long as you live."

Removing his hand from her elbow, Lissa replied evenly, "I had no intention of ever doing so." Walking away, she added, "Stick to your specialty, Jack. Evoking subtle emotional nuances from robots and crashing cars."

Only when she was outside, away from the piranha pit, did Lissa feel that she could breathe again. She stared out at the mountains, dusted with moonlight, and ached to be on the other side. On Matthew's side. But she never would be. Not in the way she had dreamed of being. Not as part of her life. Matthew had written the final chapter of their story tonight. His absence was a clear and unequivocal message that he wanted nothing further to do with her. Lissa felt a door slam shut within her. With the last flickering hope that she and Matthew might be together snuffed out, all that was left between them was the debt Lissa owed to the man who had forced her to be a true actor.

Lissa wasn't someone who was comfortable with debts. She'd owed so few in her life. She prided herself equally on having gotten where she was with almost no help from anyone and on always repaying those few who had offered her the slightest help. And now Matthew had almost single-handedly raised her above the rank of the second-tier actresses she had been milling about with.

A High, Hard Land

Though she knew she could never repay even that debt, much less the far larger one she owed him for having saved her life, Lissa knew she had to at least acknowledge it. Not to do at least that much would make her no better than the piranhas she'd left inside.

Her only thanks to Matthew had been to revile him as a betrayer and accuse him of turning her most private secrets against her. A compulsion seized her to express her gratitude properly. It was the last responsibility she had to discharge before facing the rest of her life without Matthew.

The SUV she had rented at the airport in Albuquerque hummed up the steep mountain road, almost as if the full harvest moon hanging above the peaks were a round, silver magnet drawing Lissa upward. As Lissa crested the rise above Matthew's valley, a fit of nerves worse than any case of stage fright she'd ever had overtook her. She calmed them by reminding herself sternly that it was no coy errand of unrequited love she was on. She was merely doing what any halfway decent person would do.

Still, her heart lurched as she saw lights on in his house. For a second, her courage failed her. What if Matthew refused even to speak to her? She almost turned back before she reached his property. But she drove on. She had to do what she must do, and Matthew would do what he must.

A chilly autumn wind, with a hint of winter's power,

shivered down off the mountain to catch at Lissa's dress as she strode to Matthew's door. The cold invaded her bones with an icy premonition of doom. Her initial knock was feeble. Then Lissa gathered herself up again and rapped more forcefully. Try as she might, she couldn't stifle the thrill that went through her as she heard Matthew's footsteps approach. Nor was she prepared for the way her heart ground to a stop within her when he opened the door and threw on the light.

Neither one spoke for a long, stunned moment, each wavering under the impact of the other's presence and fighting to give no sign of his or her turmoil. He was still wearing the tuxedo he'd had on for the premiere, his black tie unknotted to hang limply at his neck. She filled her eyes with the sight of him, feasting on him, filling a hunger whose extent even she hadn't known.

Matthew had thought he had gauged the depth of the despair in his life since she'd left but knew as he looked at her that he couldn't possibly have calculated how dark it had been without her radiance to illuminate it.

"Lissa."

She thought she'd never heard a sweeter sound than her name on Matthew's lips. That one sound completely undid all her strongest resolves. It slipped in past her determination and pride to the soft places within herself that only Matthew had been able to touch. Suddenly, it was all too much. The months of pretending, of putting up a bright front, of acting as if her life had a meaning without him all crumbled. She tried to pull herself together, to stop the trembling in her chin and to swallow the lump clotting up in her throat. She thought she had them under control, at least enough to return his greeting.

"Ma—" Midway through his name the trembling and the lump returned. She could have said any other word in the English language, but not that, not his name. She turned away, feeling more ridiculous than she ever had before in her life. She had to leave before he saw the tears she seemed to have lost the power of stopping.

She was hurtling across the yard when a set of strong arms stopped her flight and turned her to face him. Her tears in the moonlight cut tracks of silver across her face. All thought was banished by his presence, by his strength flowing into her, by the intensity that burned in his eyes.

"Matthew." His name was the magic word that broke an evil spell. "Matthew. Matthew. Matthew. Matthew." She babbled, incoherent in her joy as he pressed her to him, folding her slender form against the broad expanse of his chest.

"Why didn't you call?" he finally demanded, pulling her from his shirtfront.

"Call?" she echoed, incredulous. "You made it abundantly clear that you had no desire ever to see or hear from me again. Besides, you were off chasing Navajo shepherds somewhere."

"Yes, but you didn't even try. After the first few months, after the hurt cleared away enough for me to think straight, I told Vonda Kay where to reach me. If you'd really wanted to get in touch, it would have been easy enough for you to ask her how."

"Matthew, I didn't think you wanted me to try. Not after what I said, what I called you."

"I didn't. But that passed and something else stayed."

"Something else?" Lissa asked, the trembling starting again.

"Yes, something that will endure. Dammit, Lissa, I—"

Lissa covered his mouth with her hand. "Don't say it," she whispered, seized by a sudden knowledge of the awful imbalance in their relationship. "I know what I've dreamed and ached for you to say. But I can't stand back and let you say it first. That's how it's been all along. You dragging me, kicking and screaming. I have to start taking some of the risks, Matthew, if we're going to have what we both want." Lissa felt perched at the edge of a high cliff. She swallowed hard and took the plunge. "I love you, Matthew Briggs. I love you so much my heart is bursting with it."

Matthew's kiss answered her proclamation, telling Lissa more surely than words ever could of his love. "I have ached for you, Lissa. It terrifies me to think of the power you have over me."

"No more than yours over me," Lissa whispered.

"We'll have to always remember and use that power wisely."

"I'll learn from you."

"We'll learn from each other," Matthew corrected. His hand caught her jaw to tilt her head up. "I love you, Lissa Bauer, madly, without measure, I love you."

Lissa felt her heart keel over with happiness at hearing him return her words.

His grip tightened about her. "And now that I finally have you again, don't even think of trying to leave."

"Whatever will the Monroes think of your keeping a woman?" she teased back.

"Not a damned thing, especially since that woman will be my wife." He searched her face for an answer. It beamed forth with an exultant brilliance that outshone the moon. "I won't let you go again, Lissa," Matthew went on, all jesting gone from his deadly earnest tone. "Not now that I know I have no life without you."

"Matthew, I'm scared," Lissa whispered. "Scared that I won't always be strong enough for you. You demand a lot."

"And you have more to give than any woman I've ever known. I'm not promising you a life of bland contentment, Lissa. There's electricity between us and I, for one, pray that it never dims."

"Not in my lifetime," Lissa promised.

His mouth took hers, wiping away all the cruel months of separation with an aching thoroughness. He pressed her slim hips against himself with a groan of surrender. "See what you do to me, woman?" he asked. "You know how impossibly seductive you are in the moonlight, wearing that dress, don't you?" As one questing hand slid down her smooth thigh to grab hold of the hem of her dress, he asked, "You do remember what happened last time you wore that dress, don't you?"

"Um-hmm, there's a vague recollection," Lissa gibed, as shivers of delight shuddered through her at the touch of Matthew's hand inching her dress higher.

"A vague recollection, eh?" Matthew echoed, sweeping her up and into his hard arms. "I may just have to sharpen that recollection a bit then, to help your memory along."

He pushed the door open with his foot and carried Lissa into the house. He slammed the door shut and set Lissa down on wobbly legs. Slowly he drew one strong hand down over the thin jersey covering her breast, sending a shuddering warmth cascading through her body. His fingers moved to slip the strap of her dress off her shoulder. He held her eyes with his. "In order to complete this memory-sharpening experiment," he said huskily, pulling the other strap off and letting the loose-fitting dress fall away, "I may be forced to crumple your dress a bit."

"I was hoping you might," Lissa whispered, stepping into his arms. "I was just hoping you might."

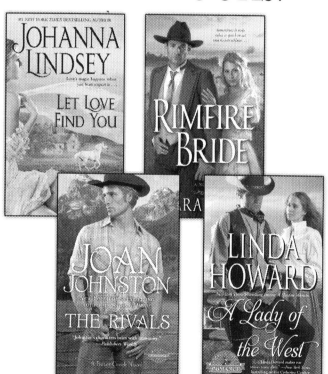

Printed in the United States
By Bookmasters